I0831509

The Book of Hamsters

W.S. Pavlich

Front cover artwork by Daisy Orellana, Instagram @flacasplacas

Graphic design by Vaughan Woods, portfolio https://vaughan-is.online/

Editing by The Cauldron Author Services

Formatting by Lana Kole

CONTENT INFORMATION

The story ahead could be classified as extreme horror.

It involves such topics as amnesia, self-harm, child abuse, body horror, hallucinations, mentions of incest, dubious consent, and cannibalism.

Read the following with comfort and care.

And thou shalt eat the fruit of thine own body, the flesh of thy sons and of thy daughters, which the Lord thy God hath given thee, in the siege, and in the straitness, wherewith thine enemies shall distress thee

Deuteronomy 28:53

THE BEGINNING

Father, guide me. I closed the front door of my family home behind me, and my hands shook. Although the air stung my eyes and froze puddles, the weather wasn't the reason for making me tremble. Today was the first day of my first job. My mother had never worked outside of the home as it was uncommon for women to do so in my community, so her parting words were merely, "Be careful." I should be careful, but I was only working at a pet store. Dusting floors and stocking shelves didn't seem too bad compared to my brother, who works in the farming district of town. However, my first day had yet to even start, so who was I to know?

The roads were icy, and I was an inexperienced driver. My knuckles pale, and my jaw clenched as I meandered down the road. It was only about a ten-minute drive, but that meant that I would no longer be driving along the dirt paths of home. The pet store was in the next closest town to ours, just on the outskirts. My parents weren't too happy that I wasn't working for our community, but since it was still relatively close, they eventually gave in, luckily, before someone else took the position.

"Women aren't to be working outside of the home!" Father declared when I had told him of my plans. I told him I was to be working with animals and that's the closest thing to being with kids, as the schoolhouse didn't need the extra help. He begrudgingly allowed me to apply only if that meant when the schoolhouse was hiring, I'd work there instead. Father told me I needed to learn how to be motherly towards children rather than animals. I told him that animals need love, too, as God made them just as He did us. Father's face reddened and I don't remember what happened after that.

It was at that moment that I realized that I actually had a job. A real-life job, just like you hear about. While pulling into the parking lot, my stomach turned over in a way where I had to focus hard on my breathing. Lord, help me. I noticed that the "Help Wanted" sign, which was there two weeks ago, was gone. I had first seen it when I had to go into town to pick up some fresh strawberries for Momma. She was baking a cake for the reverend's daughter's birthday and said she had no time to be driving so far out of the way. It sounded a little silly, as it wasn't much of a drive, but if Momma said that, then she must've meant it.

It was only seven thirty in the morning, and the front door to the store was still locked. The lights were on, however, and I saw the man who I talked to about the job, Gregory. I tapped on the glass, hoping he would see me and not be mad. When I had asked him about the job, he was rather curt with his words and unimpressed by anything I said. He seemed the type to have seen it all, and nothing phased him. I was probably nothing more than another annoying teenager for him to deal with. I stared at the building while waiting for him. The sign above me simply read "Pet Store." They weren't some big brand name store you hear cities having. It simply was what it was. The glass had scratches, the wood beaming was weathered, and the paint was severely chipped. Even so, it was exciting. It was something new. I had been born and raised in a town where everything looked all the same. The same white wood exterior with the same red roofs on every house and building was all I knew. I would only, on rare occasions, frequent the shopping center with the pet store if our market was out of something. Momma didn't like to leave town.

"Alright," Gregory said when he unlocked the front door, motioning with his head for me to hurry on inside. "Clock in." I stared up at the clock and smiled back at him with a nod. He looked at me funny and pointed to a small folder on the wall. He led me to a piece of thick paper with my name on it, and after sticking it in some machine, out came the date and time. I marveled at the technology with curious eyes. Gregory seemed regretful about hiring me, and I was not completely naïve to his exasperated sighs and condescending stares.

To some, it was just a pet store, but to me, it was a wonderland. The bird section wasn't just a row of cages; it was an orchestra. Different birds of different shapes and colors sing to the world their perfect song. The fish section wasn't just aisle two. It was enveloped by the color blue, the light bouncing off the walls, making it feel like everything was actually underwater. The hamster section wasn't merely boring glass boxes; it was warm, cozy, and homey. It was like being nested with your family, just as God intended. It was exciting to me, but then again, it was only my first day. My attitude may change as time passes and the newness wears thin, but today, I couldn't help but grin.

Gregory went to the cash register and slouched forward across the counter with a book in hand, a completely bored expression written on his face. I awkwardly looked around, having no real direction on what to do. I clasped my hands in front of my skirt and waited for a command. He turned a page. I bit off the thinnest layer of skin from my lip. His eyes focused on the next page. I stared up at the clock. It was only seven-forty.

"So what do I do?" I asked nervously, with a smile.

"Sweep," Gregory replied, his eyes still fixed on his book. I peered around the register area for a broom. "Backroom." I winced at the word. He probably thought I was stupid. I knew I worked there, but it still felt like that part of the store was off-limits. Propped against the wall right after the threshold was an old, splintered broom. Back on the sales floor, I looked around for a dirty part of the floor but struggled to find one. There appeared to be no spilled birdseed, no hay strands, or any dog food, let alone actual dirt. Without having a clear starting or ending path, I simply began sweeping mindlessly. I did so until I heard Gregory unlock the front door. It must've hit eight. I wasn't scheduled for very long, my shift ending at noon, and I stared at the front door eagerly, waiting for a parade of customers to come barreling through the door. I never thought of myself as particularly chatty, but I wanted at least one person to talk to. Obviously, Gregory wasn't going to be that person, so even if a customer in a rush came in, only saying "hello" and "goodbye," it'd be better than nothing. Seconds ticked by without even a face in the window. Knowing I had an additional four hours left seemed suddenly daunting. Time was standing still, and here I was, sweeping a floor that needn't be swept, with a coworker who wouldn't talk to me.

As more of nothing happened, I was warily unsure as to if I would be working with anyone else on this shift. While putting away the broom, I stared at the work schedule for the week, assuming Gregory wrote it. He surely had some hard-to-read handwriting. Gregory, Dinah, Virginia, Ron, and me.

That was the whole team. The next to come in for a shift was Ron. He was scheduled to arrive in thirty minutes. I hoped he would talk to me, or at least we'd get some customers.

Back out on the sales floor, I saw Gregory talking with a woman at the cash register. She was holding some item in her hand, too small to tell from where I was standing. She seemed to be going on and on about why she needed to return said item. Gregory stared at her with her new receipt in hand. Eventually, she left, and he rubbed at his temples; a sigh echoed off the walls.

A woman with a small child came through the door. The noise made my heart skip a beat, and I stood awkwardly, watching them walk down the aisles. I looked to Gregory for some guidance on what to do. His nose was back to being buried in the book. I took a deep breath and decided that it was on me to be good at my job, which I had no training in. I walked up to the pair and greeted them with a warm welcome to the store.

"Oh, we don't need any help, sugar. She just likes to look at the birds," the woman said. The young girl, maybe five or so, pointed to the bird cages with a stretched grin. I smiled and nodded before walking away. Well, I certainly tried more than Gregory did, but I suppose it didn't matter. Perhaps I should have also brought a book. I looked back at the bird girls, seeing the child jump up and down excitedly, but not so much as to scare the birds. She reminded me of my sister. I couldn't help but smile.

The bird girls left, and we went back to an empty house. The only noise that existed was the turning of pages from Gregory's book and the low humming of the fish tank motors. I felt as if my breathing were obnoxious. Suddenly, Gregory set his book down and looked up at me. He said I was to take my break in ten minutes. I knew that jobs had breaks, but I didn't really know what to do with mine. I surely hadn't worked up an appetite, and I had a warm breakfast right before I left home. It was far too cold to sit outside, so I figured I would sit in the breakroom. The name is fitting, after all.

Ten minutes eventually passed, and I walked to the back room. Papers littered the walls with different rules and laws. In the far back was a desk with a single chair in front. The desk was made of wood with different words carved into it. Names, numbers, and drawings were all a part of the top of the furniture. "Sarah was here" was scribbled in large cursive handwriting. Based on the weekly schedule, Sarah was no longer here. I started tracing my finger in the indentations of a heart with the initials R and S in it.

"So you're the new one," a voice said. Without realizing how much concentration I had poured into analyzing the desk, I jumped at the sudden break in silence, a boy now standing in the doorway.

"Yes. My name is Ema. Nice to meet you," I greeted joyfully. Oh, thank goodness there was another person here. The boy must be Ron. He didn't introduce himself; he just flashed me a quick smile. He took off his jacket, some faint traces of snow falling to the ground as he took out his arm and threw the jacket on the floor next to my feet. The scent of cigarettes quickly entered the air.

"First day, right?" he asked. His voice was similar to Gregory's with how gruff it was, but Ron's still contained an element of youthfulness. He must be a few years older than me, but it was hard to tell. I stared at him curiously, forgetting that he had asked me a question. It wasn't until he gave me a confused expression that I realized I hadn't answered.

"Oh. Yes, sorry," I said, embarrassed. He smiled again.

"Well, good luck," he said cocking his head to the side, eyes wide. I smiled instinctively. He didn't say anything funny or smart, but I wanted to keep talking to him.

"Ron, right?" I asked. It was a desperate attempt at conversation, but theoretically, it was also a good way to confirm his name. He nodded. Name confirmed. I now knew his name. I had never met a Ron before.

"Well, it was nice to meet you, Ron," I said as he was about to head for the door. He paused and chuckled,

"You already said that." I tried to think back to what I had already said, but my memory seemingly gave out.

"Oh. Sorry," I said with a slight stutter. It felt as if someone had thrown the solid wood desk against my head. It had been a while since I had made a new friend, and it appeared as if I had forgotten how to talk to new people. Then again, I didn't talk to many boys, especially outside of my community.

"Must be really nice to have met me then," he said with a slightly sarcastic tone to his voice. I felt as if I were going to sink into the chair. I felt my face warm, and all I could do was smile in response.

"It was nice to meet you, too," he said sincerely. The door shut behind him. I exhaled strongly, my shoulders slumping into my chest. I have no idea what just happened. My day was going completely fine beforehand. I acted normal when I talked to the woman with the bird-loving daughter. When talking to Gregory, everything seemed average in the few moments I had with him. Long after Ron had left the room, though, I felt my face was still smiling. *Oh no. No, no, no.* This wasn't supposed to happen. Courting a boy outside of my community was almost unheard of! I would be in so much trouble if I told my parents. They might even force me to quit the job.

Lord, help me. I met a cute boy.

I looked up at the clock. Thirty minutes had passed since the start of my break. I gasped and shot up. I immediately ran to the cash register, where no Gregory was to be seen.

His book was even gone. To the side of the counter was Ron, staring off into the distance. He must've noticed my search of the room for Gregory.

"He's out front." I looked over at the glass door. There, in fact, was Gregory, smoking a cigarette with his back to the store. "Do you need something?"

"No, I just…" I started to say before Ron met my gaze. His eyes burned into mine. "I took my break longer than allowed. I was meaning to apologize." Ron shrugged.

"It literally doesn't matter. You didn't miss anything." He wasn't wrong. The store looked exactly how I had left it. There weren't any customers on the floor, and there still wasn't anything to sweep.

Nevertheless, I still felt bad. I watched Gregory continue to smoke outside, now sitting down. I went back to trying to find things to do when the front door swung open. A woman, pink from the cold, came in and waved her arm towards me. I smiled and walked over to her, asking if I could assist her with anything.

"Oh, please, would you? I got this damn thing on and can't carry the normal bag I get," she sighed, motioning to her other arm in a sling. Having no idea what a normal bag was, I asked her what she was looking for. According to the woman, she cared for three large dogs, which meant she needed three large bags of dog food. Thankfully, whoever stocked them kept them on the lowest shelf. With as much force as I could muster, I was able to drag the bags along the floor to the register. I felt incredibly guilty for dragging the items she was to purchase all along the floor, but I simply couldn't pick them up properly. Ron saw me struggling and came over to lift them onto the counter. He flashed me a smile that made my heart race. After taking over the transaction, Ron helped the woman with the items to her car. I could hear her thanking him mercilessly until I was no longer within earshot.

It wasn't long before Gregory was back in the store. He told me that in thirty minutes, I could leave. His reasoning was that first days should be short days. Also, we were over on hours, whatever that meant. It was a Tuesday, meaning when I would be home, my sister would still be at school, and my brother and father at work. I passed the time by wiping down the windowsills of the store. Once it was time to clock out, Ron casually waved goodbye. I rushed out to my car and stared straight ahead. I couldn't do this. I wasn't allowed to do this. I could not have a crush on a boy like him. He seemed so different from the boys I had grown up with. I couldn't find the words to describe them besides just being all I knew, but what I also knew was that I liked Ron.

With a deep breath, I told myself it was okay to like a boy; I just couldn't think un-pure thoughts about one. That was definitely not allowed. What I could do, however, was think about his good qualities and character. I nodded to myself in response to my new plan. For the entire drive home, I thought to myself just how nice Ron is.

JUST AS I SUSPECTED, only my momma was home when I returned to my house. She was in the kitchen, already getting a head start on dinner. I could hear her chopping something. It didn't make much of a noise—likely being potatoes. As I kicked off my boots, she greeted me and asked how my day was. I told her fine because, realistically, it was fine. She asked if my coworkers were nice, and I told her that my coworkers were indeed, nice.

"Do you need any help with dinner, Momma?" I asked, not wanting to continue talking about my coworkers. She led me over to the potatoes that she was, in fact, dicing for me to take over so she could start dessert. She worked so effortlessly. Momma was a beautiful woman who always worked hard to care for us. She cooked each meal with such ease and grace. It all seemed to come so naturally to her, and she was the epitome of a loving, Godly wife and mother.

"So, I was talking to Susan earlier today, and she said that Joseph would be interested in the idea of you two courting," Momma said suddenly. I carefully set down the knife.

"Oh?" I asked softly, not knowing how to continue properly. Momma seldom talks about boys with me.

"What do you think I should tell her?" she asked. Susan and Joseph were neighbors of ours. We had all grown up together, me and Joseph only a few months apart in age, and Momma and Susan with close birthdays. He was a nice boy. We've exchanged words and pleasantries here and there, having gone to school together and living so close. I never found him all that special, but maybe now that I know what special can feel like, I can try to feel that way for Joseph. Maybe I just needed to see him again, and I would get that feeling.

"Oh, I don't know," I said sheepishly, which was an honest answer. I, of course, didn't want to lie, but I didn't know what to say. "I could meet him for a walk."

Momma was suddenly on the telephone with dessert quickly forgotten. I had never seen her abandon a meal she was in the middle of cooking. I wasn't sure what the urgency was all about. I didn't think we were in any sort of rush, but perhaps I shouldn't question it. Within a few short minutes, momma came back to tell me that Joseph was on his way over.

"Now?" I asked, panic in my voice. I stared down at the clothes I had worn to work. I still had my nametag on.

"Yes, now. Go on and fix your hair; I can handle the potatoes."

Suddenly, I was in my room, fixing my hair and readying myself for a date. A date! Not an hour ago, I was nearly cursing myself for having a crush on a stranger, and now I was to be set up on a date with a boy I had known forever. I felt at ease. Perhaps we would really hit it off, and I would completely forget about Ron, killing off any guilt and shame I previously felt. I unpinned my nametag and sat in on my dresser. I had never courted anyone before, so I didn't know how I was to look, but I knew I should put in a bit more effort. I was just so caught off guard by everything happening so abruptly that I didn't know what to do or how to proceed. It was all so much, so fast.

Deep down, I knew that I really didn't care that much. When pondering scenarios of courtship, it wasn't Joseph's face I saw.

"Ema, get the door!" Momma called. I sighed before walking to the door, and there in the doorway, stood Joseph. He was indeed Joseph, the same one I had known my whole life. Only this time, he had very patchy facial hair.

"So…" I started awkwardly.

"My mother said we can sit on our deck and talk." He sounded nervous, and I felt bad. We did as his mother suggested. Two chairs faced us with a pitcher of something on a table separating the two. Behind us was a window with a small face in it. I jumped at the sight before recognizing it as his younger sister.

"She really sneaks up on you, huh?" I said with a laugh.

"Oh, she's just the chaperone." I somehow forgot that courting wasn't a private process. The window was shut, so I knew she couldn't hear our conversation well, but she was there to ensure nothing inappropriate happened.

"So, what do we do?" I asked with a nervous laugh once we both had taken a seat.

"Well, last time I did this, we just talked about what we wanted within a marriage, basically." Marriage. That was surely something I was not ready for! I felt my eyes widen at the word.

"Last time?" I asked, connecting the dots once my head cleared a bit.

"Oh. Well, the last time I did one of these. My younger sister just got married, so I figured I should start courting at the least." I knew that. I forgot in the moment, but I knew that. I was at his sister's wedding; the whole town was.

"Right, of course. What did you want within a marriage?" I asked, trying desperately to break any awkward silence gaps.

"Just a normal biblical marriage, I guess. I don't really know what other there is to say."

I looked at him, and I mean really looked at him. I didn't feel anything. I concentrated on his face, the way his eyes kind of drooped downward, and the way his nostrils would flare. It was as if I were having a conversation with an empty chair, only it wasn't empty; it was with some boy Momma wanted me to marry. He wasn't rude. He didn't seem mean or cruel, and he seemed like a perfectly fine, Godly man, but the hour I spent with him on the porch felt nothing like the few minutes I had speaking with Ron.

When I got back home, momma rushed to me with questions. I told her he was friendly, which I had already known, and that was about it. She didn't seem pleased with this response. I told her that I was tired from work and just wanted to clean up. She dismissed me and I went to my room. I sat down and sighed. I simply couldn't believe that this perfectly nice boy, just a minute's walk down the road, liked me and I was stuck on this city boy. I decided to pray for some guidance. Lord knew I needed it.

At dinner, my father turned to me and asked me how my day was. I told him fine, just as I had told Momma. He said he was proud of me for getting a job, despite him thinking I was better off helping Momma around the house. It was a compliment, but it didn't really make me feel all that good. I thanked him, nonetheless. Momma then brought up me seeing Joseph earlier this afternoon. Father lowered his glasses and stared directly at me and a chill ran up my spine. I was confused. Momma basically sent me out the door with this boy, but Father looked mad. I quickly glanced at Momma for reassurance, but her gaze was fixed on my father.

"Well, you better behave yourself. You know what happens if you don't act right. I hope you had a good time," he said solemnly. I nodded and kept eating.

THE NEXT DAY, I headed back to the pet store. Luckily, my shift started a little later, so I had time to eat breakfast with my family without rushing. I sat between each of my siblings, my brother Isaiah on my left and my sister Judith on my right. I watched Jude shovel food into her mouth before she asked to be excused. School was to be starting soon, and she always liked to be early. I heard the shuffling of her grabbing her backpack and boots before heading out the door. Then there were four. It wasn't long before Isaiah and my father also left. I knew that Father didn't mind being a little late to work if he could spend extra time with Momma. She was his absolute everything. They had such a perfect marriage in my eyes. Isaiah admired them also, being older and far more ready to follow in their footsteps.

When it was my turn to head out the door, Momma stopped me. In her hand was a neatly wrapped paper bag. I gave her a confused look, to which she answered that inside was a sandwich if I got hungry. It was the same thing she'd pack me for school. A simple gesture, but being that I hadn't been in school for a little bit, I forgot how nice it was. I thanked her for the food and headed out. The drive to work wasn't a long one. You basically drive past a few houses, some greenery, farmland, and a few shops, making for a boring drive. It doesn't take long before the roads are nice, and you're at the stop sign taking you into the next town.

Pulling into the same spot I parked in yesterday, I took a deep breath. I couldn't remember if Ron was to be working with me or not, but in any case, I told myself that I had only acted the way I did because I must've been hungry. I was acting differently because I was hungry, and hungry people act funny. I had a nice, full meal this morning, so it wouldn't make sense for me to act that way. Plus, I had my sandwich. Everything was going to be great.

I entered the shop and saw a girl at the counter instead of Ron or Gregory. She was tall, with absolutely captivating eyes. A girl like her should be in the movies! I clocked in, and she didn't even look up at me. Her gaze was fixed on a magazine. Another Gregory, it seemed. I tried not to sigh audibly in disappointment, but I wanted someone to talk to. The schedule was placed on the counter. I casually eyed it so I could figure out her name. Virginia. I asked her what I should do today as, once again, there was not one customer in the store. She shrugged before saying that I really didn't have to do anything. Bewildered, I stared at her wide-eyed asking if I should go home. She let out a laugh before saying, "You wish." I sighed softly, realizing that learning how to operate the cash register would be for another day.

I realized that something was different and then it hit me.

There was music playing in the store. I wasn't completely enveloped in deafening silence. This was already a strong improvement. I could take the no one talking to me if music played. I tried to get a listen, but it sounded like nothing I had heard before. I wasn't really familiar with secular music, as it was something that wasn't played at home. It was something that my family protested against, but it really didn't seem all that bad. The instruments were actually pretty catchy!

A few customers came into the store as time passed. I got to have multiple conversations with multiple strangers. I didn't realize until that moment that was something I seldom did. I knew everyone who worked at my town's food market, I knew the schoolhouse teachers, and I knew everyone who worked within the church. Not being able to easily predict what people were going to say was enlightening. I was on the edge of my seat and I listened intently. Everything was so curious. It was all so new.

"Hey, stranger," a voice behind me whispered. I jumped, my heart in my throat. Ron passed me by, on his way to clock in.

"Fucking finally!" Virginia exclaimed. "I've had this headache for hours. What took you so long?" She rubbed her temples and grabbed her coat from behind the counter.

"Hey, I'm here," he replied, his tone clearly annoyed.

"Whatever. I called Dinah. She said she can close with you." Ron headed straight for the back room, replying only with a thumbs up. I could hear Virginia mutter obscenities under her breath before storming out of the store. My eyes nervously darted around, realizing I was the only one on the sales floor. Theoretically, I was in charge. What a feeling, but it made my stomach turn. Ron came back, his pace rather slow as there really was nothing important to do at the moment. Once he was back at the cash register, he eyed a piece of paper. I assumed it to be the schedule.

"Gonna cut you. Is that alright?" he asked, his eyes fixed on mine. My eyes widened, unsure of how to respond.

"Schedules a mess. Is it alright if I send you home at around two-thirty instead of five?" I nodded in response, and he scribbled some adjustments on the paper. I walked back over to the rodent section. The hamsters ran on their wheels, their little legs going faster than I could comprehend. I put my finger to the glass, but that didn't deter them.

"Hey, what are you doing later?" Ron asked. Well, not working, apparently. I shrugged and told him that I didn't have any plans besides the routine dinner with my family. He nodded, seemingly processing what I told him before asking if I wanted to meet up later.

"Okay," I replied shyly, before nervously walking away.

What had I just done? I wasn't allowed to hang out with a strange boy! Especially without any supervision! My parents would be so concerned. They surely wouldn't allow it. My stomach turned over far worse than when I was alone on the sales floor. Luckily for me, there were actual real-life customers who came into the store and needed my assistance, which managed to stave off the volcano of anxiety looming in my body. It was time for my break, where I sat in the back room and picked at my cuticles. Was I doing something bad? Would God think I was sinning for spending time with Ron alone? I couldn't think of any verse that would back that up, but I knew my parents wouldn't approve, and surely that was enough, right?

Time was not on my side as the minutes, for once, seemed to tick faster than average. The sooner I left the store, the sooner I'd be home and have to tell my parents what was going on.

Back on the sales floor, from a break that felt far from refreshing, I watched Ron. He was talking to a customer, his eyes filled with boredom. Looking at him made me nervous, so I walked to the opposite end of the store and began reorganizing shelves.

I looked up at the clock, and it was two-fifteen. I wrung my hands and walked away from the shelves. I saw a girl come into the store with a strong look of displeasure and walk immediately into the back room; the door slamming behind her. That must've been Dinah. That meant my shift was over. I tried to run out of the store after clocking out, but Ron caught me. He asked where I lived and seemed confused when I tried giving directions. I watched him mentally map out where my house is, before his eyes widened.

"Oh. You live over there," he said solemnly. I wasn't sure why he seemed so morose about it, but I nodded with a smile.

BACK AT HOME, I sat on my bed. Momma wasn't home. She must've been out at the store and it'd be a few hours before Father was home from work. I could hear shuffling in Judith's room, but she wasn't who I needed to confess to. The shuffling grew louder until Judith was standing in my doorway. She remarked that I was home early, to which I replied that it wasn't busy enough for me to stay as long. She was fine with that answer and left me alone. I heard the front door close and the faint sounds of two girls talking. I wished Isaiah was home. Him being older than me, I could ask if he had ever been on a date with a girl from out of town. Not sure where he would've met her but I kind of just wanted to talk to someone. It wasn't long before the front door opened again, and I could hear the sighs of my mother carrying in groceries.

"Momma?" I called while walking out towards the kitchen. She turned her head to me, greeting me with a kind smile.

"Momma, I must tell you something." I began. She turned her back to the groceries and asked me what was the matter. I thought about Ron. I thought about his eyes. The little spark that would shine when he would talk to me. The smirk that would dent his cheek. The way my heart felt so out of my body when talking to him.

"I'm meeting Jill Meyers for dinner tonight, so I won't be home. Is that alright?"

Lord, help me. I lied to my parents for the first time in my life. Back in my room, I collapsed to my knees and clasped my hands.

Oh Lord, please forgive me as I lied to my mother. Not just lied to my mother, Lord, but lied to her about meeting a boy! I'm so sorry. Please forgive me. Oh, no. I'm sorry.

I climbed into bed as I felt a wave of nausea come over me. I've heard that people lie all the time. How can they possibly muster this? What an absolutely terrible feeling! I cannot believe that I allowed my emotions to cloud my judgement in such a way. I glanced at my clock, and it read a bit past four. Ron said he would pick me up at six-thirty, right after work. I had two and a half hours to calm down.

I stared down at my clothes: a long brown skirt, a beige blouse and my work nametag. Well, for starters, I should remove my nametag. I didn't know if I should change my outfit completely. My parents thought I was seeing an old friend from school, and there was no real reason to dress up for that. My hair was long, so when at work, I had it tied up. I undid my hair for it to fall like water, down far past my shoulders. I thought it was too long, like I was drowning in it, but Father wouldn't allow me to cut it. I created a compromise hairstyle of half up, half down. That was something that was new for Ron to see me in. I kicked off my boots and changed them out for a nice heel, something I really only wore for special church services or weddings. I looked at the clock. *Four-fifteen*. Time surely is a fickle thing now, isn't it?

I stared at myself in a handheld mirror. My parents didn't really like mirrors as they said they promoted vanity, but I've seen Momma apply lipstick with her compact. It's only fair for me to have one, too, by that logic. I didn't have any makeup; I didn't know where to get it, and I surely didn't know how to use it. I pinched my cheeks to add a little color. I set down the mirror and bounced my leg furiously.

I couldn't believe I was going on a real date. Not courting, no supervisors, but a date, like they do in the movies. *Six o'clock*. I could hear Momma setting up the dinner table. Muffled chatter occurred, but it was too far away for me to decipher anything. I heard the oven door creak open. This was my one opportunity. I dashed to my parents' bathroom and stole a spritz of Momma's nicest perfume. Well, not stealing, really, as she let me wear it many times in the past. It made me feel pretty. She wouldn't mind. *Five past six*.

There was a knock at the front door, and my heart seemingly stopped. My breathing came to an immediate halt. I told Ron to wait outside in his car for me. Footsteps approached to get the door, and a girl's voice was on the other side. I couldn't quite tell who it was, but I knew it wasn't Jill's, and that's all that really mattered. I took a deep breath to try and fix my heartbeat. *Six fifteen*.

I peered out my bedroom window. Night had fallen, so no one would be able to see Ron's car. Thank goodness. It wasn't long before it was officially time. I nodded to myself for a few seconds before leaving my bedroom.

"Well, I'll be off at Jill's. I'll be home before nine," I called, holding my breath as I walked to the front door. Momma was still setting up the table and talking to the guest. She told me to be safe and be home no later than that. I closed the door behind me.

I did it. I made it out of the house. Ron's car, however, was nowhere in sight. Our roads stretched long, and there were no headlights on either end. I walked away from my house and out of any view that could be seen from any window. My feet began to hurt as I stood motionless in my heels, shifting my weight every so often.

Growing colder and more disappointed with every fleeting moment, I checked my watch to read it was nearly seven. My heart began to sink slowly. It wasn't fast, like immediate sorrow. It was a pulsating wave of steady heartache. I suppose it was silly of me to get so caught up in the idea of a boy I barely knew, but everything about him seemed so exciting. I couldn't help but be completely drawn in.

Right before any tears were shed, I saw a car pull up. Within fragments of a second, my heart began to flutter. The car's engine was quite clamorous and could easily be heard from my parents' bedroom. I saw that it was him, and I quickly shuffled into the car, hoping to be light on my feet. Expecting an immediate apology for the delay, I furrowed my brow at Ron's seemingly cavalier attitude. In place of an apology, he complimented my hair, which was enough to make me blush. *I am so weak.*

"Where are we going?" I asked nervously, trepidation dancing on my words.

"Friend's house," he replied as he made a hard right turn. I braced myself against the side of the door and let out a soft gasp. I had conflicting feelings about the idea of being in a group setting. For one, I was a bit disappointed. I was hoping for a more quiet, private environment where we could talk and get to know one another better. The idea of there being distractions was a bit frustrating. On the other hand, however, I clung to the idea of being with his friends. The concept of being completely alone with Ron in a private setting was daunting. I didn't know what he exactly wanted to do or try, and I didn't know what I wanted, for that matter. He was exciting and new. All of this was.

The car ride was awkwardly electric. Words weren't exchanged; I couldn't think of anything to say. Every rudimentary "getting to know you" style question was something I couldn't wrap my mind around. We simply sat in silence. It wasn't completely awkward, but it surely wasn't familiar grounds in this moment of pause, of hesitation, and trepidation. Knowing that something was likely to come, but uncertain of when or what.

Ron was still rather unknown to me, so it's not like with a family member where we could be both silent and it be normal. There was this urge for communication to learn about one another. Neither of us, however, took the plunge. Every so often, I would look at him and smile, and every so often, he would do the same.

I placed my hands in my lap, not knowing what to do with them. I wanted nothing more than for him to reach out and grab my hand, interlocking fingers, just as I saw my parents do, but considering I barely knew him, I suppose it was a bit out of place for now.

Ron's friend's house wasn't far, as we were there before I knew it. The house was small, with an unkept yard. It was hard to make much of the surrounding area considering it being dark out, but it appeared to be in a neighborhood that I had never been to before. Perhaps it was merely the night sky, and if it were morning, I would have known where I was.

Ron simply opened the door without a knock or ring of the doorbell. My eyes widened in surprise, but I walked on in with him.

The room was plainly decorated. A thick shag carpet spread across the room and showed signs of age with the amount of stains and dirt. The furniture was simple: a couch and matching chair set facing a television. A man, somewhere in his twenties, sat on the couch with a drink in hand. His eyes seemed lost somewhere else, and he nodded slowly when we entered. Ron and the man exchanged greetings, and I sheepishly waved. I suppose it was a bit more private than expected. Here I was, getting all twisted over the idea of a party I wasn't enthralled to attend.

"Do you want a drink?" Ron asked. I nervously accepted, not knowing exactly what he was offering but not wanting to seem rude. Rummaging through the refrigerator, Ron came back with two silver cans of something.

"Soda-pop?" I asked curiously, looking at the design with a sense of unfamiliarity.

"Beer," he said, correcting me. My eyes widened before I smiled politely. The can opened similarly to that of soda and had that same burst of carbonation. Without thinking, I took a small sip and tried not to recoil at the taste. I forced a smile as I swallowed hard. I don't know if I was supposed to do that.

Ron took my hand and led me into a back room of the house. The room was small and cramped, with a tall stack of books placed precariously on top of one another. The only light that ignited the room came from the window, only allowing me to see the most prominent features on Ron's face. We smiled at one another, our eyes meeting at the same time. The butterflies from before returned at full volume. We both sat on the bed and began arbitrary conversations.

The "getting to know you" questions were now in full force. Since we went to different schools, that was Ron's first question. He had many after that, as it quickly dawned on him that we had very different schooling experiences. I felt as my mouth fell open when he told me that his school didn't teach anything from the Bible.

We then bonded over our enjoyment of music. I told him that I played piano for quite a few years. When he asked why I stopped, I told him that my father said I wasn't good enough and was wasting his money. When I saw his face drop, I froze, suddenly guilty that I may have spoilt the mood. I didn't realize my little anecdote could be interpreted badly. He then talked about his love for playing the guitar and how he wanted to pursue playing in a band in the northeast.

As the conversation continued, his left leg slowly inched closer to my right. A quiet lull slipped between us but quickly broke when he told me I looked beautiful.

I suddenly understood why my mother would grin ear to ear every time my father would share the same sentiment. It felt as if he could tell me a million times, and I would still be utterly bursting each and every time. I don't know what it was; family members and friends had complimented me throughout the years with no physical reaction on my behalf. This time, however, euphoria burst from the center of my stomach in a way I had simply never felt before.

As he leaned in and kissed me, I sat there motionless on the bed with my eyes open, completely caught off guard even though the situation was clearly leading to that. It felt like fireworks, but ones that I couldn't quite see. The moment was something I knew to be theoretically exhilarating, but it was simply odd. It wasn't bad, but I felt incapable—like I didn't know what I was doing. The act was unbalanced; as I could easily tell he had more experience than me. Nerves blinded a moment of what could have been a crashing wave of bliss.

I tried to focus on something, anything, at that moment; I just didn't know where to look. He wore a thin necklace with dog tags at the end. The silver gleamed when the moon would hit it just right. A framed photograph of a woman by the beach hung just behind Ron's head. She posed in what looked to be underwear blowing a kiss to the camera. I probably looked so strange, my eyes darting around the room in the attempt to calm down while being kissed.

Was this okay? Was I supposed to be doing this? If my parents found out, boy, would I be in trouble... First kiss jitters transformed from stomach butterflies to cold sweats. This was probably bad. Was this bad? Am I a bad person? I was doing something wrong wasn't I? *I'm sorry.*

What once was sweet, soft kisses that I would see my parents exchange were now turning aggressive. A dizzying sensation came over me, not from feelings of elation, but merely a lack of oxygen. I broke away, leading Ron to have a puzzled look on his face. He asked if I was okay, and I said that I was because I didn't think I had any other option. Catching my breath and analyzing the situation, I allowed myself to mostly fall back into his embrace, my spine still tense.

I felt his hands touch parts of my body that no one had dared to touch. I felt scared but, at the same time, invigorated. I felt curious but at the same time deeply shameful. It was moving faster than desired, but I suddenly was very small and incapable of saying no. I lay silent in the dark as I felt his fingers fumble with the buttons on my blouse. My heart raced wildly below my flesh, and I prayed that he didn't notice. With the rate at which it was going though, it seemed impossible for him not to. It felt as though my heart slammed into my bones with each beat. A devilish grin spread across his face when my top lay only upon my bare shoulders. Exhilaration radiated off of Ron, pairing in contrast with my anxiety. It wasn't long before all clothes were a background item, and we were all but skin and sound. I bled while he moaned.

ONE

The night I lost my virginity, I lay in my bed, staring woefully at the ceiling. I didn't know what to feel. I wasn't sure how I was supposed to feel. Girls at the schoolhouse had gossiped on the topic in passing, very few saying it meant nothing. However, many said it meant everything. If I had to choose, I would fall somewhere in the middle. I didn't expect to have such an apathetic approach. I didn't necessarily intend to have sex that night, so I did not have much time for mental preparation.

Most notably, everyone often spoke about how it is something you reserve for marriage. All my life, that was what I had heard. It was taught to me at a young age with a more watered-down description, using phrases and metaphors that I could comprehend. As I got older, the messages became more frank and straightforward. It's simple, really: fall in love, get married, and then you can have sex. It is God's gift to the married couple for abstaining. Starting backward left a bad taste in my mouth. While I didn't feel like a new person, I felt I had suddenly experienced this huge life thing, but because I went about it improperly, I now had this huge secret.

Such a burden it would be to carry, the words to hang consistently on the tip of my tongue until one day, I slip. I had essentially turned my back on everything I had learned and grown up to uphold in a sheer matter of moments. How did it happen all so quickly?

I had never done anything wrong before. My parents, the schoolhouse teachers, and the church elders all warned us kids how a child can so easily disobey the word of the Lord. It just seemed like silly stories. Of course, I wouldn't do such a thing! That wasn't me! But it was me. Within such a short time period, it was me. I was the warning story. I had betrayed God. There was no coming back from that. Was there?

I slipped out of my bed and fell onto my knees, clasping my hands together. Typically, when I would go to pray, I would do it in bed, hands together, and my body relaxed. This time was different. My fingers twitched, my lower lip trembled, and I began to cry.

"I'm sorry," I whispered. I didn't want to wake my parents. I couldn't even imagine how they would react. My body flinched at the idea.

"I'm sorry, Lord. I'm sorry." I wept. I had nothing else to say. Sorrow was all I felt, so sorry was all I spoke.

Stifling my sobs, I climbed back into my bed. My pillowcase grew damp with my tears. With my blanket pulled up to my mouth, I buried my face into the fabric. I deserved this, the anguish. Every tear, every sob was brought on by my own lust. My mouth curved downward into a disgusted scowl, my teeth grinding into each other. This was all my fault. I did it all wrong. If I had simply followed in my parents' footsteps, I would have been fine. There were plenty of kind Godly men in our community that I could be paired with. Why did I have to do this?

Now, none of them would want me, a mere plucked flower. I balled up my fists, my fingernails digging deep into my palms. My brow furrowed with the pain, but I deserved it. I squeezed harder. My wrists grew tired quickly. Fed up with my weakness, I scraped my nails into the skin of my forearms. A dark pink line quickly rose from my action, with fragments of white tissue on my torn skin. The area was hot to the touch, but in the darkness, I saw no blood.

WALKING into the pet store the next day, I saw Virginia in Ron's place. Confused, I scoped the store layout to find no one else there. I wanted to brush it off. Perhaps he caught a cold or simply had something else going on, but I couldn't help but feel that he was gone because of me. In the back room, I stared at the schedule. I had begun to notice that whenever there were alterations made, they would be written in red ink. By the looks of the sheet, no changes were documented. As I walked back to the sales floor, Virginia nodded in my direction, to which I awkwardly waved back. She had a perturbed look noticeably written across her face.

"Where's Ron?" I asked.

"Bailed," she muttered, her tone of voice telling far more than her one word. Not wanting to pester her further, I walked to the back of the store with the birdcages. Some were missing from the last time I saw them. I suppose that was a good thing, but it made me just the slightest bit glum that I couldn't hang out with them.

I didn't go out—I didn't know where or who to go with. If I wasn't at work, I was with my family. Friends from school I kept only mild contact with, so my colleagues were the only non-family members I saw on a regular basis. I was bursting at the seams holding in the news of Ron and me having sex, but it felt as if there was no one to share it with. As much as Virginia seemed perfectly content with not talking, I walked up to her anyway. Not knowing how to introduce the topic, I simply stared at her feet before she asked me what I needed.

"Ron and I had sex a few days ago," I blurted out. Well, so much for the plan of secrecy. This was enough to pique her interest as her eyebrow raised in curiosity.

"Wow. Well, how was it?" She prompted with a faint air of condescendence. I gathered from her tone that she didn't exactly believe me.

"Okay, I guess?" I said, delivering the statement in the tone of a question. This provoked a stifled laugh from her, and she shook her head. Virginia stopped and stared at me for a moment, her eyes dancing across my every piece of my flesh.

"Was that your first?" she asked quietly. I nodded sheepishly, not knowing what her response would be. She smiled earnestly and we talked about the subject for quite some time. Only two customers showed that day, so we had the afternoon to discuss as much as we pleased. It was comforting.

Over a matter of a few hours, she turned into the older sister I never had. A part of me felt a tinge of guilt that I wasn't having this conversation with my mom, but for some odd reason, it felt more natural to open up to someone I hardly knew. Plus, to have the conversation with my mother would have included unwanted parenting. While I couldn't predict her exact answer, there was a chance I was to be scolded, punished, or something along those lines. It was refreshing to speak in a neutral environment. She was an outsider to the rest of my life, but I felt safe.

~

THE NEXT DAY, my family and I woke up early for church. Our home was located close to the building, near the beginning of the neighborhood, making it a rather short walk. Considering the mild weather, it was quite a peaceful scene. My mother and father had their arms interlocking as us kids followed behind like a line of ducks. For years, we would walk, holding one another's hands, but I suppose one day we simply grew out of it. It was likely around the time when Judith had lost a bit of her child-like spark that inspired her to run everywhere, always out of reach.

Walking into church, I saw the same faces I grew up with, but with years layered upon their flesh. Faces that were once round and soft turned angular and mature, and those who were already grown grew withered and wise.

The reverend began his introductions, making note of the number of young adults in his flock. With that in mind, he started reciting sermons that spoke of abstinence. How apt that he would. I mean, why speak of literally anything else? If I hadn't slept with Ron, it would have been about any other old topic and passage, but the stars aligned in an irksome coincidence.

I nervously wrung my hands and looked at the ground. I couldn't have made myself look more guilty if I tried.

"Flee from sexual immorality. All other sins a person commits are outside the body, but whoever sins sexually, sins against their own body." Corinthians 6:18.

My body was reacting to the words spoken as if the reverend were spitting the words at me directly, calling me by name. My body grew hot, spreading from the nape of my neck outward before turning into a cold sweat. My stomach grew nauseous with every passing second. Even sitting, I was stuck with a dizzying sensation. The light emerging from the windows was utterly blinding. Everything simply felt too much. Judith noticed and asked if I was alright. I smiled weakly and nodded despite my appearance, likely suggesting otherwise. She didn't need to know.

I stared down at the floor. Deep maroon carpeting stared back. I tried to calm my body down but I had no idea what was happening. I said a silent prayer. Whether that would help or hinder, I was still willing to try. Would He even listen to me anymore?

The world around me was closing in, and in response, I felt myself start to cry. I pressed my lips together to conceal them from quivering and let my hair fall in front of my face to hide my red eyes. It was really quite obvious that I was crying, but I had to at least attempt to mask it.

After the service, my parents thanked the reverend and commended him on his words. Feeling slightly better, I stood by their side and smiled despite hardly paying any attention to their conversation. I primarily concentrated on my breathing to help ease my nausea.

Thinking back to breakfast, nothing I had eaten was out of the ordinary or seemed off. Even if, perhaps, I had eaten spoiled food, no one else appeared to be having a similar reaction. I looked at Isaiah, and he seemed himself. My parents were fine and well enough to be engaging in conversations, and Judith, if anything, seemed bored. Comparing myself to my siblings, I was obviously the odd one out. Trying my hardest, I attempted to compose my fallen face and my trembling body. I figured that the harder I tried to emulate being fine, the more it would come true.

The reverend smiled a humble smile at my parents. I knew very little about our reverend, but from what I did, I knew he was a kind man. His wife quickly walked over to us, slithering her hand onto his shoulder. I always remembered his wife for one of two reasons. The first was her name, Judy, so similar to Judith that it was impossible to forget. The second is her eyes. Her entire demeanor was a bit unsettling, but her eyes really solidified that. Large and blue, always staring as if consistently looking for something. Her mascara was smudged, making it look as if she had just wiped away tears. I would be more concerned if she didn't always look like that.

When we returned home, my mother entered my bedroom and gracefully sat on my bed. I looked at her curiously, not knowing what brought her.

"You know…" She started with a shy smile. What followed was not at all what I expected to fall from her lips, but considering what today's sermon included, I shouldn't have been as surprised as I was. She began to ask me if any of the boys in our town piqued my interest. I was being taunted.

I remember going to school and, every once in a while, having a crush on a fellow classmate. I never became close friends with any of them, but I knew if I said any of their names, my mother would take the initiative to speak to them for me or, worse yet, talk to their parents. That scenario, however, was far better than telling her about the random boy at the pet store I had barely known before sleeping with him.

I said nothing in return, not knowing what to say. She then went on to tell me about a friend of hers who has a son my age, as if I didn't grow up knowing who he was. We were never really friends, nor was he a classmate I ever looked at in such a way, but we were always friendly to one another. He was just another Joseph. She left my room not long after that, leaving an odd lingering energy that stayed after she left. I wondered if she had a similar conversation with Isaiah, considering he was two years my senior.

~

I DID my best to appear normal, like I wasn't sitting on a massive secret. I participated in nightly dinner conversations with my family. I would help my mother with meals and setting the table. Judith and I would laugh together as she would recount her day at school to me. Nothing was out of line. As days turned to weeks, no one asked if anything was the matter. The guilt, however, never went away. I would retire to my bedroom after a night of merriment only for my face to fall, remembering what I had done. Some nights were worse than others. When I got too overwhelmed, I would pull at my hair to stop myself from crying. If my eyes were to be swollen the next day, someone was bound to notice. That all was in the darkness, though, when no one was looking. On the surface, I thought I hid it all quite well. That was until I couldn't.

A couple of weeks after the incident, I began to feel sick. Luckily, Virginia was working with me that day, so I could lament to her about it. As I stood up to get dressed, I felt as if every fragment of energy had been sucked out of me. My body felt near lifeless. The mere act of putting on my work clothes seemed unnecessarily strenuous. I attempted to simply shake it off, but it lingered with me like an unwelcome shadow always close behind.

Driving to work only seemed to increase my ailments. My knuckles were pale as I gripped the steering wheel with all my force. I tried my best to concentrate on the road, but my efforts were futile. I watched in dismay at the weathered road conditions, physically bracing myself for every crack in the road. As I continued, my vision began to relax and became blurry due to mere exhaustion. It was a relatively straight drive from my home to the pet store, so I wasn't terribly worried despite it still being abhorrently dangerous.

As the car seemingly drove itself, a shocking jolt brought me back to reality as I realized I must have driven over a pothole in the road. The abrupt jerk caused my stomach to feel as if every organ inside of me shifted.

Nausea was no longer a mild sensation, but a crippling one. My mouth quickly grew full with saliva, which I uncomfortably swallowed. As I began to feel myself grow sicker with every passing second, I pulled over to the side of the road, my tires rolling to a halt. I threw my body against the car door, leading it to open with such a mighty force as I came stumbling out. The side of the road was nothing but gritty dirt, a noise usually quite noticeable when walking along it, but my senses were so distorted that I didn't hear that familiar sound. I did, however, feel that granular sensation under my shoes, one I always liked for some reason. Standing along the side of the road, I crouched down, my hands gripping my legs. My hair fell in my face as I was positioned downward, blocking my view. The last thing in the world I wanted to do at that moment was go to work, but I felt as if I had no other option. It would get worse before it would get better. That was the moment when I threw up heavily all along the dirt path.

"Hey!" Virginia shouted when I entered the store. Her delighted expression quickly turned into concern under closer inspection. She asked if I had heard from Ron, since he hadn't been showing up to any of his scheduled shifts. I weakly shook my head and told her I didn't have his phone number. Noticing my distress, she asked if I was feeling alright. She brought the back of her hand to my forehead. Sweat had melted into my skin, so although my head wasn't wet to the touch, it wasn't completely dry. I shrugged before saying that I must've caught a stomach bug. Virginia seemed satisfied with the answer, but only for a second before a look of shock washed over her face.

"You don't think?" she asked, trailing off. I stood motionless, waiting for her to finish her sentence. When I didn't respond she made a face as if I were supposed to answer her incomplete question.

"You don't think you're pregnant, do you?"

Sexual education was something you learned in city schools. It was a worldly topic not meant to be taught at our schoolhouse. It spoke of unnatural acts with unnecessary information, or so I was told. At the schoolhouse, the girls would learn how to read, write, and do basic math problems. There was a concentration on how to cook, clean, and maintain a suitable home for children, though. I knew how to get pregnant, but a lot of the signs and symptoms I didn't know as well. The most basic definition was taught to us, leaving out anything that might be helpful to know.

Many of the girls I had gone to school with were already mothers and, in some cases, to multiple children. My mother had Isaiah at my age, with my father only a year older. Knowing that most women in my town had children at or around my age didn't dissolve the fact that I couldn't see myself as a mother, and I couldn't comprehend the possibility of being pregnant. I still felt quite like a child myself.

"I don't know," I said meekly. My voice was soft, frightened like that of a child who was just scolded. No one else was scheduled until hours later, but considering it was a weekday morning, our slowest time during store hours, Virginia took my hand and locked up the store. She and I walked down the street to a corner market. She wrapped her arm around my shoulders and walked with me at a speed that didn't upset my stomach heavily. I looked over my shoulder consistently in case any patrons tried to enter the pet store, but none ever did.

The store only had one pregnancy test kit cradled in a bulky box with a thin layer of dust covering it. I found myself standing in our store's restroom, Virginia hovering right outside. My fingers, numb from the cold, fumbled trying to remove the test from its packaging. As my eyes scanned the instructions, I realized that I hadn't understood a word of what I was reading. I softly shook my head before rereading each word carefully. Once completed, I stared feverishly at the instructions making sure I did everything correctly. According to the papers, the test took about two hours to give an answer. I was surely in no mental state to work, but considering we had no customers, I could fret in peace.

TWO HOURS. One hundred and twenty minutes. Seven thousand two hundred seconds.

I STOOD next to the register and anxiously wrung my hands. There was nothing else in the world I could possibly attempt to concentrate on. The world had narrowed into such a minute measurement that everything else appeared nonexistent.

The nausea came in waves. If I stood perfectly still, it was almost as if I were okay, but if I were to merely turn my head, all progress had seemingly been lost. I wanted to place my hand on my stomach, but I knew if I did, Virginia would say something, and I wasn't in the mood for talking.

I began to read about the ingredients contained in the fish food. I stared at the keys on the register. My eyes darted around the store to find something interesting, but nothing was distracting.

I wanted a customer to come into the store with not much in mind to buy but simply wanting to talk off the ear of the closest store employee. Tell me what store existed before this one, tell me what this city used to be named when you were young, and tell me the names, ages and hobbies of each of your grandchildren. I wanted someone to walk in who talked simply to hear their own voice, someone who thought they were the wisest and most interesting person in the vicinity.

After glancing at my watch, I saw that I still had another hour before I would find out the result. I both wanted time to stop in order not to know the answer, as well as speed to the point where I would already know. I wanted the hard truth but also blissful ignorance.

I had a 50/50 chance, and considering how my body was behaving, it gave away what the likely outcome was. I felt as my stomach began to turn, even though I was positive there was nothing left inside it.

Before I knew it, Virginia shook my shoulders, telling me it was time. Goodness, why would she shake my shoulders? We walked into the back room of the store together, and she squeezed my hand reassuringly. I truly appreciated the support she had shown me, but there was no act or gesture that would calm what I was feeling. After looking at the test and the instructions, I had my answer.

A solemn silence slipped over the room. My body went cold, starting from my hands and feet, before all meeting in the middle. I didn't know whether to laugh or cry, so I simply stood there, motionlessly. The stillness of the room was omnipresent, with the only thing breaking it being my jagged breathing. With my body turned to ice, I was incapable of anything but staring at my fate.

"What are you going to do?" Virginia whispered. I shook my head, unable to speak. There were no words to be found. "Are you gonna get an abortion?"

That was a word that I had heard in passing. Thinking it was never applicable to me, I never took the time to research an exact definition as I only knew it to have a negative connotation from those around me. I looked to Virginia to educate me on the term, which she did, answering my each and every question. I asked her if she ever had one, to which she replied no, but a close friend of hers did whom she accompanied. After mulling over the idea, I found it to be the logical option.

Virginia let me leave the store early as it wasn't too long before Gregory was to come in. My hands shook, feeling as if there were no way to ease my nerves. I don't know how I drove home; I truly couldn't remember. One moment, I was sitting in the store's parking lot, and the next, I was pulled up to the side of my home. Checking the time, it wouldn't be a long wait before my father was to be home from work. Although far more daunting, I preferred to have one large conversation as opposed to repeating myself to each parent.

I sat outside my house, unable to leave the car. Both hands continued clutching the wheel despite being parked and having turned the car off. My fingers had become one with the steering wheel, both molded from the same slab of metal. My clothes, stitched together with the fabric of the seat. I existed to be the centerpiece, with the car being my frame. There was no going anywhere. Sobs began to ripple out of me like ocean currents. How could I have done this? How could I have let this happen? I was weak. Babies are supposed to be a gift from God, but it felt like He was punishing me. I committed a sin, so now I had to face the consequences. I sobbed, sobbed till my face was red, and I was gasping for breath.

"I'm sorry, Lord. I'm so sorry." I wept, choking on air.

It took a while to collect myself. My emotions were unusually high, but perhaps given the circumstances, it was usual. I checked my face in the rearview mirror. My nose was red, and my face was spotty. I looked like a complete wreck. There was no way I could just walk into the house like this; my family would think something happened. Sure, something surely was happening, but I at least wanted to start out with a voice that didn't waver and eyes that weren't swollen.

Two young kids ran together in the street. One fell to his knees, and I expected an outburst, but it was within a second that he was back to chasing the other. Braver than I, that little one. If I had fallen, acquiring a small pain, I would surely be in tears. The mind games pregnancy pulls were cruel, and I was only a few short weeks in.

After sitting in my car for some time, I realized I would have to get this over with sooner or later. Checking my reflection and seeing it was back to normal, I took that as my go-ahead.

As I shut the car door behind me, my heart skipped a beat. Oh God. I was actually going to do this. I'm going to tell my parents that I got pregnant. I stopped for a moment. Should Ron be with me? Should we tell my parents together? Should I tell him first? My plan stopped resembling a plan the more questions I asked myself. I didn't know how to do this. It was all so adult. I had been to baby showers and the mom always seemed so together, so confident. Tears welled in my eyes and I sighed in defeat. I would be out here all day.

After slipping into my parents' house, I immediately went to my room, unseen by anyone. I exhaled slowly. I went from one confinement to another. At least this one had a bed to lay on. I removed my work nametag and set it on my bedside table. As I lay in bed, I felt the nausea return. My body really wanted to kick me while I was down. I propped my feet up on the bed, my knees to the sky, hoping to ease my stomach. It wasn't a cure, but I didn't throw up, so I considered it a victory.

I slowly ambled to my bookcase to retrieve the Bible I used in school. The stitching was worn, with many pages weathered from time. There had to be something in there to ease all of it.

Why are you cast down, O my soul,
and why are you disquieted within me?
Hope in God; for I shall again praise him,
my help and my God. Psalm 42:11

I SUPPOSE THAT WAS APPLICABLE. The words on those thin paper pages had once been my ultimate saving grace. On nights when I let my emotions overtake me, I would turn to His word for peace. So often did it work; I simply allowed myself to let whatever issue I suffered from at that moment ripple through me, trusting that the Lord would ease my suffering. This was a much larger, more complicated situation. It's not that I didn't trust Him; I just was a bit unsure of how I would become calm.

Before saying a silent prayer to myself, I decided it was time. I opened my bedroom door and hoped that I would not vomit. My entire family was in the same general area of the dining room. I was hoping this conversation would be limited to just my parents. Obviously, Isaiah and Judith were to know at some point, but I wanted to speak to my parents privately first.

"Can I talk to them alone for a second?" I asked in a hushed tone to my siblings, nodding toward my parents. My mother adjusted her posture, and my father cocked his head. Isaiah, without any hesitation, exited the room with Judith right behind.

"What's on your mind, Ema?" my father asked kindly. Now that the spotlight was on me, I felt as if I were to be sick. My entire body grew warm and my palms became sweaty. As I stared at each parent with love and care in their eyes, I felt my throat close and my vision blurred with tears. It had to be said, but my body was shutting down immediately. Avoiding eye contact was the way to go. I looked down, away from their concerned stares. I eyed the floor, the perfectly manicured floor.

"I'm sorry," I whispered before a tear fell down my face. My breathing grew rapidly, and it felt as if the world were spinning too fast. My father took my wrist and led me to a chair. I couldn't quite concentrate on their expressions as concentrating on anything felt impossible in those moments. Holding back only meant I was delaying the inevitable. The sooner it was said, the sooner it was over. Dragging this out would only make it worse. I had to just say it. Lord, guide me.

"I'm pregnant."

The words, spoken in a hushed tone, echoed through the halls. The world felt uncomfortably silent; it was as if I had the entire world as my audience. I held my breath as I thought that my own breathing was too loud. At that moment, a pin dropping would shatter eardrums.

THE FIRST PART WAS DONE. I said it. I let the words spill out of my mouth and float into the air with a lack of gravity. My mother's face twisted into a confused stare before breaking into some kind of smile. My mother was a beautiful woman, but that expression was so strange. My father wore a blank expression giving no indication of any specific emotion. I sat in the most painfully awkward silence, mentally begging for someone to speak up. To comfort, to yell, it truly did not matter, I simply wanted noise. The deafening silence was driving me mad.

"Where is the man who did this?" my father asked coldly. I swallowed hard before adjusting myself in the chair. I don't know why I expected a more loving response, but his tone unnerved me further. This was not ideal, but not off the rails yet.

"I do not know. I have not seen him in some time." I spoke each word slowly, trying not to allow my emotions to overflow into my voice. They didn't need to see that.

"Does he not know you are carrying his child?" my mother asked softly.

"Not that I'm aware of, no." My father stared at me with eyes holding a meaning that I couldn't quite decipher. The closest thing I could come up with is disgust, like he couldn't look at me as his child anymore now that I had sex. I couldn't break my gaze from his face. His expression read so many emotions: angry, hurt, betrayed, worried, confused. There was surely not a positive emotion in there. I held my breath, waiting for him to speak. I needed to know what he was thinking.

"What's done is done, and before we know it, we'll be holding our first grandchild!" my mother said, breaking the silence instead. I took my eyes off of my father and looked at her. She was simply glowing. Her smile appeared a bit forced, but otherwise, she was happier than I expected.

"Wait, no, I don't want to have the baby!" I exclaimed, my voice quivering, panic rising.

"Of course you do! You're just nervous. Every woman feels that way; it's completely normal." She waved me off and snickered at my fear.

"Momma, I'm only eighteen, I don't want a baby," I said. Tears that had once dried had now reformed.

Despite there being no actual interruptions, I felt as if I were being talked over. In my peripheral vision, I saw Judith and Isaiah come into the kitchen. Judith was bouncing with elation, clearly not picking up on my or our father's emotions. Isaiah looked stunned, his gaze only on me with question marks in his eyes. He almost appeared hurt, as if wishing I had told him first before telling our parents. A part of me wishes I had done that as well. He was my first friend in the world, and he and I used to tell each other everything. I had left him out of so much of my life recently that it felt natural to exclude him from this. I don't even know if he knew where the pet store was. I mentally promised myself, and him, we would reconnect and talk about it all together. I would catch him up on my life and give him a more detailed view of what was happening.

"Is he from that job of yours?" my father asked solemnly. I nodded quickly. He stood up and sighed, rubbing his forehead. My mom stood up and clapped, squealing with joy. My body shrank down, feeling like I was a mere child again. Truthfully, I was still a child, but larger, with my perception distorted. Everyone began speaking all at once except for my father. Baby names, baby showers, and things of that nature were brought up at rapid speed.

"No, you're not listening to me!" I said. And no one was.

"We're having a baby!" my mother exclaimed, and the whole family crowded on top of me in the most sinister hug.

WEEK 7. MONTH 1

I stared into the kitchen to see my family sitting at the table. Confused as to why I wasn't asked to join, I tentatively stood in the shadows, waiting for someone to turn around. Each person's back was to me, and all I could hear was a slow mumbling, too quiet for me to pinpoint anything specific. What they were muttering didn't even sound like words, but just an ongoing noise as if they were machines. As I approached, the sound increased naturally, and I realized they were praying with their hands clasped together. It made sense for them to do it without me, as I had recently become a bit of a controversial figure. I felt rather arrogant to assume that they were praying for me, though I couldn't help but smile, as the notion warmed my heart. I waited cautiously for them to finish, but their prayer seemed never-ending. My smile slowly slipped from my lips. Being the controversial figure did not warrant me warm wishes but exclusion instead.

I felt as my stomach slowly dropped, and my face fell. I knew that my parents would be unhappy with me, but I didn't expect to be treated as if I weren't even present. It was physically shocking, leaving me with a cold feeling in the pit of my stomach. The taste of rejection was unfamiliar to me. All I knew from my family was warmth and love; I never once saw my parents fight and I never got into an altercation with a sibling. My days from infancy to childhood to adolescence had been nothing short of rainbows and sunshine, from what my memory allows. My life was never short of familial care and praise. The sudden shift was jarring.

Fed up with how long it was taking, I walked around to see them but gasped in horror. Each one of their faces had become morbidly distorted. Their eye sockets sagged down to where their noses should be. Their mouths fell agape but done so in such an exaggerated way that could only be done if their jaws had been broken. It looked as if each person's face was melting in slightly different ways. Their eyes were all vacant. They were open, but not really looking at anything. All light or any spark of life had dimmed completely. There was a glossy haze to it, making it appear as if they had been stuck in this position for quite some time now. The prayers came out of their mouths, but not one of their lips moved. The noise simply echoed out of each person's throat as if their mouths were but a radio, the noise even having a slightly tinny quality.

The situation posed an uncomfortable number of questions. For example, who did this? Where was I? What had happened? Upon close inspection, none of my family members seemed hurt. There were no bruises, cuts, or any other signs of harm. It was as if someone had sculpted each family member out of clay and left them out in the sun. I rushed to their sides despite my trepidation. I cautiously went to touch their faces. They felt slick, like the side of a candle, waxy too. Their skin had a slight sheen when the light reflected just right. What were they? The noise emitted from their mouths was indeed coming from their mouths but how?

Judith, being the closest person to me, I stared at her. Her mouth fell slightly askew, favoring the right. Nervously, I reached my hand to her mouth. The noise didn't waver. I extended my hand forward, my fingertips touching her lips. There was no warmth or sign of breathing. I lost confidence and quickly drew back my hand, the hair on my arms sticking up straight. Each person's face was terrifying to witness; I tried to concentrate on anything else. It felt impossible, but I averted my eyes to the rest of the kitchen. From spices to kitchen towels to utensils, each and every item was in its proper place, with the only deviation being the obvious. I stared in disbelief at the perfection of everything around me. It felt too realistic to be a dream, but then there was no explanation for my family. I began rummaging through each drawer in the kitchen, and not one single item was out of place or unusual. As I searched, the sound of their prayers increased in volume. Each second, it only grew louder, to the point of it being deafening. I covered my ears with my hands, wincing at the sound. Trying to be as far from it as possible, I walked backward, further into the kitchen. As I did, I accidentally knocked a knife off of the counter. As it clamored to the floor, I gasped awake.

I FOUND myself wrapped in the comforts of my bedroom. I listened intently for the ominous chanting but was met with ameliorating silence. Rubbing at my eyes, to rid myself of the images from my nightmare, I couldn't shake off the feeling of dread. Obviously, having experienced nightmares before, I knew the difference between reality and my subconscious, but something about it felt so uncomfortably familiar. The distortions often seen in dreams of mundane things were not to be found.

Climbing out of bed, I anxiously left my bedroom. The sounds of my mom clearing away a few dishes and humming softly to herself found me before formally seeing her. As I stepped into the kitchen, a rush of smells wrapped around me. It was all so pungent. It smelled so abhorrently greasy. What likely was a simple breakfast for Judith smelled of a bustling kitchen that had never been cleaned. My stomach instantly turned, and just as my mother noticed me standing there, I rushed to the bathroom to reject what little I had in me. I felt my mother's hands collect my hair from my face and rub at my back. Once done, I leaned back into her arms, recoiling at the sour taste left on my tongue.

"You're okay," she cooed and I groaned in response. I felt anything but okay.

"Momma, I don't want the baby," I said weakly.

"Sure, you do. The first few months are always hard, but, hey, they go by fast," she responded with a grin. I knew it would be hard to convince her, considering she had her first child at my age, but it was worth a try.

"This girl at work said I could get an abortion. I think I want to do that," I said in a small voice. My mother's face twisted into a disapproving scowl.

"Oh, no, no, no, honey. You don't need to do that." Her voice turned shocked, the voice I expected her to use when I initially broke the news to her of the pregnancy.

"I don't think I can raise the baby. I'm scared, and I don't know where the boy is," I said, trailing off. I felt odd for simply calling him "the boy." I didn't really want them to know his name and he wasn't by any means my boyfriend, so a mere boy was all he was.

"It takes a village to raise a child, and you've got one all under the same roof," she said with a smile, her tone now warm and motherly again. Without missing a beat, her smile then disappeared as she announced, "I don't like the ideas the people at your work are saying. I don't want you going back there."

"You want me to quit my job?" I asked, dumbfounded.

"If you aren't too sick, I'd do it today. Plus, you'll be feeling like this for quite some time. It'd be rude of you to be always calling out sick. Really, you'd be doing them and yourself a big favor."

I went back to bed not long after that conversation. I pondered over the idea of not working anymore and grew sad. I had really grown fond of Virginia as well as simply getting out of the house. While my mother had a valid point of me being likely too sick to show up for work some days, I wasn't sure if I wanted to leave. As I curled up in my bedsheets, I felt my face fall in sorrow.

Later on that day, I got up to go to work. My nausea subsided enough for me to drive, but there were moments when I had to pull over to the side of the road in case I was to get sick again. Thankfully, the roads weren't busy or else I likely would've been in an accident.

Walking into the store, I saw Gregory and Virginia talking at the front register. I didn't recall ever seeing them interact with each other. When I really thought about it, I couldn't recall Gregory talking to anyone. I was thankful that each of them was there; as with Gregory, I needed to inform him of my resignation, and, as with Virginia, to simply see a friendly face.

"I need to speak with you both," I said, my voice small, lacking confidence. I felt my hands tremble, so I clasped them in front of my stomach. Neither said a word and simply stared at me, waiting for me to speak up. Virginia's expression turned rather grim, likely aware of what was to come.

"I'm sorry, but I have to quit," I blurted out. Gregory raised an eyebrow. Virginia shut her eyes briefly and sighed.

"Why?" Gregory asked, his voice near a perfect monotone.

"I'm pregnant. My mom said it would be best for me to stay home."

Once Gregory left for his lunch break, Virginia approached me, asking why I was keeping the baby. I told her that my parents wouldn't let me do anything else besides continue through with the pregnancy. I bit my tongue to stop tears from forming, but that proved little aid. I barely even knew her for a month, but I knew I would miss her terribly.

The shift flew by like a breeze. It made sense. The days where I didn't exactly want to be there or have people to talk to, the days dragged, but when I wanted to soak in as much as possible, it was as if time had been altered to accelerate wildly. With Gregory being there, Virginia and I couldn't spend nearly as much time together talking. Frustrating, but understandable.

They had me stationed next to the rodents. A few of the mice were missing, likely bought by a snake owner or perhaps a classroom teacher. The rats were all the same, scurrying around with no discernable differences. The hamsters were the same in terms of quantity, but one of them appeared a bit larger around its midsection. I peered at it woefully, hoping that it was alright and wasn't sick or in pain. I continued standing in the same position, yawning like clockwork. It felt as if I hadn't slept in a fortnight, and I had to yawn to reignite my consciousness. Virginia passed by me at one point with a broom. The sudden appearance of a person made me jump ever so slightly.

"Have you heard from Ron?" I blurted out. Considering it

was now my last day, and I had no way of contacting him, I wanted to know so I could tell him of the situation. She shook her head and said that due to the lack of contact and the number of missed shifts, they'd taken him off the schedule. I asked her if she knew where he lived but was once again met with uncertainty. Gregory was more likely to know but disclosing information like that would be a breach of privacy.

It felt unwittingly wrong not to tell Ron. I felt he deserved to know, and it was driving me mad having no form of communication to reach him. Knowing that he wasn't picking up his phone, wasn't showing up to work, and not having his address made the dynamic difficult. Although he drove me to his friend's home that one time, I knew I wouldn't be able to remember exactly how to get there. It was dark, I wasn't paying close attention, and I didn't really even meet his friend to be able to recognize him. The chances of Ron never finding out felt astronomically high. It's not that I expected him to step into a fatherly role; I simply felt bad about his lack of awareness. Not knowing that somewhere out there, you have a child. Fifty percent of your DNA existing somewhere in the world. Perhaps one day I would get the opportunity to tell him, or he would find out through rumors. It wasn't my fault after all that he didn't know. I tried.

As my shift came to an end, I felt my chest grow heavy. Gregory could not have been more indifferent to the situation, but Virginia had a look of worry painted on her face. I assured her that I would be fine, but I knew she didn't believe me. Hell, I hardly believed me. She wrapped me in a tight hug. The scent of cigarettes flooded my nostrils, and I quickly held my breath. I was already perturbed by how sensitive I was becoming to scents. She told me to visit, and I told her I would, knowing I likely wouldn't. If my mother demanded me to quit so suddenly, if she knew I were to visit, there'd be a price to pay.

Walking out of the store, I allowed my emotions to escape. I didn't want to cry in front of them. For one, I felt it may look a bit silly, as I only worked there for such a short time. I also simply didn't want to allow that slip of vulnerability. I knew I could simply blame my being pregnant for the emotions, but I knew that wasn't all of it.

As I climbed inside my car, I cried angry tears, angry at my mother for making me quit. While I suppose it made perfect sense in her eyes, I found it wildly unfair. Mother knows best. Do not disobey.

Once home, as I walked to the front door, the wind stung my eyes, and my skin felt tight across my face. Inside, Judith was drawing on a piece of paper, a bored expression on her face. As I sat my bag on the floor, my mother came rushing over towards me with a look of controlled fire in her eyes.

"Where have you been? I've been absolutely worried sick!" she exclaimed. Judith cowered in the corner, shooting me a sheepish look.

"I was at the pet store. You told me to quit," I said softly, unaccustomed to her scolding tone of voice.

"For five hours?" Her voice holds motherly concern but her face doesn't display any motherly love.

"Momma, I had a shift to work," I said with a slight chuckle. "I couldn't just quit and leave." In reality, I could have, but she didn't need to know that.

"Well, as long as you quit," she said, losing her anger. As she realized her outburst was a bit of an exaggeration, she coyly ambled back to the kitchen. Once gone, I sat in the living room with Judith. She looked up from her drawing and smiled at me.

"So, are you gonna marry him?" Judith asked, her feet swaying in the air as she colored while on her stomach.

"What?" I asked with a laugh.

"The guy! Who made you pregnant!" The explanation wasn't exactly necessary.

"Well, probably not. He, well, he doesn't even know that I'm pregnant." Her eyes widened. She seemed to revel in the gossip at my expense.

"Why not?"

"Well, I don't have his telephone number and I don't know where he lives."

"Is he from your job?" she asked, her head tilted.

"Yes. He doesn't work there anymore though, so it's not like I can just go back there and find him."

"Mm." Her interest was waning and her eyes broke my gaze. I glanced over at her drawing. My blood ran cold as she was drawing the family as how I saw them in my nightmare. Their eyes were blackened out, their mouths unnaturally agape, melting into the floor.

"Jude, what is that?" I asked, taking the piece of paper out from under her.

"It's us?" she replied, confused. As I held the paper in my hands, she was right. It was us. There was nothing strange about it. The paper I saw two seconds prior was not the one I was holding in my grasp. It was the family sitting in the kitchen, but we looked normal. Judith was no special artist, so normal is used a bit loosely, but there was nothing unnatural about our appearances. We were a typical family in a child's drawing. I glanced at Judith, who wore an incredibly weirded out expression. I had no idea how to defend myself.

"Sorry, I thought I saw something," I muttered.

"Well anyway, you should try and find the guy. It'd be fun, like having another brother." Her innocence was starting to wear on me so I merely smirked in response before excusing myself.

~

Now alone in my room, I stood facing my mirror. I stripped down to nothing but my skin and stared at my stomach, as if it were to balloon in a matter of mere seconds. Nonetheless, I stared at my body, which was no stranger to me. I looked the same as I did a month ago. Placing my hands on my stomach, I felt nothing but a sense of anxiety. Immense dread seemed to spread throughout my entire being, all stemming from my core. Wrapping myself in a heavy robe, I felt protected and comforted, more so than my family had provided me since hearing the news.

A soft tapping at my door startled me, leading me to flinch as if someone had struck me. After taking a second to compose myself and let my heart rate return to normal, I opened the door. Judith stood curiously before me and greeted me with a smile. Perhaps she was about to apologize for her inane questions. She walked across the threshold without an invitation and sat on my bed. I stared at her silently, waiting for her to speak, while in the meantime, letting a mildly awkward silence drift through the room.

"What will you name the baby?" she finally asked, breaking the silence. Her legs kicked with a sort of child-like curiosity. I tried not to groan and roll my eyes. I didn't think I could mentally handle a round two of questions I didn't feel like answering.

On top of that, I had no answer for her. I hadn't even thought that far ahead to when it would eventually be born. I simply saw it as the thing inside of me, as if it were a new organ in my body. I didn't care to name it just as much as I didn't care to raise it. It did make me realize I wasn't just sick but was growing something that one day would be moving and breathing. I would have to name it, clothe it, bathe it, feed it, calm its cries, and teach it words. The idea made my eye twitch. I would think all of that over later.

"Well, I'm not quite sure. Have you got any suggestions?" I asked, trying to cover the fear in my voice. It wasn't Judith's fault that I was so anxious. I didn't want to project that onto her. If she wanted to be over the moon excited about my pregnancy, who was I to try and stop her? I could, however, do without a million questions.

"Name her after me!" she exclaimed with her on-brand enthusiasm. I smiled softly without saying much else. It's not that I didn't want her in my room; I just didn't have anything to say. She must have sensed that I wasn't up for much of an ongoing conversation, so she left not much after.

Watching her close the door behind her, I thought about her question, forcing myself to be calmer this time around. I suppose it was a logical question. I was pregnant, and you usually start to think of names before you have the baby. Having a baby shower and picking out items was also something I would likely have to embark upon as well the further I progressed. I remember when my mother was pregnant with Judith. I wouldn't have even known she was if it weren't for her protruding stomach. She carried on with her tasks effortlessly and never appeared to complain. I never once remember her being sick in the toilet or displaying any other common pregnancy signs. That seemed so odd to me, considering I felt like I was plagued by the flu nearly every moment.

I sat down on my bed and tried to make myself comfortable. I felt a headache coming, so I closed the blinds, sheathing the sun. As I tried to find a suitable position to lie in bed, I was bothered by a faint ringing noise. Furrowing my brow, I opened my eyes and looked around the room. There was no light on or anything to be making that noise. It was likely coming from another room and would hopefully cease shortly. As I tossed and turned, unable to nap properly, I sat upright in bed, willfully annoyed. The ringing noise grew louder and sharper. I opened my bedroom door with a fervor, hoping to find the cause.

In the kitchen, the piercing noise continued and grew far louder. It bounced off the cabinets, off the floors and the ceiling. It flooded my brain, and I felt it underneath my skin. I winced, perhaps even screamed; it was hard to tell exactly what was happening or what I was doing. I blinked hard and was back in my bedroom. The windows were dark, the blinds not drawn.

I lay motionless in bed, nearly breathless. What did I just do? How did I do that? Was it all a dream? Peering out the window, I saw it was surely nighttime. When I had laid down, it must've only been around four or so, right? I looked at my clock, and it read eleven. Aghast, I stared at the time. Did I miss dinner? My mother would surely have woken me up for that! If not her, then most definitely Judith. The gap in my doorway showed no light was on in the hallway. I really slept right through dinner! I suppose I really needed the sleep.

I WAS in the bathroom I shared with my siblings. I looked around, unsure of how I ended up there. The carpet felt dirty under me, as if it hadn't ever been cleaned and years of feet had worn it flat into the ground. The world felt hazy, like I wasn't properly awake yet. Chances are, I wasn't. I grabbed my hairbrush from the counter to untangle any knots. As I looked at myself in the mirror, I saw a woman standing behind me. My heart may have actually stopped. My body froze, incapable of running or screaming. I stood there in fear. I quickly looked behind me to find no one there. It made sense. The bathroom was quite small, and no one would be able to fit right behind me without needing a rib or two removed to make way for the towel rack. The woman, however, was still there. The mirror was dirty and foggy like someone just showered, but as I approached the reflection, I recognized the woman. It was Virginia. She had a concerned but encouraging look on her face. I once again looked back behind me as if, this time, she was about to show.

"Virginia?" I asked, but I was back in bed.

I was unaware that pregnancy gives you consistent, incredibly realistic dreams. That was something to not look forward to. As I gathered my bearings, my stomach churned. How was this even possible? I didn't eat dinner. I didn't even remember eating lunch! What was there to throw up? Gosh, and I was nowhere near the end. Feeling paralyzed by exhaustion, I couldn't muster the strength to get out of bed, so I threw up on my sheets. I was still stuck in a slumber haze that I didn't even see it, I simply felt my body reject whatever was left in my stomach. The putrid smell instigated a stronger reaction, leading me to throw up more. There wasn't much left in my body to expel, so I simply dry-heaved for what felt like an eternity. Sweat collected at the root of my hair and dripped down my face. My body felt so weak, like there was nothing I could do at that moment to help myself. Knowing I had a glass of water sitting on my bedside table, I reached for it, but in doing so, knocked the glass over. It didn't shatter as the carpet cradled its fall, but every last drop then absorbed into the floor.

Incapable of being near the smell of my own vomit, I began to very slowly roll myself onto the floor. In doing so, I landed right in the center of where I spilled my water. With water quickly seeping through my nightgown and touching my skin, I moved a bit further to a dry section of the carpet.

The situation was laughable, a series of ridiculous events one after another, but I simply couldn't do anything but groan.

After closing my eyes, the images I saw lingered with me long after. Pictures in my mind flashed rapidly. It was hard to concentrate on what exactly I was seeing, but something about it felt so foreboding. A few of the images I could decipher were the pregnancy test I took, Ron grinning devilishly, and a very bloodied blanket. The images gained speed and appeared almost as if they were all circling around me. It was such a dizzying experience; when I awoke, it felt as if my body were spinning. I placed my hands on my head as some kind of defensive tactic and whimpered like a wounded puppy, as the images I knew were only a dream continued to flash behind my eyes, despite my being fully awake. I think I was awake, at least.

WEEK 10. MONTH 2

I rubbed at my eyes to fully process what I was seeing. The room is bathed in red. It was as if a traditional lightbulb had been replaced with one with a dark red tint. There, before me, in my childhood bedroom, was Ron. His hair was as messy as it always was and he stared at me with such a deeply passionate expression. I couldn't quite tell if that was a good thing, however. It wasn't a loving expression. It wasn't quite a hateful one either. Ron simply looked like a lion, ready to pounce on its prey. I then began to look around the room to observe my surroundings. Everything, for the most part, was in its correct place. My bed was against the wall beside the window, my nightstand stood near my headboard, and the bookshelf my father built for me was placed in the corner as it has, was and always will be. Every little detail was in place, except it felt completely different. I glanced out the window, unsure of the time. It was dark out, but not pitch black. I was able to see neighboring trees swaying in the wind. Branches swung violently, looking as if they were about to snap off at any minute.

Windstorms weren't uncommon where I lived, but they always had a way of unsettling me.

It took me a moment to realize he was naked. I was confused as to why I didn't realize that immediately, but once I saw it, it was impossible to avoid. His body was more muscular than I remembered him being, with strong, broad shoulders and a sculpted stomach. He resembled a statue, with his skin hard as marble. Without walking to him, I was suddenly in his embrace. His body was warm against my skin. This revelation led me to realize that I, too, wasn't wearing any clothing. Nervously, I stared around at the room, my eyes focusing on the floor. There was no way I was allowed to have Ron over at my family's house, especially with the pair of us being in the state of undress that we were! I listened nervously for any signs of my family being nearby, but no clues of their presence were given. The room wasn't silent, however. There was a dull humming, like the sounds of a permanent bass guitar singing, echoing off the walls. While it wasn't deafening by any means, it was difficult to tune out. Wind, likely.

Within a blink, we went from standing facing one another to me lying on the bed. My childhood bed, the one where I hid every single tooth under my pillow and where my mother would sing me lullabies. A place of virtue and purity now corrupted by lust and sin. It was hard to really conceptualize at the moment. All I knew then was it felt dirty. The trepidation I exuded during our first encounter had almost completely vanished. Something felt a bit off, but otherwise I found myself drawn to him magnetically. It felt good to have my shoulders drop and not have my knees locked. Everything seemed to merely come naturally. Not only did I allow myself to relax; but I enjoyed the experience. Making love wasn't the right word. It wasn't the right word for the first time, and it certainly wasn't the right word now.

It was not soft and tender with sweet kisses and terms of endearment. With the little knowledge I had, I knew this wasn't the act of love saved for husband and wife. It was fast and hard, with strong winds circling around us.

Ron took a lock of my hair in his fist and pulled. Naturally, my head jerked back in response. While having my head closer to his mouth, he whispered obscenities in my ear, something that at one time would have led me to gasp in shock, but in that moment led me to smile lecherously.

"I'm going to breed you, you stupid fucking cow."

Startled, I awoke, realizing it was all but a dream. With my heart racing, I tentatively looked about my room. It was how it always was. There was no red tint to the room, nor was Ron standing at the foot of my bed with a salacious look in his eye. Recalling back on the images my subconscious had created, I was not fully certain if that was a nightmare or not. As I sat back and replayed the fragments of the dream that I was still able to easily visualize, I caught myself smiling.

I managed to sit up, but in doing so, I felt as if my entire stomach had turned upside down. I exhaled slowly. It was a Saturday, so I knew my whole family was to be home. My deep breathing provided me no help as it wasn't long before I expelled last night's dinner onto part of my bedding. I sighed and slowly ambled out of bed. Just as predicted, everyone was sitting together in the living room. When my father noticed me, he stood up with concerned eyes.

"Are you doing alright?" he asked. Considering I likely looked exhausted and smelled of sick, his question seemed unnecessary.

"Fine, why?" I muttered, not feeling well enough to be more happily social.

"You were making an awful lot of noise in your sleep," my mother chimed in. I did my best to keep my cheeks from burning crimson. I merely shrugged and helped myself to a glass of water. As I walked back to my room, ready to clean the sheets, I was startled to find nothing. There was no vomit or even the smell of it within my room. I peered at my bed, which was not freshly cleaned, and ran my hand along the duvet. I stared in disbelief. I remember distinctly throwing up on the covers! It wasn't even five minutes ago. As I glanced at my bedside table, a tall glass of water faced me. I could've sworn I didn't have one last night. Cautiously, I placed the new water glass next to the old.

"Momma!" I called from my bedroom. My bedroom was the closest to the living room, so I was rather confident that she could hear me.

"Yes?" she asked, her voice closer than I had predicted. A second passed and she was standing in the doorway. I asked her if she cleaned the bedding, to which she replied she had about a week ago. I nodded in a staged understanding.

"Would you like for me to wash it again?" she asked with the kindest sincerity. I shook my head and assured her that everything was fine and that I was merely confused. She smiled sweetly before exiting. I climbed into my bed, held the blankets to my face, and inhaled deeply. There was hardly any particular scent, but if I really concentrated, I could pick out a slight sweat smell. I wrapped the blanket around my shoulders and fell back into bed. Staring lazily around my bedroom, I saw flashes of Ron standing there. Although a part of me surely hated him for leaving without a trace, another part of me wished that he actually was standing there. It's not like I didn't sleep with him with no cause.

As I daydreamed about the father he would never be, my bedroom door opening spun me back into reality. My mother walked in holding a bright blue dress. It appeared to be a soft gingham, stopping just at the calves with a white collar. It looked like a dress I would wear to Easter dinner, beaming in bright springtime tones.

"What do you think?" my mother asked excitedly.

"It's very nice." My voice was dry and plain.

"Good, well try it on. Make sure it fits. If not, we'll have to go shopping tomorrow," she said.

"Why?" I asked, unsure of the severity of my liking the garment.

"For Sunday," she replied. My blank expression garnered her to then say, "Adam and Hannah's wedding!"

Adam and Hannah. They were my age, kids I went to the schoolhouse with. Hannah was a sweet girl; we enjoyed each other's company. I remember the days when we would make mud pies and look at bugs together. Adam I was less close to, but yet still quite familiar with. His family owned our local market. Last I heard, he was training to become a butcher there. I tried to recall how long they had been courting for, but eight months sounded about right. They seemed like a happy enough couple. They looked quite similar too. Both having hair of gold and eyes like the ocean was one thing, but their smiles and noses were nearly the same. I thought it was always a bit funny that they looked like they could be siblings, but it didn't seem to bother them. When I sat back and thought about it, it was wild that my childhood friends were growing up and getting married. I could theoretically see them having children not long after. It felt as if, just yesterday, we were all a bunch of toddlers running about in the tall grassy fields. Surely, it had been years since we interacted with such whimsy and wonder, but it was hard to come to terms with a now rapid sense of growing up. Maybe they felt weird, too. Or perhaps I was just behind.

I tried on the dress. It was itchy and uncomfortable. Beautiful, but something I dreaded wearing. As I stood in front of the mirror, someone I hardly knew stared back. My face was different; I looked older. Not necessarily wrinkles carved into my skin, but my eyes seemed to sit differently, and my cheekbones appeared more pronounced. It was as if I shed the last remains of childhood roundness from my face. It was likely that I wasn't, in fact, aging rapidly, but simply losing weight from being so sick over the past few weeks. Regardless of the logic, the difference in my face was present. Not only that, but the dress hugged my curves, showing off a figure I didn't realize that I had. Perhaps the garment was too small? I didn't remember clothes fitting that way before. I turned, showing different angles of my body, allowing me to notice that my hips appeared a bit wider. As I stared at my hips, my eyes fell down my legs. This led me to notice my ankles were larger as well as my wrists. Acne stained my chin and jawline, breaking out more in the last few days than I had ever had throughout my early teenage years.

I had often heard that you're supposed to glow when pregnant, but I surely did not see it. I looked tired because I was. Being plagued with hyper-realistic dreams, as well as feeling sick constantly, proved to disrupt my usual sleep patterns. In addition to looking tired, I looked unhappy. A permanent frown sat upon my face as I felt no emotion to change it. This wasn't what I wanted, so naturally, I was unhappy. There was a heavy dullness that washed over my body. All radiance I had once exuded had dimmed like a candle as its wick slowly died.

As I stared in the mirror, out of the corner of my eye, I could have sworn to see a figure behind me. It was tall, tall enough to be a person for sure. Any details beyond that were beyond me. It was simply a shape that I got the quickest glance at. My heart raced as I froze, as I wasn't sure what else I was supposed to do. When I ultimately turned, it vanished. However, even with it gone, I still felt like it was there. Any sense of privacy I felt I once had was diminished. Whatever it was, it didn't feel good. My every move felt watched by invisible eyes. I really needed quality sleep.

It continued for the rest of the day; that need to look behind my shoulder. Sitting in my bedroom, I wrung my hands and tried to focus on anything else, but it felt near impossible. It was resemblant of someone mouthing words but without making a sound. You can't hear anything, but the presence is there and a message is received. Or similar to wearing a blindfold when standing next to someone. You know they're there because you can feel them. You can't feel them physically, but you can sense them.

Adam and Hannah's wedding was not a day to be remembered. I sat on hard wooden church pews in the itchy blue dress, wanting nothing more than to peel off my skin. I watched as two kids I grew up with stood at the altar before God, confessing their devotion to each other. They still looked like kids. Perhaps it was merely bias from knowing them for such a long time. I bet their parents saw them as just kids too. They looked so awkward up there as if they were meeting for the first time. As they went to kiss, I felt my face frown. I hoped I didn't look like that when I was with Ron. I guess it didn't really matter anyhow.

The reception was held just outside the church. The skies were vibrant blue with faint streaks of white for clouds. It was perfect weather for the newlyweds. Hannah was enveloped by her dress; it practically ate her alive. With the puffs, the ruffles, the gloves and the tule, her little face just barely stuck out in the pounds of fabric wrapped around her. The community gathered around various tables set up. Her family had made the majority of the food, enough to feed all of us and then some. Staring at the serving platters spread across rows of tables, I tried to imagine how long it took them to cook everything. I remembered Hannah's mom being a pretty good cook from my time spent at her house.

My uncle on my father's side approached me. He was an awkwardly tall man who didn't come around often. He was nice enough, but I only remember seeing him for significant events. I don't know exactly where he lived either, never having gone to his house. I knew he lived within the community, but he kept somewhat to himself. Crumbs of hors d'oeuvres sat nestled in his beard. He proceeded to ask me when it was my turn.

I laughed nervously, saying, "I'm not sure."

Afterall, what else was I supposed to say? He then told me it was only a matter of time before a ripe peach like me would be snatched off the streets. I didn't know what to say to that, but I knew it made me feel weird. As soon as the conversation came to a lull I found an empty table to stand at. I felt my face frozen in a permanent scowl.

I don't like being called a fruit. I am not to be eaten.

Standing in my corner, I felt my jaw drop as I saw a man enter. Dressed in a tan linen suit, Ron walked in next to whom I could only assume to be his parents. My heart stopped. The whole world felt like it stopped. Gasping back to life, I calmed myself down by slowly sipping water. I knew by doing so, I would have to use the restroom at least twice while there, but I figured that was a problem for later. What was he doing here? He didn't live within the community, and I couldn't imagine a reality where he would be friends with either Hannah or Adam. No one ever really left town.

Continuing to stare at the man, I waited for him to notice me. He mingled and hugged other guests he seemed to know. His hair, typically messy and rugged, was brushed back a bit. It wasn't completely clean-cut, but it was more groomed than I remembered him looking at work. With my eyes digging into his existence, he still didn't appear to notice me. Frustrated, I walked through a crowd of people to approach him.

"Hey," I said, my tone pointed and my voice out of breath. I was no longer afraid of making a scene.

"Hello," he said awkwardly, with a shy smile. With me waiting for him to say more, a silence spread between us. Eventually, he asked, "So, do you know the bride or the groom?"

"Can we talk?" My voice made it clear this was a command and not a question, yet my voice still quavered. Nervously, he followed me behind a nearby tree, where there was a bit more privacy. My hands shook. I hardly knew what I was doing. I had no script to go off of or had anything planned and ready to say.

"Well, I'm pregnant," I stated bluntly. God, that felt good. He raised an eyebrow before staring at my midsection.

"Oh, well, congratulations," he said before pausing.

"You don't seem too happy about it." His words came with a nervous chuckle, very obviously uncomfortable in the situation I placed him in.

"Why would I be?"

"Well, typically, women are excited to become mothers, you know," he stammered. His nervousness was beyond palpable.

"Well, I'm not," I retorted coldly. My heart raced against my chest, feeling guilty for being rude, never having behaved in such a way before.

"I, uh, can see that. Sorry," he said. "Is this what you wanted to talk to me about?"

"Of course it is. It's your baby!" I exclaimed. Multiple heads turned.

"Excuse me?" His voice was now raised. "Who are you?"

"Don't act like you don't know me," I said, my voice now quiet. I was losing confidence by the second. I was now the nervous one, and he spoke with firmness.

"I think you may have confused me for someone else," he said calmly.

"Ron?" I whispered, now very much doubting myself. He shook his head with a laugh.

"Not Ron. Peter."

Peter apologized for my unwanted pregnancy before walking away. I stared, my mouth agape, not knowing what just happened. As I looked at him again, I realized that he, in fact, was not Ron. Peter's nose was a different shape from Ron's, and Ron had a slight chip in his front tooth that Peter didn't. The more I stared, the more I realized that aside from hair color, approximate height, and eye color, there weren't too many similarities between the two and as time passed, even those things weren't accurate. I knew I had seen Ron, so suddenly, seeing this stranger who hardly resembled him made me feel as if I were going crazy. Now mortified, I kept my head down and avoided speaking to anyone.

Isaiah came over to me with a plate of food, asking if I wanted to share. I shrugged him off, leading him to ask what was wrong. Without telling him I hallucinated the man who got me pregnant, I merely told him I wasn't feeling too well. It wasn't a lie. He once again offered me food from his plate, and I reluctantly tore off a piece of bread. I wanted more, and my body craved more, but my stomach was still in knots over the encounter with Peter, so I calmly ate plain bread in an attempt to soothe myself.

"Do you ever want this?" Isaiah asked. We looked out at the newlyweds. They posed for photographs, his arm around her waist, bouquet in her hands.

"I don't know. Don't we all want this?"

"I think it's nice," he said softly. It wasn't long before Judith skipped by and completed our sibling loner corner. She asked why we were by ourselves, to which Isaiah replied saying that I wasn't feeling well. Bored by our unprecedented lethargy, she soon left to join other kids her age. I rested my head against Isaiah's arm, waiting for the moment our parents gave us the go-ahead to start walking back home. At that moment, I realized I hadn't even spoken to neither Hannah nor Adam. A part of me didn't care and my stomach twisted with guilt. She was my friend. I should care. I waited around for her to eventually make eye contact with me. It took time, but she did. Her eyes sparkled and she waved me over.

"Ema!" She beamed as she hugged me tightly.

"Congratulations, Hannah! You look beautiful!" She truly did. Her eyes shone like stars in a summer night sky, twinkling continuously. Her skin glowed, rosy red cheeks that the sun simply bounced off of. She wore a little bit of makeup for the wedding, her eyelashes were more pronounced than usual, and a slight gloss stained her lips. She thanked me with a strong tone of sincerity.

"Hey, it could be you next. I heard you went out with Joseph?" she asked—small town things. Everyone knows everything.

"Oh! Well, yes, maybe two months ago we did."

"Oh no, what happened? You two didn't show up together, I saw."

"It was just a one-time thing, I guess," I said awkwardly. I quickly glanced around to spot Joseph, not even thinking about the idea of running into him.

"You'll find your man somewhere around here! And soon, too! Look, we got to catch up, okay? I'll see you around! Call me!" she said as her grandmother pulled her away.

I looked back to find Isaiah talking to a girl named Abagail. I remembered her from the schoolhouse. She didn't get the best grades and once she asked me to tutor her. Little did she know that I got a worse grade that semester than she did. We had a laugh about it. Besides that, I didn't know that much. I think her mom worked at the bakery in the market. Abagail stood, her hands awkwardly holding one another in front of her dress. Isaiah told her something that made her cheeks burn crimson.

"Go tell your brother we're leaving," my father told me curtly. I was shocked that he asked me to deliver the message, as I felt as if we weren't exactly on speaking terms that much as of late.

"Hey, Abagail, sorry to interrupt," I said sheepishly before turning to Isaiah. "Dad's telling us it's time to go."

"We'll talk later, okay?" Isaiah said as he turned to leave with me.

"Okay! Bye, Ema!" Her voice rang like bells. I smiled and waved goodbye before walking off to the rest of my family.

"Well, did everyone have a good time?" Momma asked as we walked together. A resounding "yes" followed from each of our mouths.

"So, is Ema going to have a wedding since she's pregnant?" Judith asked excitedly.

"Hush now!" Momma said under her breath, touching Judith's shoulder.

"Keep your voice *down*!" Father commanded, speaking between his teeth. I wasn't even the one getting scolded, and my heart raced wildly.

"I don't understand," Judith murmured, her voice shaken.

"We'll discuss this at home, baby, okay?" Momma replied sweetly. Judith looked back over her shoulder at me as I was a couple of feet behind. Her eyes pooled with tears, pulling the corners of my mouth down into a frown.

"I don't know." I mouthed to her, trying to give her my most sympathetic gaze.

Once home, I happily tore off my dress, beyond bothered by the material and how it irritated my skin. I casually tossed it to a corner in my room, but in reality, I wanted to throw it with all of my strength. It didn't really matter though, because at that point, I was at least no longer wearing it. I stared at my body; it was red and itchy. I traced my finger along a patch of skin that was dimpled in the same pattern as the fabric when my door opened. My mother stood in the doorway with clean laundry in her arms.

"Ema! Stop staring at yourself now! Go put some clothes on!" she commanded, slamming my door shut. I nervously threw on a nightgown, my hands trembling and fumbling with the sleeves. I wasn't sure what made her so mad, but I obeyed and approached the door as soon as I was dressed. My heart thudded against my chest, and my face warmed, unsure if I should be embarrassed or scared. I opened my door, and my mother handed me my clothes without saying a word.

At dinner, I nervously sat down at the kitchen table, unsure how my mother would behave towards me. I watched as she set the table, placing plates down in a fluid motion. She wore a serene smile and hummed ever so softly to herself. Her humming was so faint that if any other noise occurred, it would be fully masked. Based on her behavior, everything seemed fine, making her sudden lashing out seem even more strange. I still kept my composure around her, wary of my mother's seemingly unpredictable temperament.

I sat nervously while the whole family was present at the table. The remaining sparks of adrenaline ran through my veins as I noticed my finger twitching ever so slightly. My plate consisted of food I was too on edge to eat, but my stomach groaned in hunger. Ever since becoming pregnant, my entire eating schedule was thrown way off course. I toyed with my fork, every so often taking a bite.

"My favorite part was her dress!" Judith exclaimed when asked what was her favorite part of the whole day—a valid answer. My mother agreed, saying how lovely she looked.

"Ema should wear a dress like that when she gets married!" Judith then said. That comment slipped silence over the room. I smiled politely, not knowing really what to say. My parents exchanged uncomfortable glances, making the awkward air in the room feel all the more present.

"I'm sure she will," my mother said curtly but with a smile. She didn't need to add to the tension, but she did so anyway. To attempt to break some of the discomfort, I nodded in agreement.

That night, I lay in my bed, staring up at my ceiling. Replaying over and over in my head was my mother getting quite upset at my simply standing naked. She was seemingly more upset from that compared to when I told her I was pregnant.

I placed my hands on my stomach and shut my eyes. I was a body, but existing within it felt sinful. I ran my hands up and down my legs, feeling the warm stretches of skin that held me whole. It was the first place where Ron had touched me on our date. I eventually began to place my hands in the same order where Ron had touched me, going from my legs to my hips to my breasts. It felt nicer than when Ron did it, but perhaps that was due to nerves. I began feeling between my legs, and my heart began to beat wildly. Such euphoric pleasure was unknown to me; I only ever truly experienced it in my most guilt-ridden dreams.

While in mid-pleasure, my bedroom door opened, with both my parents standing in the doorway. I tried to hide my actions to the best of my abilities, but what I was doing was likely obvious. My father angrily marched towards me and grabbed my arms. I felt his fingers pressing into my bone. I cried out in pain and had no choice but to follow his grip as he dragged me out of my bedroom. He was far stronger than I had imagined and I was unable to escape his grasp, no matter how much I tried. I had no idea what was happening.

Breathing hard, I looked around for clues as to what exactly was going on. My heart fell into my stomach as he threw my body into the bathroom. My knees hit the tile floor with an aching thud and my ribcage smacked into the bathtub. I was in too much shock to register the pain at first, but it wasn't long before the aches hit me.

I looked behind me to see my father grabbing a long object. It appeared to be a stick of some unknown material. It slightly resembled a towel rack. Suddenly, he pushed my upper back with his foot, leading me to hit my body into the base of the bathtub again. Holding me by the back of my neck with one hand, he lifted up my nightgown with the other. I did not know what he was about to do, but without even realizing it, I began to piss myself. Whimpering in fear, I knelt there motionlessly as my father began to hit my backside with the metal rod.

Paralyzed by endless emotions, I did not speak or move. I merely gasped with each strike to my body. It was a dull pain, something I felt deep within my muscles. It wasn't sharp like that of a cut. He struck me five times before he angrily threw my nightgown back into place and stood up. I looked up at him with pleading eyes, not knowing what to say but not knowing the man standing before me. This was not the father I had grown up with. That man always smiled, hugged his wife, and played with his kids. This was not the man who taught me to ride a bike or who bought all of my birthday presents. This was a man who looked at his child with hate in his eyes.

"Never do that again," he spat before exiting and going to his bedroom.

Back in bed, I lay curled in a ball. I was too shaken to cry; the most I could muster was jagged breathing. My heart did not slow down for what felt like the longest time. That was the first time that I felt unsafe in my own home. As I began to close my eyes, I heard muddled whispers. I'd assume them to be from my parents, but their room was at the opposite end of the hallway. I nestled myself further into the bed and they got louder.

SIN IS A DEMON LURKING.

A RUSH of birds flocked together in a formation similar to a tornado. Heavy rain fell onto the roof, and strong winds ripped through the air. Branches fell to the earth, and a choir of wailing echoed through the sky. Screams from the tormented, moans from the freed. On all sides was the thrashing of water, and that was when I saw his tail.

THE NEXT DAY, I did not eat breakfast with my family. I got in my car to drive to the pet store. I needed to see Ron or, at the very least, find his contact information. I felt like I was going absolutely crazy and was being eaten alive with guilt for his not knowing of my pregnancy. In hindsight, I knew that it wasn't my fault. He was absent before I got the chance to tell him. Nonetheless, I still had an obligation.

The roads were wet with springtime showers, and I was back to being nauseous, an unfortunate combination. I was a bit distracted as it was wildly uncomfortable to sit after what happened the night prior.

It was ten in the morning. Whether it be Gregory or Virginia, someone must have been in the store as it was store hours. Few cars were parked in the lot.

I saw a woman, perhaps around my mother's age, taping a sign to a telephone pole. Normally, something I would want to investigate is now something I could hardly pay attention to. As I approached the front door, I saw that the cash wrap was empty, with no bored employee manning the station. Confused, I opened the door with hesitation, not sure if it would be locked or not. The store, upon entering, was completely quiet with no signs of life. Even with no customers being present, you could usually hear the sound of one of the employees walking about, eating, smoking, or doing really anything to pass the time. An eerie energy lingered. At that moment, I truly understood the concept of "too quiet." I started moving so I could hear something, even if it were just my footsteps. As I peered around, the stock was in place and the shelves were filled, but neither employee nor patron existed within. I anxiously peeked my head around every aisle in the hopes of finding someone. When no one was found, I ambled over to the register, sweat forming on my temple. A million scenarios played through my head. What if there was a robbery? What if there was a kidnapping? What if something had happened the night prior and no one was around to witness it? Was Ron involved? Was anyone hurt? As more hypothetical scenarios came to mind, I began to make myself dizzy. A small bell sat on the counter to alert one of the salespeople for assistance. I smacked my hand against it, and the bell chimed and danced off the hollow walls. My breathing had become rapid, and I nervously looked over my shoulder. The silent whispers were back.

A shadow stood behind me. I couldn't fully see it or hear it, but I felt it. Whatever it was, it was there. Whatever it was, it followed me. It was not confined to my house. It moved when I moved, truly as if it were my shadow. If only it were as simple and pure as that. I wanted to glance behind my shoulder to confront it; on the other hand, I wanted to cower, to hide, and run. I smacked the bell at the counter again. The chime echoed up to the ceiling. I wrung my hands nervously before walking away from the register.

I looked over at the rodents. The hamster that was once round and always sleeping was now surrounded by her litter. I smiled softly, watching the tiny rodents flail around in the cage. They were so small, maybe half the size of my index finger. The mother approached one of her littlest babies and, without missing a beat, began to chew on its body. I gasped, holding my hands up to my face, watching in horror. She proceeded to eat at its meat, leaving behind bits of reddened bone. Trembling, I backed away from the cages and walked into a person. Turning around, I saw it was Virginia. With tear-stained cheeks, I collapsed into her arms.

"Ema! What happened?" she exclaimed.

"I need to see Ron," I sobbed. After providing some context on what was happening, she pulled up a folding chair from the back room and sat me down.

"What has your doctor said? About the hallucinations and stuff?" she asked.

"I haven't been to a doctor," I said. Her eyes shot wide open.

"Dude, you're like, kind of showing. You haven't been to a doctor at all?"

"Am I supposed to?" I asked nervously. I looked down at my stomach. Was I starting to show?

"Yes! You're supposed to see one every few weeks or something. What have you been doing in the meantime?"

"My mom just has me lying in bed all day and gives me water or bread for when I'm nauseous," I said, trailing off. Virginia made a face equal to if I had just slapped her.

"Okay, well, find yourself a doctor. There's a clinic if you need one about twenty minutes up this road," she said as she pointed towards the larger city.

"But about Ron, I don't know." Her face turned grim. She

wore a look of dread, and concern filled her eyes. "He hasn't been back or called or anything. And um... Well, there are these posters now. I don't know how long ago it started, but, I mean he's too old for his face to be on a milk carton."

"What do you mean?" I asked quietly, my voice hardly a voice.

"His mom came in the other day asking about him. She doesn't know where he is." I sat there frozen, my mouth slightly agape.

"Okay, Ema, I know you like, told me about that night, but god, is there anything you can think of that seemed weird?" I sat just staring at Virginia for a while before I could muster up an answer.

"I don't know. I think it was all normal?" I whispered. We then sat there, me in the folding chair, and Virginia sitting at the cash register. Our silence spoke for us.

"Could you still give me his telephone number?" I asked sheepishly. Virginia climbed off the counter and grabbed a thick binder. After carelessly flipping through, she motioned for me to come take a look. Written down after Virginia's name and number was Ron's.

"I'm honestly not sure what good it'll do, but I hope this helps you."

As I pulled up to my house, I walked casually up to the door. If my mother knew where I was, oh, would she yell. Something, for some reason, couldn't bring me to care. I know I should. I know I should obey my parents; that's what I was brought up to do. Nevertheless, I walked normally into the house with a blank expression. I didn't hear anything as I opened the door. Perhaps no one was home. I dialed the number that was written across my arm in marker. I ran my fingers through the phone cord, attempting to give myself some kind of distraction. With the receiver pressed into my ear, I waited and waited for the line to pick up. After hanging up, I tried once more, hoping that this time around would be different. With a heavy hand and heart, I hung up the phone after being met with nothing. The guilt of not having told him had quickly been replaced with fear for his well-being.

Disappointed and worried, I decided I would call later. Standing in the living room, my mother came in from the kitchen, avoiding all eye contact with me. I felt as if my body physically fell. I didn't think she was home. She was so silent. I tried to control my face from looking like I just got caught. She looked at me with a mix of suspicion and disdain. She couldn't have possibly known where I had just come from, had she?

"Momma, when should I go see a doctor?" I asked, breaking the silence only met me with continued silence. I waited patiently, assuming she was thinking of a good day for me to go. The longer I waited for her to answer, the more I realized she wasn't going to. Frustrated, I repeated and asked her again, my tone more urgent.

"You don't need one," she said curtly. I made a face out of confusion and annoyance.

"But Momma, I heard when you're pregnant, you need to get check-ups to make sure you're okay," I muttered softly. I wanted to stand my ground and see a doctor, but at the same time she had been in my position before so I trusted her opinion. I had no choice but to.

"And where did you hear that from?" Her tone was sharp and cold. It contrasted so heavily with the motherly personality she always displayed. Each word was like a swift strike to my heart.

"I don't know. I just heard it around. School, I guess." I was losing confidence in my argument, and it was noticeable. She knew she was winning but tried not to display her pride too overtly.

"Well, you heard wrong; everything you need is at home." After speaking, she immediately turned and walked away.

Once she was out of earshot, I tried to call Ron once more. I got my hopes up for nothing as I was met with the same answer as before. I squeezed the phone in my hand and fought back tears. I felt annoying for calling consistently, not wanting to bother his family, but I tried once more. As the rings sounded through the holes in the phone, I realized that I would have to learn to live without the closure. I slowly hung up the phone and walked back to my bedroom, my body feeling completely numb. It felt like I had floated, not feeling the carpet beneath my feet. When I closed my bedroom door, I felt my body collapse into a hurricane of emotions. Tears fell from my eyes for what felt like years, and sobs echoed through my chest. Having nothing else to do, I simply wrapped myself in my favorite blanket, hoping to find some peace in the small, comfortable things.

"Whore," Ron spat. The red tint bounced off the walls. What sounded like a hurricane made the windows rattle angrily. I turned my head to look at the storm, but Ron gripped my chin, forcing me to look at him. I gasped myself awake, finding myself still in bed with things being back to normal. My hair was chaos and my heartbeat was everywhere. I calmly shut my eyes and said a small prayer of forgiveness. I shouldn't be dreaming about such things, but those things were such fun to dream of.

WEEK 13. MONTH 3

With my vision blurred, the world was dark. It was similar to trying to look through eyes clouded by tears. I couldn't quite comprehend where I was, but I could tell it was outside. Winds mixed with rain were strong, ripping through my skin like butterfly needles left out in the cold. I tried to cover my arms, but that gave no comfort. All I could do was suffer and observe.

The ground was thick and wet, like sand from the ocean. Trudging through it was difficult but not impossible. The texture was quite vile, appearing similar to vomit mixed with mud. It was of a thick viscosity with chunks of an unknown substance littered throughout. It was nearly impossible to decipher what exactly it was as my vision was distorted and there wasn't any light around me. Walking through it, however, made me grow nauseous. It was hard to determine how much of the substance lay upon the earth, or if it was the earth, and it continued until you hit a rocky layer of the earth's surface. I tried to push my foot further in and although met with resistance, the substance swallowed my leg up to my calf. The sensation was vile, and I tried to shake off the particles after pulling my leg out of the slop.

I tried to look around for a place to go. I wanted to escape the darkness and the conditions that surrounded it. It felt like I was standing in the eye of a storm, and all hell was about to break loose. It was obvious that I was outside, but no streetlamps illuminated the ground around me. No cars with their headlights drove past. No porchlight flickered. It was seemingly nothing short of a desolate flatland.

Suddenly, emerging from the earth, was a monstrous creature. A long centipede-like entity rose far above me. It was no bug; however, the longer I stared, the more I realized that it was made of people. The body of the creature was mud and flesh, with dozens of random arms and legs of varying sizes and skin tones flailing wildly. What wasn't severed appendages were full, intact bodies, their torsos melted and sewn into the creature's skin. Bodies that were low to the ground grabbed at the sludge of the earth and readily ingested it. The filth ran down their mouths and stained their faces. Some of the faces continuously retched up the slop to then eat more. The harder I looked, the more people looked familiar. I couldn't put names to faces, and even the faces were hard to view through the storm, but there was a level of familiarity that existed.

A thick sheen existed on the creature, looking like translucent slime. Occasionally, it would drip down and splash into the slop below. As I looked at one of the bodies, I saw one face that I seemed to recognize more than the others. If I looked hard enough he appeared to resemble my uncle. I was too horrified to feel sick. All I could do was stare at the creature, watching as it ambled slowly through the sludge. Arms swung wildly, legs kicked with no direction, and the bodies that were whole each struggled in their own manner. Some screamed in agony as they tried to rip themselves off from the beast. Others were too far gone to care and moved along with the current, rain pouring down their faces. The rest had their way with the slop of the earth.

It was moving almost away from me. Despite it not actively hurting me, I tried to be as quiet and careful as possible not to bother it, whatever "it" was anyway. The weather conditions only grew worse, the winds picking up speed, and the rain became accompanied by hail and snow. Despite now having said hail and snow, the overall temperature of the place didn't feel cold. It all just felt so wrong. I stared, mouth agape, as the creature sauntered about. The winds suddenly changed direction, causing everything to fall towards my line of vision. A piece of hail struck my eye and I cried out. The creature stopped and changed its path. It was slow, but it was on its way over to me. There was nowhere to run or hide. The mud of the earth was growing to my knees, and there was no object I could see to hide behind. Dread filled my core, and I instinctively clasped my hands.

Do not fear nor be dismayed, for the Lord, your God, is with you wherever you go.

I whispered these words under the torrents of rain blinding my gaze. I whispered over and over, hoping he'd hear me. Please hear me.

Waking up in a cold sweat, I sat up in bed, hyperventilating. I anxiously looked around the room, getting a grip on my safe surroundings. As the initial adrenaline rush ceased, I began to pick at my cuticles as I stared into nothingness. I wasn't sure if wildly vivid nightmares were common with pregnancy or if I was going mad. Regardless, nearly three months of this was really wearing on me. As I stood up out of bed, I was hit with a strong wave of vertigo. It felt as if I had stepped upon a small boat sustaining through rippling currents. I stumbled back into bed. The dizziness did not cease, and I felt as if the bed was floating on top of the ocean. I shut my eyes and buried my face into my pillow for a semblance of comfort.

Trying again, I very carefully placed my foot on the ground and began to lift myself into a standing position. The vertigo was still quite noticeable, but using a wall to hold a bit of balance, made the process a bit easier. As long as I walked slowly, I was fine. My mother was fixing breakfast for my father and Judith when she noticed my struggling to walk. She walked over to me and led me to the dining room table. The change from the stationary wall to my mother, who was walking, was unfortunate. The world seemed to flip sideways as if someone had manually rolled the Earth like a globe. My mother caught me by the waist without faltering and successfully placed me in a chair.

"Momma, I'm really dizzy. I should go to the doctor," I mumbled, my words slurring a bit. I wasn't sure if that was due to just waking up, or a larger problem. As I sat down and smelled the aroma of breakfast, my stomach growled on cue. I was pleased that the smell of food didn't bring about nausea, as it had been doing for the past few weeks.

"Oh, hush. You just need some food in you," she said with a smile and fixed me a plate. Meats, grains, fruits and eggs were all served to me on one inviting plate. I instinctively grabbed my fork fervently, wanting to eat to cure my dizziness. My father smacked my hand and looked at me as if I cursed the entire table.

"Wait," he ordered. I shrunk back into my seat and shut my eyes as my father began the prayer.

"Heavenly Father, we thank thee for this meal. May this food restore our strength, may this drink restore our souls, and may you bless us in always finding better ways in honoring you. Amen."

My mother was right, to an extent at least. Eating did, in fact, help things, and once fully nourished, the dizziness started to subside. Once back in my room, I fell back into my blankets, wanting nothing more than to be enveloped in the comfort of my bed. Just as I had begun to get into a comfortable position, the whispers began. They felt distant at first, like they were across the room watching me. I could feel its eyes on me, leering and judging. I pulled the covers over my eyes as a means of childlike protection. Much to my dismay, the blanket did not shield me from the invisible forces at hand. They grew closer with every passing minute. I couldn't see them, and I couldn't exactly hear them, but I knew they were all around me. Closing in and swallowing me whole.

As I shuddered under my blanket, my stomach grew warm, as if I were resting a bowl of soup on my lap. I placed my hands on my skin and felt a dull electric sensation. I couldn't feel anything specifically moving per se; it wasn't a kick that many parents speak of, but more of a subdued vibration. I rubbed my stomach soothingly in an attempt to calm whatever was happening, tracing my hand in small circles as if what I was feeling were merely digestion issues. What went from a warm vibration turned to a hot, thunderous rumbling. Wrapping my arms around my stomach I began to sob, not knowing what my body was doing and, more so, not knowing how to fix things.

My mother must've heard my cries. I didn't know how loud I had been, but I wasn't totally surprised when she entered my room. Pulling the blankets from my face, she cradled my head and brushed my hair tenderly. I grabbed her arms with what little strength I had in fear of her leaving. I had become fearful of being alone. The whispers were most noticeable when I was alone.

"Momma, what's wrong with me?" I wailed. She shushed my cries and rocked me back and forth.

"It's okay. Everyone goes a bit crazy when they're pregnant," she said reassuringly.

"No, no, there's something wrong with me. The baby is evil or something," I sobbed.

"Not possible, sweets. You're probably just tired," she said. I heard a smile bleed through her words. She probably held back a laugh. Thinking your unborn baby is evil probably sounds absolutely crazy, but to me, it felt very real. She wasn't entirely wrong, though. I was sleep-deprived, but I didn't understand how sleep deprivation would lead to what all I was experiencing. A lack of sleep could eventually lead to being dizzy, sure, but feeling as if my stomach was being lit aflame and feeling as if invisible beings were following and watching me seemed highly illogical.

"Momma, I want it out!" I cried. My sobs tore through my trachea, making it feel as if I had a sore throat. A warmth quickly crept up along every inch of my skin until I was sweating from every pore. I felt as if I were slowly coming into closer contact with a raging fire, only I couldn't quite tell if the fire was external or internal.

"Oh, Ema, honey. You know that can't happen." Her voice sounded soothing, but her words provided no comfort. It was like talking to a wall. I stared at my bulging stomach and wondered if she was correct in that statement. Virginia never divulged the specifics with me about the timeline of abortions. I wasn't sure if it was too late, but considering that my mother wouldn't even take me to the doctor, I wouldn't likely find out.

My mother confined me to bedrest, placing a damp washcloth on my forehead to ease my rising temperatures. She told me if I needed anything to simply shout her name, as I shouldn't have to engage in anything physical or have to think about things. I lay in bed in a pool of my sweat, mindlessly picking at my cuticles, being as that I was instructed not to read or participate in any activity. I didn't know the logic in her reasoning, as that stripping me of any distraction felt counterproductive.

Across from my bed was a tall bookcase holding a range of items, ironically not too many books. A snow globe sat next to a few other random knickknacks, all collecting dust as many hadn't been touched in years. The bottom shelf held a lofty encyclopedia that I had used once for a paper in school. It had been my father's, and I forgot to return it to him. He never asked for it back, so I suppose it's partially mine. I very carefully sat up, frightful in the case that I had another episode of the spins. Easing my way to the book, I slowly grabbed it and placed it on my lap.

I remembered when my father had gotten it; it was maybe three years prior. He was overjoyed, always having wanted a set of his own. For days after the purchase, he would spend hours at night sitting in his chair and flipping through each and every page. He never talked about the words in it to any of us in the family, but I knew he was reading it as he would occasionally smile when looking at the pages. When I had asked to borrow the book for school, he seemed so enthusiastic to share it with me. Neither Isaiah nor Judith took any interest, so I knew it pleased him greatly to know that I seemingly shared his hobby, even if it were only for school.

Holding it in my lap, I flipped a few pages in. Abortion, being quite early into the alphabet, wasn't far in before I found it. It was described as being a medical procedure to terminate a pregnancy before the person is full term. It did not describe how the procedure was carried out or if it could be performed at home. I didn't know exactly how far along I was, so I wasn't even sure if I could have one still performed. My mother said it was too late, so I gathered that I had no option but to trust her. Dejected, I placed the book back on the shelf and fell back into bed.

I continued to lie in bed and stare at the ceiling. Boredom was an egregious understatement. There was the feeling of being bored, simply having nothing to do, and then there was the feeling that I was unable to do anything.

I was subjected to permanent bedrest and not allowed to partake in any casual hobbies to help pass the time.

I knew that if I were to go into the living room and ask to play a board game with Judith, my mother would shoo me back into my room.

If she saw me reading, she would tell me I was straining my eyes.

If she saw me walking about my room, picking things up off the floor, she would instruct me to get back to bed and get as much physical rest as possible.

I knew she was doing it out of care, saying words likely her mother told her, but I couldn't help but grow impatient.

The books I did have sat on my shelf with a thick layer of dust and have never looked so enticing. The dirty laundry scattered across my bedroom carpet seemed laughably interesting. The idea of mopping the floor or plunging the toilet seemed utterly remarkable. The prospect of simply looking at something other than the ceiling seemed so out of reach but nice to daydream of.

It wasn't even the idea of being at home that was bothersome; it was the bed. Sure, my mother telling me to leave my job wasn't something I was happy about. Not having any activities to do outside the home was a bit dull, but it wasn't the worst fate. I could even tolerate it if I couldn't leave my bedroom, but the fact I was essentially instructed to lie motionless in bed drove me mad. Sure, there were days I was so sick that the idea of doing nothing, absolutely nothing, and being waited on hand and foot sounded rather nice and something I would want to take advantage of. However, for the rest of the days when I was capable of caring for myself, I wanted to do so. Guilt began to grow due to my growing annoyance. My mother was taking care of my every need. If I ever were to be sick, I could count the seconds on one hand before I felt my mother at my side, holding back my hair. If I were suddenly ravenous, she'd instantly cook me a meal. If I were too sick to eat, she would nod and save the food for leftovers. Her patience seemed never-ending.

The foul waters poured unrelentingly upon my rain-soaked body. I could no longer see the world around me. All I could do was feel. My nightgown grew heavy as it continuously soaked up water. The muddy floors ran up to my thighs now. Was I to drown? Was I going to die here? I tried to trudge through, but I was growing weaker with every passing moment.

I tried to walk backward, away from where I knew the creature to be—not like I could even see it anymore. I felt something grab my arm, and I screamed.

I woke up with my eyes glazed over, as if I hadn't slept in years. I heard voices outside in the living room. There was a new voice, a new tone. I can always recognize voices from my bedroom without listening to the words, but there was someone else here. It was a girl. What time even was it that I was just waking up, and we had company? I looked over, and my clock read four in the afternoon. I furrowed my brow as I expected to read something close to eight in the morning. Not having time to deal with the concept of time, I rolled out of bed to see who was visiting.

I walked into the living room to see my parents with Isaiah and Abagail. My mother and Abagail shared excited expressions, rosy cheeks sitting above their wide grins. Isaiah seemed pleased, content. He looked like he was at peace. My father wore an expression I couldn't quite read. If I had to try and describe it, it appeared to be some mix between frustrated, worried, and yet also pleased. He was smiling, but his eyes weren't. I stepped further into the room and all four heads turned. I nervously smiled, not knowing exactly what I had walked into.

"Hi, Ema!" Abagail greeted politely. I returned the greeting and asked what was going on. Abagail looked to Isaiah to speak.

"I was bringing Abagail by here to formally introduce her to everyone and announce our courtship," he said with a half-grin.

"Oh, congratulations," I said calmly. Courtships were quite common in our community. Some would work and turn into marriages; others would fall through quickly. This was Isaiah's first time courting anyone, so I could see it being quite a big deal in the eyes of my parents. My mother's exuberant expression matched the situation, but my father's was still up for debate.

Abagail wasn't at the house for much longer. After maybe five minutes or so, Isaiah walked her back home. Momma asked if I needed anything, to which I replied that I needed some water. My father had stormed off to my parents' bedroom. I carefully tiptoed closer into the kitchen, where my mother was pouring my glass.

"Is he okay?" I whispered to momma. She turned to me and smiled.

"Oh, he's just not feeling too great today. Bit of a headache, sweets, nothing to worry about," she replied, her voice calm but low. My expression must've not changed from her words as she then said, "He's okay, I promise! Now, come along. Let's get you back to your room." She guided me back into my bedroom and closed the door behind me. She was still holding my water. I heard her bedroom door close. Voices became loud. I cautiously opened my bedroom door in order to not make a sound.

"How could this happen?!" Father shouted. I flinched at how angry he sounded.

"It was bound to happen. Especially with Ema's…situation," Momma replied, her voice nervous but even.

"It wasn't supposed to go this way."

"Well, what can we do now? I mean, really? Sure, this wasn't what we wanted, but it will all work itself out in the way that it was meant to. God is good." Her voice was pleading. There was a pause. "Oh, hold on." I heard their bedroom door open, and I bolted to my bed, not even bothering to try and close my door.

"I'm so sorry, bunny, I have your water! Gosh, I feel so silly," she said, her voice fast and higher pitched than usual. She set the glass down on my nightstand. Her hand shook ever so slightly.

"That's okay," I murmured, not knowing what else to say. She quickly left, her eyes not once meeting mine. There were more noises, but the yelling had ceased. My head hung in shame. While obviously, my situation was a big one, I didn't think they'd fight about it. I didn't think they'd still be talking about it. They probably saw Isiah as the perfect child. He was better in school than I was. He met a nice girl to court and based on how the pair acted, I wouldn't be surprised if they ended up engaged to be wed. He was doing it the right way, unlike me. My parents' first grandchild would be born without a marriage or a father. Isaiah and Abagail were the salt in the wound I created.

I SLOWLY RESTED my head on my pillow, too tired to want to keep thinking such sad thoughts. Although I had spent much time here, I noticed small changes. I couldn't quite pinpoint what exactly I was seeing or feeling, but I had such an overwhelming feeling that something was off. Over the next few days, I would scan the room, waiting for that moment when I would finally notice what the problem was. I would laugh and observe the change, and then that weight would be lifted. The issue was, that moment never happened. I would get out of bed and stare at it, stare at the exact position that it was in. I began to measure the bed in conjunction with the rest of the furniture and its placement against the wall. The bed never moved. The curtains veiling my window remained in the same position, no matter the time of day. I would then look out the window to see if an object was outside, perhaps obstructing the view of how light would normally enter my room. Nothing was ever there.

I knew in my heart that I wasn't simply imagining things, that something was truly altered. I would go on to inspect smaller items in my room. The books placed on my bookshelf never moved. My lamp on my bedside table sat in the same spot it always did. There was no physical change to my room, but it simply felt different. At times, I would feel too small, and other times, I would feel too large. There was an aspect to it that felt ever-changing, as if I existed within a home of water, and my every movement disrupted the natural flow of things.

I would talk to my mom occasionally about these sensations. Feeling alone in my experiences, I thought it would make sense to ask her about what I was going through, considering she had been through pregnancy three times. Every time I would bring up something, she'd simply smile and tell me it was normal. However, when I would ask her if she had gone through it as well, she would avoid giving me a direct answer. She would then have me pray with her, over and over. It became quite a frustrating thing, talking to my mom, as every single odd thing she deemed to be normal she seemed to miraculously avoid. I began to ask her to take me to a doctor to confirm if the nightmares, the paranoia, and every other sensation I experienced were to be expected, but she said it was unnecessary. The longer it persisted, the more I wanted to see a doctor to get out of the house. After all, if everything was so normal, why was she having me pray over it?

Apart from Adam and Hannah's wedding and visiting the pet store, I was always inside my bedroom. It reached the point where if I would exit my bedroom to go into the kitchen, my mom would ask if I needed help, as she could do for me whatever I needed. To an extent, I appreciated her efforts. She likely didn't have that kind of help when she was pregnant, so it was possible that she simply wanted to treat me the way she wished she was treated. On the other hand, I greatly felt like I was losing my autonomy, and although I was to become a mother within less than a year's time, I felt as if I were being forced back into childhood.

Lying in bed was beginning to hurt my neck and back, so I started sitting. This was somehow worse. At least with lying down, it felt more like resting. As I was staring at the wall in front of me, I heard the whispers. They felt loud today, loud and fast. I shut my eyes like a scared child and waited for them to leave. They circled me, jumping about in erratic motions like mice. A cramp hit me in my stomach, similar to someone physically striking me. I recoiled and breathed through the pain. Was I dying? Was I giving birth? I had no idea, but everything was far too overwhelming. I balled my fists and scrunched my face, as if that were to help. Just as quickly as it had arrived, the pain vanished. The whispers were now gone. It was like flipping on a light switch.

The back and forth of it all was exhausting. Paranoia whiplash, erratic stress-induced ailments, whatever term you could possibly give it, was burdening. It was always unexpected despite slowly picking up some similarities. In those moments, however, it felt like an instant death sentence. I didn't even bother asking my mom anymore if she had experienced what I was going through because I knew she would dance around my question, but in a nutshell, say no. Having known girls in school who were now mothers, I figured it wasn't a bad idea to try and reach out and compare experiences. Jill Meyers was a friend of mine during school who was now married with a baby. I began riffling through old notebooks and loose papers, hoping to have her telephone number written down somewhere. Although her house wasn't far from mine, I had a feeling my mom wouldn't be thrilled with my leaving the house.

After searching for some time, I found her number scribbled on the forward page of a book she had lent me. I made a face, realizing that I had never returned it, not even remembering when exactly she had lent it to me. I casually walked into the living room where the phone was hung. Judith was sitting on the couch, book in hand. My mom was in the backyard. The coast was clear enough. My fingers trembled slightly as I punched in each number. Sure, we were friends, but I hadn't exactly reached out in a while and felt a tinge of guilt for calling for my own peace of mind. Of course, I would extend niceties and ask her how she was, but I truly didn't care. I didn't need to know what words her son was beginning to babble or how devoted her husband was.

"Hello?" she answered, her voice on the other line. She sounded a bit tired but still spoke in a voice sweet as sugar.

"Jill?" I asked, despite instantly recognizing her voice.

"Oh, Ema?" she squealed with enthusiasm. My heart was instantly warmed. I didn't even care about my inquiry anymore; simply hearing her voice, a voice other than my family's, was a treat. I didn't realize how comforting it was to speak to someone who wasn't from my house. That made me feel guilty. I made a mental note to pray for appreciation for my family later. I conveniently never did.

"Hey, how's it going?" I said, a smile stretching across my face for the first time in weeks.

"Oh gosh, good! It's been so long. How are you?" I could see her saying these words, beaming up and down, clasping her hands, a twinkle in her eye.

"I'm okay." Lies. I didn't know how convincing I sounded, but she would soon hear how not okay I actually was.

"How are things with you?" I asked. I did want to know. I more so wanted to hear her speak. Her voice was a warm bath, and I was so cold. Jill rambled on for some time. She spoke of her family, who I hadn't realized how dearly I had missed. She spoke of her husband, who I had seen randomly throughout school, a mere face in the halls as he was older than us. She spoke of her son, who was three months old, and how he was an absolute joy. She missed Hannah's wedding due to a cold that hit all three of them.

I was so elated to hear all of it. She really deserved the happiness in her life. I remembered her family as being nothing short of the kindest people. I could only imagine what kind of child the pair of them created.

"So, uh, I'm pregnant," I said with a forced laugh. There was not a full beat of silence before she burst on the other line.

"Oh, why didn't you say so sooner? Congratulations!"

"Thank you," I said uncomfortably. That was the first time I remember someone congratulating me. I had only told my parents, Virginia and Abagail likely found out through Isaiah.

"Who's your husband? I didn't know you got married!"

Here it comes. I grit my teeth.

"I'm actually not married. I met the guy at a job I got after graduating," I said nervously. I didn't expect her to say anything rude, but nonetheless, I was still nervous.

"Oh wow, that's great, Ema! So you both have been together for a few months now, right? Since you graduated back in, what, January?" Her voice was definitely shocked but not rude. Jill was a grade above me. We tried to keep in touch after her graduation, but life started going fast for her. Now and then, we would meet up or see each other at church, but over time, it became less and less frequent.

"We're not together anymore, actually," I said sheepishly.

"Oh, I'm sorry to hear that," she said genuinely. Empathy bled through her words.

"Thanks, it's okay. I've been having some strange pregnancy symptoms, though. Were you ever like that?" I asked, hoping she'd have similar experiences, and I wasn't simply mad.

"Oh gosh, of course. I mean, I feel that's awfully common right?"

"Mm, right," I muttered. She was starting to sound like my mom and that wasn't what I was hoping for.

"Morning sickness?" she guessed.

"Definitely. I've been having terrible nightmares too, like, really vivid ones. I've been jumpier, like every little thing just…really frightens me. Did you have that?" Pause. I could hear her murmur on the other line. My chances weren't looking great that we shared common ground.

"Hm, I mean, I suppose. I was more tired so I'd sleep more and I remember having pretty realistic dreams. Nothing too out of the ordinary, though."

My stomach sank. While I was happy she didn't have to experience what I existed through, I really wanted company. I wanted someone to tell me they were like me, too. I didn't want someone to gloss over it and say it was normal. I wanted shared experiences and similar stories. I wanted to know that I wasn't alone. Biting my tongue, I listened to her continue until we eventually hung up. She said she'd visit and help take care of me anytime I needed, and for that I was incredibly grateful. It would be great to see her and be a nice change in routine. Nonetheless, I was still missing answers. There had to have been billions of other pregnant people before me, ones with worse symptoms. I could not have been the only one to experience what I was experiencing.

Back in my bedroom, I stood before my bed with a look of trepidation. I didn't want to sleep anymore. There had not been a single night since becoming pregnant that I had slept well, that I had slept without being in the other world. Every dream was a constant continuation of itself, even if it was relatively short. Begrudgingly, I slipped beneath my sheets. I reminded myself that these were dreams; nothing could physically harm me in any way, and that if I were to get too frightened, I could force my body awake. As I nestled my head into the pillows, I was pulled beneath my bed into the realm of nightmares.

WEEK 17. MONTH 4

I awoke on a large boulder, triple the size of my bed. Gaining my bearings, I tried to observe where exactly I was. The sky was dark, not a deep navy of a clear night, but a blackened maroon, resembling the sky of a city that had been burnt to the ground. There were no stars, nor were there clouds. It was simply an even layer of warm darkness. Crawling towards the boulder's edge, I peered below at what was beneath me. There were people! Far below my gaze, to the land down below, were dozens of bodies walking aimlessly about, all of which were unclothed. Not wanting to catch their attention, I pulled back from the edge. Looking behind me and finding nothing, I realized that my awakening point was at the top of this world, and the only way forward was down.

Peering over the edge, I quickly realized that climbing down the side of a large rock was going to be no easy task. I didn't even have shoes. I sat as close as I could to the boulder's edge, with my legs swinging off. With my feet, I tried to paw at the side of the rock, attempting to find a divot that could hold my weight. I quickly found one and began the awkward process of turning my body in order to climb down. Suddenly, I was rock climbing, something I had no experience with. I was rather slow at it but felt that being overly careful was the smartest course of action. Managing to make progress downward, I quickly grew too cocky. I placed my foot in a crevasse that felt a little snug. As I transferred my weight to that foot, the rock beneath began to crumble within seconds. It was all so fast. I tried to grab onto something, but the velocity that I was falling at was far too fast for me to attempt finding a piece of wall I could hold onto. My fingers, at times, ran down the sides of the wall, tearing through my fingernails until I was left with nothing but bloodied hands.

Once I finally landed, I hit the ground with a deafening thud, my head smacking against the gritty rock. Confused, as I expected pain but felt none at all. Disoriented and out of breath, I crawled woefully to the side of the boulder from which I fell. Despite it casting no shadow or providing any shelter, I felt it protected me from being seen by the wandering bodies. Now, closer to them, I noticed that something was seriously distorted about them. They appeared tall, not ridiculously tall, but surely taller than the average man I've met. If I had to estimate, it'd be somewhere around seven or so feet tall. They walked a bit unusually, perhaps suffering from an injury of sorts. It would be understandable if they had fallen from where I had, too. I crept alongside the wall; what lay beyond it, I didn't know, but it seemed to keep these people inside trapped, as climbing up the boulder seemed nearly impossible.

As I moved along, one of the people noticed me. As it turned its head, I gasped. Most of its facial features were seemingly smeared away. Only its eyes remained. There was no nose, no mouth, ears, or even a distorted orifice to make for an airway. Along the sides of its torso, where a ribcage would be, were hands, three on each side. They weren't attached to any arms but a short wrist, allowing for small movements. Its fingers were long and thin, almost skeletal-like. I stood frozen in fear, having no way to defend myself and nowhere to run. I thought that perhaps if I stood perfectly still, it wouldn't see me as a threat. After all, I wasn't a threat—I was just there.

I wanted to cry, to sob. What I was seeing was so foreboding, so unsettling. I wanted my mom. It stepped towards me, and its fingers all extended outward, further than before it was bothered. I held my breath, not wanting to create any disruption. There was nothing I could do but wait and see if it would keep walking towards me or turn away. It was far too big for me to contemplate whether I could fight it or not. As it drew closer, I inspected its eyes. They looked human, so normal, despite everything. As the creature took another step closer, one of its hands swiped at the air, like a cat pawing at a bird. I recoiled, only to hit my back into the wall behind me. As I made impact, pebbles fell, and debris dripped into my hair like raindrops. This led the monster to grow wild, walking faster towards me. It wasn't a run, as its legs were bent in a way where it wouldn't be able to. As it eventually approached me, I felt a deep scratch sting my forearm, and I cried out.

SUDDENLY, I was back in reality; I looked around my room, realizing that it wasn't quite morning yet. Groggily glancing at my watch, I had to rub a bit of sleep away from my eyes before focusing my vision on reading the small print numbers. I shook my head in confusion as my watch read seven-thirty. My bed, being right next to the window, led me to believe that my watch was wildly inaccurate. As I stared out the dark window, I glanced back at my watch. It then read quarter after five. I stared blankly at the time presented, not knowing how to handle the sudden change of information. Outside, it was still dark out. It was a clear night with a few stars visible. There was no indication I could find that the sun was about to rise. I shook my head and snorted; my vision was likely clouded from having just awoken. I looked at my watch again. *Six-fifty.*

I unlatched the watch from my wrist and stared at it feverishly. I watched as the second hand moved as it normally would. Only now, within the fraction of a second that it took for me to blink, the time was saying it was three-thirty. Frustrated, I tore the blankets off of me and walked out of my bedroom. As I left, I began to feel quite warm, as if my room was a completely different temperature than the rest of the house. Although possible in some scenarios, this one wasn't too likely. My window wasn't open like the one in the living room. The sun wasn't out, so it wasn't as if the sun were positioned to hit a room differently than others. I decided to set aside the temperature changes and find the clock in the living room. The clock read three-thirty, just as my watch now did. Feeling mildly comforted by some fragment of consistency, I left to go back to bed.

Back in my bed, I placed my arms across my ribs. It was then when I glanced at my forearm, which showed a faint scratch. I carefully traced my finger along my skin. In doing so with such a light touch, I gave myself goosebumps. I stared furiously at my arm. There's no way that the monster that attacked me in my dream created some real-life evidence. It was preposterous! I had to have merely scratched myself while sleeping. I tossed and turned restlessly, unable to calm my mind.

I must have fallen asleep, as when I opened my eyes next, sunshine had flooded my room. Comforted by light, I looked at my watch. It was just a bit after eight. The time matched perfectly with how the light entered through my window. As I stood up and stretched, a wave of dizziness hit me, causing my balance to sway. I stumbled sideways into my side table, hitting my hip right into the corner. As the impact of the hit surged through my body, I knew that within only a few hours, I would have the nastiest bruise.

Thinking I was in the clear with no immediate rush of nausea, I planned out what food sounded good for breakfast. I began to grow queasy as I ran through a list of traditional breakfast foods we would eat as a family. The simple idea of buttered toast made me nearly gag. I wasn't sure if it was the bread that sounded foul, the butter, or the entire package deal, but the mere concept of it all was revolting. Suddenly, I sat very still on the edge of my bed, not wanting to make any sudden movements that may unsettle my stomach further. Heat. All I felt was heat, but when I touched my skin, it felt quite cold. It felt as if the overall room temperature went up one degree every second. These feelings weren't strange to me, as during the first few weeks of my pregnancy, overheating paired with nausea were staple symptoms.

My body needed something. I had a deep desire, but that desire was unknown. I carefully sipped at a glass of water that sat on my nightstand. Drinking in small sips helped ease the overheated feeling over time, but it didn't satiate me. Being that it was morning, I was likely hungry. It was hard to tell considering that I had to think past my nausea and that was nearly impossible, but the odds were likely that my body needed food.

I wanted to walk to the kitchen, but doing so without throwing up seemed futile. I sat dejectedly on my bed staring longingly at my bedroom door, wishing I knew how to escape successfully. I began to hear the sounds of my mother starting breakfast. Pots and pans clanged together, and the sizzling of food echoed through the halls. Some kind of meat was being cooked, bacon or sausage; it was difficult to tell. The smell made my stomach growl, and I instinctively got up, as if I weren't on the verge of being sick a mere few seconds prior.

Walking into the kitchen, I watched as my mom prepared breakfast for the house. She cheerfully greeted me as she noticed my presence, and I replied by telling her that the kitchen smelled wonderful. She told me to return to my room and she would soon bring me a plate once everything was finished. I obliged and walked back into my room without thinking twice.

As it was springtime, I opened my window for some fresh air. The sound of birds chirping danced into my bedroom as a sweet melody. The smell of freshly cut grass mixed with a light spring rain flooded in. It wasn't long before staring out the window gave me a headache. Wincing away, I shut the drapes closed and shut my eyes. It seemed that doing any minor task was going to ail me in some way. It was an awfully defeated feeling, giving me little options to occupy myself with. It seemed like the only doable hobby was sleeping, but it surely wasn't enjoyable. I couldn't remember the last time I had a pleasant dream, one that wasn't ridiculously vivid or startled me awake. I suppose if I thought about it, the dreams with Ron weren't all that bad.

My mom brought me my plate of food with a wide smile to match. I kindly thanked her, instantly grabbing a piece of bacon and began to eat it ravenously. It didn't quite stop the craving, but it was close. Everything else on the plate didn't interest me, but the bacon was good enough. The other foods simply seemed too bland. The mouthwatering saltiness of the bacon strips was easily the best thing I had eaten in what felt like months. With my nausea at bay and my hunger satiated, I felt almost completely at peace. I likely just had some protein or iron deficiency.

Finishing up with my breakfast, I set the plate aside. I stared down at my stomach, as if a few pieces of bacon and a couple bites of toast were responsible for my ever-growing pelvis. As I placed my hand on my bump, I felt a warm sensation. It started underneath my hand, similar to if I had gone out during the winter without mittens and tried to warm up my hands by placing them on my warmer skin. The warmth then grew, spreading slowly from every direction to every stretch of skin. Once it finally reached my entire body, it was still warmest at my stomach. Trying to calm my panic, I took a few deep breaths. I inhaled slowly from my mouth, mentally counting the seconds as they passed. As I exhaled, I stretched out my hands and lifted my head to face the ceiling. I tried not to be scared. Sure, nine months is quite some time for your body to do a list of new things, but it felt like I was going mad, that no one else had ever gone through it but me. My mom said it was just nerves, but God, it felt like I was growing a demon.

Later that day, I was back to cradling my stomach. Thankfully, I was no longer overheating, but it wasn't long before my stomach began to feel strange. A hollowing sensation was happening, like blowing a bubble that grew larger with every passing second. The pop was imminent, and I was quite startled when it happened. It wasn't strong but like a quick tap on a doorknocker. I gasped, and my heart began to race. Every new sensation was almost always panic-inducing, and this was no exception. Holding my breath, I waited for something, whether it be another burst or something else. I sat, quivering, dreading. A look of trepidation crept upon my face and I tentatively placed my hands in the shape of a diamond over my stomach.

A few minutes passed, and the sensation happened again. It was softer this time. Rather than a doorknocker being used, it felt like a balled-up piece of parchment was flying inside of me. I grimaced at the feeling. It didn't hurt, and I supposed it wasn't inherently harmful, but the feeling made me want to crawl out of my skin. I wanted nothing more than to slip away from my body and never feel that specific feeling again. My face grew hot, and my vision blurred with tears. I hated the trajectory of where this was going, as I knew that the further the pregnancy progressed, the more things would happen.

I began crying and mumbling to myself incoherently. It wasn't a sob. I wasn't completely overcome with tears, but I felt very fragile. I was a small glass statue that held a deep crack. Shattering was in my future and would only be a matter of time. I dug my nails into my skin until my mother, concern on her face, stopped me. She grabbed my hands and held them in hers. She brushed my hair out of my face and hushed my words. She asked me what the matter was, and I told her that I felt it kicking me. Overjoyed, she covered her mouth with her hands and let out a small squeal. She bounced with a childish glee and called in the rest of my family. Overwhelmed by the rush of them coming into my room, I sat on my bed, incapable of moving. I had stopped crying, not because I was feeling better, but because I no longer knew what was happening and watched every event as it played out. It was mere seconds before my sister, father, brother, and Abagail crowded into my bedroom, a room unequipped to hold that many people. I felt as hands were placed on my stomach and words overlapped.

Everything felt so tight. My bedroom, where I once found nothing but comfort and solace, quickly felt like a cage. I was an animal at the zoo, and my family were patrons. I was to be gawked at, photographed, and made fun of. I was the show pony of entertainment being thrown peanuts to continue the amusement. I resented my captivity, and piece by piece, I was starting to resent my captors. With every adoring grin spread across the faces of my family members, I felt less like a member of the family and simply its piece of entertainment. Long gone were the days of being a carefree child, nurtured by her mother and cradled by her father. Long gone were the days of playing for hours with my brother, my former partner in crime. Long gone were the days of helping to raise my sister when each of my parents were too busy. To replace those memories was the picture of each family member extending their claws to place upon my swollen stomach. I was far too put off by the concept of my nightmare being their amusement.

Once finally in solitude, I lay uncomfortably in bed. I felt as if someone had stared at my naked body. I wanted to cry, but I couldn't, so my face was frozen in a permanent scowl. Too upset to eat, I went to bed hungry, my stomach angrily crying at my decision. In an attempt to calm it, I drank water and switched positions, but that had no effect. Running my hand through my hair, my fingers were left with a coat of oil. Showering was difficult and I couldn't remember the last time I did it. Realizing that I was more than past due to take one, I sighed. I slowly ambled out of bed and picked out clothes to change into. I have gone from one nightgown to the next for quite some time now. The more billowy, the better.

The bathroom was so incredibly neutral. The rest of the house had what I believed to be an average amount of decorations: family photographs, random knick-knacks, heirlooms. Shelves were stocked, and the walls were bright. It was inviting and homey. The bathroom did not get that same treatment. The walls were white tiled with cracks scattered throughout. The appliances were yellowing with age and sun damage. If it weren't as small as it was, one might confuse it for a public restroom based on its pure neutrality. I stared at the bathtub with exhausted eyes. Despite standing in the bathroom, the pure idea of taking a shower sounded impossible. I knew it was physically doable. I wouldn't die from the act, but actually getting around to doing it was laborious.

An unknown number of minutes passed before I took a step forward. I turned on the water, letting it run rapidly from its faucet. I placed my hand underneath the water and waited for it to reach a comfortable temperature. I liked my showers lukewarm. Cold showers were far too shocking, and I simply couldn't do it. Hot showers, where the water is so warm that your veins pop through and you grow weary, were too much for me. It didn't take long before the water rose to the right temperature, but bringing myself to get undressed and step inside was a lot.

I sat on the edge of the bathtub with my hand under the running water, staring into nothing while also feeling too, like nothing.

Like being in a trance, I took off each piece of clothing and stepped inside the shower.

Letting the water soak through my hair, I felt cleaner already, like a layer of grime had been washed off within only seconds. I stood motionless, letting the water strike against the back of my body in small pellets, and pressed my hands into the depths of my skin, my body ever-changing.

My stomach wasn't plump and round like you may commonly associate with pregnancy. I was still rather small, but the protrusions were more square and aligned with my ribcage. I had a more cylindrical shadow than a curvaceous one. My breasts weren't larger, but my nipples had darkened and gotten slightly bigger. That was all that was larger about my body. I was hardly eating enough for one, let alone two. The bones in my shoulders stood out in ways they never did before. My collarbones jutted forward, sticking beyond the rest of my skin. My hands appeared skeletal, but when I asked Judith if she noticed a difference, she simply shrugged me off. I don't know how long I was in the shower before exiting. It could have been minutes, or it could have been hours. I didn't remember if I used soap or shampoo. I was simply in the shower one second, and the next, I was a dripping figure back in my bedroom.

The people with the hands visited me again in my dreams. They looked the same as they did the previous time I had dreamt of them, still towering over me. The height difference was comparable to a small child with their father. Even with seeing the creatures in dreams prior, I couldn't help but be just as terrified as I was the first time. Despite having a slight human-esque appearance, my mind couldn't comprehend any of them as being a person. Their presence felt too menacing, too otherworldly, too threatening, too other. Animalistic isn't the right word; predatory would be more accurate. After each of these dreams, I always wonder how I could have possibly imagined such wild creatures. All the books I owned were never that fantastical, and I had never seen a movie even close to being as horrific as what I saw in my dreams. It all seemed so wildly out of nowhere, leading me to fear my imagination.

The next day, I awoke with more pain than I was accustomed to. It, not surprisingly, stemmed from my stomach. Still writhing in a dream-like state, I didn't attend to my ailment with fervor but took my time and allowed myself to continue waking up. Sleep slowly faded from my eyes, and the bright colors of reality flooded in. Now that life was no longer blurred by the haziness of rest, I pulled up my nightgown to expose my torso. Dozens of scratches marked my stomach. Some seemed more faint and soft, whereas others were obviously deep enough to have drawn blood. I stared in horror, not remembering having done that to myself but not knowing of any other cause for the crime. I daintily traced my fingers over each scar. They were fresh, tender. I winced each time. After staring at my stomach, I looked at my fingernails. They were short, to the skin, short. I could have sworn that just the day prior, my nails were rather long and healthy. Running my thumb along the tips of each finger, I found them to be sore, as if each finger had a bruise. I stared in utter confusion, not knowing what had happened.

As I began to get out of bed, I noticed something at the foot of my bedside table. Upon further inspection, it appeared to be a few fingernail clippings. I tried to think back to the night prior, if I had cut them without remembering or if I had peeled them off in my sleep. No matter what narrative was accurate, it didn't make sense. How could I have forgotten cutting my nails when it had only happened the night prior? Sure, it's a rather rudimentary task that isn't really worth remembering, but the fact that I had possibly forgotten it so easily was something that raised concern. If I had ripped them off in my sleep, then that would make sense as to why I didn't remember, but that's just as strange behavior. I looked back at the loose fingernails on the carpet and saw that it was only three clippings. It was as if someone had done a poor job of cleaning up their mess. I called my mom into the room, wondering if she would provide any insight. She entered my room with a smile and slightly darker circles than usual. She looked tired, but she had been taking care of me more so than she's done in years. Her fatigue was rather warranted. However, as much as she did around the house, her face, on average, seldom showed exhaustion. Even when Judith was a newborn, I remember her glowing.

As my mother stood before me with her kind hazel eyes, I dawdled on asking what happened. I bit at the skin on my lip as she absentmindedly grabbed dirty dishes from my bedside table. After much deliberation, I asked her if I had cut my fingernails last night, trying to phrase my words as carefully as possible without sounding mad.

"Well, yes, we helped you last night," my mom said softly.

"Helped me with what?"

"With your fingernails," she said without missing a beat. I stared at her silently, trying to recall a memory I couldn't place.

I remember feeling sick when it was kicking and crying, feeling immensely overwhelmed. I was in bed when it happened, sometime in the early evening. I hadn't had dinner yet; in fact, I didn't remember having dinner at all that night. Crying in my bed was the last memory I had before taking a shower. I couldn't even remember going to bed. There were simply hours cut from my day that seemingly floated out of existence.

My mom walked out of my bedroom with my old dishes and to fix me breakfast. Despite not having dinner the night prior, I wasn't too focused on the concept of eating. As much as I was aware that my body craved food, I was utterly consumed by nerves with my mind racing at a speed I couldn't comprehend. While doing so, I stared blankly at the wall. My body felt frozen and stimulated somehow at the same time. Even with being perfectly still, my heart raced against my chest. My stomach was knotted, and the smell of the food only furthered my discomfort. Everything simply felt wrong.

From my bedroom, I heard the usual noises of breakfast being prepared. I didn't care. My mind was somewhere else which led my stomach to a familiar path of unease. My mom often made the same meals with some rotation, so there wouldn't be any repeat days. There had been a time when each meal made my mouth water despite my having it all throughout my life. That time had come to an end as the repetition, while innocuous in intention, had begun to aggravate me. Having had the same meals on rotation for nearly nineteen years was growing tiresome. I looked at the plate of food my mom left me and felt my face scowl. Turning my nose up, I slowly pushed the plate out of my reach, all the while knowing that the smell had completely infested my room. I let the plate sit and grow cold, unimpressed by a meal I once craved each and every morning. As I stared at the ceiling with nothing to do, I heard my mother escort Judith out the door in time for school. On most days, my mom would just walk her out the door, but as I heard the jingling of her keys, I knew that she must've had errands to run as well. With Isaiah and my father at work, and now my mom and Judith gone, it was a moment where I could enjoy the house to myself.

The house was quiet. Stirrings of life were nonexistent and the rustling of chores decamped. Despite what should be a calm and tranquil state, it felt oddly foreboding. Even though everyone who lived in the house was gone, I didn't quite feel alone. There was literally no evidence of anyone else nearby, but there was this energy humming around me. It was a silent bass tone, an intangible touch, and an invisible shadow. Whatever it was, it felt suffocating. It felt like this pressure was suddenly omnipresent and crushing me in every direction. As I began to feel overwhelmed, I fell out of bed and started nervously pacing around my room. I wrung my hands and cracked each knuckle. I ran into the kitchen and aggressively turned on the sink to splash some water on my face. The water, being room temperature, didn't feel as shocking as I hoped. Although surprising, it was merely a wet sensation that didn't wake me up and out of my panic state. I splashed the water against my skin once more, feeling the small beads run down my face before scaling my neck. I sighed before turning off the faucet and placing my elbows on the counter. I likely just needed to get some food in me. Uninterested in the plate of breakfast sitting somewhere in my room, I searched through the refrigerator for some kind of nourishment. Just as I had been for the past few days, I heavily craved meat. The colorful array of fruits and vegetables was irrelevant to me. It might as well have been all artificial, mere decoration.

There didn't appear to be much in the house, likely why my mother was out shopping, but I did notice one lone chicken breast sitting in its bloodied packaging that once held an entire family dinner's worth. I grabbed it and thought of different ways I could prepare it. It could be grilled, baked, or breaded, but the thought of doing the prep work sounded tiresome. I tore off the packaging, the smell flooded my nostrils. I was expecting it to have no scent, or worst-case scenario, smell rotted. Neither was the case and instead, it smelled delicious. What looked to be a cold, slimy chicken breast smelled like a fully cooked meal.

I felt as my mouth began to salivate, as if I were a dog with a steak in front of it. Without thinking, I took a bite. The texture, I'll admit, was bizarre, but also, in a way, satisfying. It was something I wasn't at all used to, but it felt so right. The act felt very primal, like this was what my body wanted. Something still felt a bit off, likely because of how cold it was, but I hadn't been that satisfied by food in I couldn't place how long. I felt as my body fell into the cabinetry, overcome with elation. The fluids of the chicken ran down from my wrist. Just before it could drip onto the floor, I licked my arm ravenously, as if I hadn't eaten in days. My teeth shred into the piece of meat as if it were bread. It all slid so easily down my throat. Once finished, I sucked my fingers clean, once again, acting as if I had been starved. After sighing contently, I noticed my mother standing across from me. One of her grocery bags slipped from her grip as she stared at me in horror.

~

I LAY SPRAWLED out across my bed. Blankets were a burden. Even my top sheet felt suffocating. I writhed and winced as my body felt like it was shutting down. This wasn't too different from how pregnancy had been treating me. Every inch of my body felt dirty, as I had been lying in my own sweat for hours. The only solace I had was a damp washcloth, but the tap water was seemingly replaced by my sweat, so it was simply a washcloth that smelt of old laundry. I felt too weak to shower; the idea of standing for so long made me tired thinking about it. A bucket was placed next to my bed at the ready, just in case. It was the very same one that had been by my side during my first few weeks of pregnancy. Dinner was highly out of the question, and all I wanted to do was sleep. There was no position that would allow me to relax and be comfortable, however, as no matter what I did, I suffered.

I felt dazed. I felt as if I were barely alive. I wanted nothing more than to slip into a deep sleep and wake when I felt like myself again. Alas, life wasn't that kind, and my body kept me awake during the entirety of my sickness. I thought back to my mom and her words about her easy pregnancies. While too weak to grow overcome with emotion, I lay still and seething. I knew it was wrong to be upset over someone's lack of suffering, especially my own mother's, but that's all I felt. Why was it she only spoke highly of that time of her life when mine was nothing short of awful? We were related, so one would think we would have similar experiences. That is, unless she lied. Perhaps she had positively awful pregnancies and wanted to try and be positive to make me feel better. Clearly, that backfired, but who was she to know? I tried desperately to think back to when she was pregnant with Judith. She glowed. Her dresses fit snugly around her belly and flared out around her petite frame. She continued to make the family meals, do the bulk of the housework, and have time to raise Isaiah and me when my father was off at work. Nearing the time when Judith was born, I remember her slowing down but only a bit. This was the time when myself and Isaiah were expected to step up, as we were both to be now big siblings. Regardless, if my mom had any ailments along the way, that would have been news to me.

It wasn't fair. I didn't understand what was happening to me. I didn't understand why I felt so terrible both physically and mentally. Growing up, abstinence was preached heavily. I woefully wondered if this was the result of having sex prior to marriage and if this was some curse I had brought on myself. I knew that pregnancy came with a list of unwanted symptoms, but it couldn't be this bad for everyone, could it? Why would couples have multiple kids? God wouldn't do this to them, would he? Was this all my fault? If I had done things the proper way, would I be suffering as greatly? This just wasn't normal. I knew deep down that none of this was.

The more I thought about it, the more emotional I became. I felt like a disappointment, a burden, something to be ashamed of. I was the mess of the family, the black sheep. I imagined the lies my parents told their friends at church about why I wasn't with them at service. Hot tears ran down my face, and I felt my lip begin to tremble. I didn't want my parents to hate me. I didn't want to be looked down upon. I wish I knew someone else who was in my position. There had to have been someone else near my age who had a child out of wedlock somewhere in the world. I ran through a list in my head of all the people I knew who had children: parents, old classmates, teachers, farmers, shop owners, and the church elders. While it was possible that someone somewhere on that list had been in the same boat as I was, not one name came to mind. I wish there were a way to look up these people. The drive out of town isn't long, but the idea of driving seemed rather laborious. However, for peace of mind, it may be worth it.

After my tears had dried and my mind calmed down, I positioned myself in a comfortable spot in bed. I waited for my eyelids to droop, for my mind to slowly shut off, and slip into sleep as I could tell my body craved it. I laid there and laid there, yet to no avail. I waited and waited and nothing. Growing more frustrated, I tossed and turned, desperately trying to rest, even if it was just for an hour. I stared at my clock.

Midnight.

There were so many of them now. Their heads bounced wildly from every direction, as if their neck did absolutely nothing in support. There had to have been dozens of them at this point. They walked in flocks, their bones stretching out over their greyed skin, jutting out at every angle.

The terrain was rocky. I watched as they would paw at the jagged stone walls that held us in. I, too, placed my hand on the wall, which, in reality, was just the side of the boulder I first saw myself on. I lightly picked at the rock, and small fragments fell to the ground, bouncing off beyond my view. A glint in the stone caught my eye. There was a soft light. Intrigued, I took one of the fallen fragments and used it to hit around the light. Little by little, the gleaming stone became loose. It wasn't long before it sat in the palm of my hand. It was gold. Lumpy and a bit dull, it rolled around until it slipped from my grasp. It hit the ground with an unimpressive noise, but as I went to pick it up, every eye was on me. Every creature within my line of vision went on high alert. Their eyes widened and chests flared, they all began to run towards me, their fingers extending far beyond their being. They ran like cattle; their stampede echoed within the wind. I stood there, my back against the wall, with nowhere to run, having nothing to do but accept my fate. They were going to kill me. There were so many of them. I braced myself, my arms clutching my chest, preparing for the inevitable.

I woke up with a gasp as I had a tendency to do. I took a deep breath in an attempt to soothe my racing heart. Glancing over, I noticed my clock sitting on my bedside table.

1 a.m.

I got the hour of sleep I wanted so bad. Then the kicking started. It does that now after the nightmares.

WEEK 21. MONTH 5

The hex-handed monsters were no longer. I was still tucked away next to the boulder where a thick smoke sat in the air. More of the monsters existed in the distance but far enough from me not to be in their line of vision. Right where the monsters attacked me was a peculiar crack in the ground. I slowly got to my knees and traced my finger along the divot to get a closer inspection. Hot air came out of the crack, which, paired with the fact that the crack was perfectly straight, gave me the realization that it was likely a trap door to a new room. I managed to jimmy my fingers under the ground and expose a weathered step ladder made of rope and aged wood.

The wood planks creaked heavily under my feet and felt rather brittle. I tried to be light on my feet, as it felt as if the wood were to snap. Lowering myself into the next room, a strong odor danced around me. It smelt oddly clean yet sharp, like a fountain with hundreds of pennies tossed inside. The step ladder led me to a landing, which, as soon as I stepped off of the ladder, it had disappeared. Standing on the lone landing, I looked around, and a fog replaced the ladder and door. Rather than a traditional, even layer of white, the fog looked wispy in some areas, whereas more condensed in others. It looked as if I were floating in the sky above the clouds. The more I looked around, I eventually realized that was the case. The skies above were dark, made up of thunderous dark grey clouds. Light was limited, and it was hard to determine where exactly I was. I had to crawl around on my hands and knees to determine the edge of what I was standing on. As I moved my hands along the ground, I realized how gritty it was, almost as if it were covered in sand. My hands crawled forward, leading me through the clouds at a downward slope. I treaded carefully in order to not fall forward. Taking small steps, I felt as I passed through clouds, mist kissing my face so delicately.

The ground felt colder the lower I went and more malleable, similar to the feeling of wet dirt. The further I descended, the more noise there was. It sounded similar to a storm: a chaotic whirl of wind, a dull rumbling of thunder and what sounded like a rainstorm, only there was no rain. Meandering through was difficult. I no longer crawled through the unknown terrain but still kept my body low to the ground. I was unable to keep my eyes open, or else sand and debris would sting my eyes, not that even having my eyes open in the first place would be helpful. It was incredibly dark, and for the life of me, my eyes wouldn't adjust to the level of darkness. It was similar to the sensation of being in strong daylight for hours, only to walk into a dark room and barely be able to make out furniture.

Considering I didn't know exactly where I was walking, I obviously wanted to be cautious. It wasn't until I crawled to a point where I felt shallow waters that I attempted to open my eyes. Still unaccustomed to the darkness, I squinted, barely able to make out anything before me. It took quite some time to realize I was placed on a river bank. The waters before me ran rapidly and angrily forward, waves consistently crashing into one another. The river extended as far as I could see. There appeared to be a never-ending amount of objects being carried along the current. Bottles and cans were littered throughout, floating vagrantly along.

As I knelt at the riverbank, a stuffed bear floated towards me. I honestly didn't think anything of it until more toys continued passing me by. Cracked baby dolls, stuffed animals with matted fur, and blocks with the paint chipped away. I stared blankly, growing more bored with each passing toy. The symbolism was not lost on me. As I felt a mighty kick, I put my hand on my stomach in a similar fashion as if someone were to cover another's mouth when speaking rudely.

I squinted toward the distance, trying to determine if the shape beyond the horizon was land or if my mind was playing tricks. Considering I was currently at a small riverbank with nowhere else to go but beyond, if that were, in fact, land, that was clearly where I was supposed to continue toward. However, due to having no boat, there was no safe way for me to cross the river. I didn't have much faith in my ability to swim, and even then, the current was quite strong. The longer I looked, the more I realized that I was likely imagining what I wanted to see and that there was no plot of land in the distance. I sat dejectedly on the dirt, staring at the river before me. Aside from not having a clue as to where I was, I felt utterly lost. I felt oddly unprepared despite my not knowing where I was or how I ended up there in the first place. I had a sense of guilt, like I should have known better.

The ground was made up of very clay-like soil that crumbled easily when held in my hands. Surrounding me were these tall string-like vines. The shape was similar to that of a tree, but the object didn't feel alive. It didn't look like any plant that I had seen before. It had no greenery or leaves, just a dark brown stump that extended far above my height and broke up into multiple jagged branches. The "trees" could have been used to make a raft of some sort, but I had no way of cutting it down. I merely sat on the dirt, having no sense of direction or plan of action. Slowly, I began to move my hand closer to the water's edge. As my hand was inches away, I experienced a sharp pain in my lower stomach. I recoiled back, wrapping both arms around my torso. As my body seemed to settle, I once again reached out to touch the water. Just as it had done before, the pain returned. It wasn't like a strong kick or a stomach cramp. It was a precise pain, like the sharpest blade directly plunged into my lower abdomen. It was the kind of pain to make your entire body wince in response.

I knew I would have to cross the river as there was nothing left for me at the water's edge. It was impossible to tell just how deep the water was, but if I had to guess, I knew it would be deep enough to swallow me whole. I stood up and gazed across the horizon. My heart raced at a speed that felt infeasible. My pulse echoed throughout my body, allowing me to feel it in every limb. Baby steps drew me closer to the water's edge. I knew it was a bad idea but something compelled me to continue onward. Just as I began to place my right foot in the water, a hand reached out and pulled me in.

Naturally, I tripped and fell face-first into the river. The touch of the water was shocking. I could not fully identify if the water was blistering hot or freezing cold, but somehow, an intertwinement of both burned my skin. Writhing at the touch, I struggled to get my head above the water. Gasping for air, it wasn't long before I was soon pulled further under the water's surface. The water was too murky to see through before being underwater, yet for whatever reason, I attempted to open my eyes whilst submerged. The water scalded my eyes and felt like acid poured into them. Naturally, I opened my mouth to cry out in pain, only to allow the water to enter my mouth. I thrashed and fought, unknowing of what I was even fighting. Flailing in the voided waters blind, my skin ached. I was on fire. I was frozen. My skin was melting off. The poison entered my throat, searing away whatever was in its path. Everything was dark, and I could not breathe. I could not breathe at all. God, I was going to die. Death by the creatures seemed far kinder, but that was then, and this is now. My legs tried to kick away whatever was trying to harm me, but the water prohibited any fighting from happening. I was only tiring out my body at an incredible speed. I was out of air. I grew weak. My body grew limp, unable to fight anymore.

I WOKE UP CHOKING. It was as if I had actually started drowning and had water in my lungs. I thrashed on my bed, panicked before adjusting my perception to knowing I was safe. I checked my watch and realized it was a bit past ten, far later than I typically wake up. School was out for Judith, so I knew it was almost a guarantee for her to be home with me. Curious as to what she was up to, I ambled out of bed. My morning nausea had almost completely subsided, with only a few random days where I felt sick. Hunger fueling my motion, I quickly slipped out of my room and headed for the kitchen.

"What are you doing?" Judith asked in a tone of worry, stopping me before I could exit the hallway. Confused as to why she seemed so concerned, I stared at her with a puzzled look.

"I'm hungry," I replied plainly. She didn't say anything else, but she followed me as I walked into the kitchen. The kitchen had been cleared, and all but one dish put away.

Wrapped in foil was a small plate, presumably for me. I asked Judith if it was mine, and she nodded in response. I unraveled the foil, revealing a pretty standard breakfast. As I turned from the dish and approached the refrigerator, Judith followed not far behind.

"What is it?" I asked, confused by her behavior. She looked at the floor and scrunched up her nose. I narrowed my eyes at her actions, as she was never anything but honest. Her energy was anxious, apprehensive. She was uncomfortable with her own actions and it was alarmingly apparent.

"Jude, what's wrong?" I asked, concerned. She refused to speak or make eye contact, behavior far different from how she regularly portrays herself. Something was surely wrong, and her dawdling was killing me.

"Momma said you couldn't be in the kitchen alone anymore," she finally blurted out. I raised my brow, shocked and incapable of words.

Processing the words she spoke, I slowly picked up the dish my mom left for me and walked back into my room. I slammed my door shut and immediately started to cry. I grabbed the plate of food and slammed it onto the floor repeatedly. Pieces of egg and other loose crumbs bounced onto the floor until everything was littered everywhere. They saw me so differently than how they once did. It was almost hard to comprehend how life was prior to my pregnancy. The loving, the nurturing, the warmth was now a caricature of what was once presented to me. They said "I love you" and smiled when I entered a room, but their eyes contradicted their actions. Their energy negated their words. In their eyes, I was now the problem child.

I laid back in bed after picking up each piece of food. It had grown quite cold and lost some of its flavoring, but it didn't even matter. Almost every piece had fuzz or a stray hair stuck to it that I had to meticulously remove. It humbled my outburst as it was clearly not worth all the trouble. Despite it all, I had begun to grow ravenously hungry as each week passed by, so putting in the work to replate my food was worth it. Each cold piece of egg, each piece of buttered toast that now homed a stray thread, was simply mouthwatering. Perhaps my standards were lowered. I truly didn't care.

As I lay in bed, I lifted my nightgown, exposing my stomach. Small red lines were now present near my pelvis. As I looked closer, the lines changed positions ever so slightly. Furrowing my brow, I looked once more, and they were moving. The stretch marks appeared as if they were vibrating. It wasn't significant movement; in fact, it was just barely noticeable. I watched in horror as my skin danced to an impossible reality. I rubbed at the lines softly, thinking it would either stop the movements or erase the lines altogether. Neither was the conclusion, and the pulsating motions of my skin only made me grow more anxious. It began to feel as if something were physically on me and I could feel the marks on my skin move. It felt like ants were running continuously across my stomach. Placing my hand on top of my skin didn't alleviate the agitation. Growing more worried, I scratched at the marks, hoping it would ease the rising discomfort. It was quite literally an itch I couldn't quite scratch. Digging my nails into my skin, I began to apply strong amounts of pressure in the hopes of stopping the sensation. While it didn't worsen, it continued to persist. I watched as ants ran across my stomach in a perfect little line. They emerged from my flesh to run across my protruding stomach, only to melt back into my skin right above my pelvis. I pulled down my nightgown and pressed my forearms into my stomach.

"It's not real," I whispered to myself over and over. As I continued whispering, the sensation did not stop. The bugs grew larger and continued along my skin. Every hair on my body was upright, and my stomach quickly turned. I lay in bed as the bugs ran up and down my body.

That night at dinner, I sat at the table with my family. Isaiah and Abagail had joined us. Things seemed to be going well for them. She looked at him as if he hung the stars, and he matched her gaze tenderly. They really seemed like a fit pair. Sitting at the table with all of them somehow made me feel more lonely than when I was to eat meals by my lonesome in my bedroom. They laughed and conversed amongst themselves and, despite my being right there, didn't appear to make the effort to include me. It wasn't obvious to an onlooker, but being a part of the family, I could feel a shift.

Was it sad that I was surprised at being asked to join them for dinner? I couldn't remember the last time I had enjoyed a meal with them.

Normally, my mother would simply drop off a plate in my room and take it away an hour or so later. I would still bless my meals even when by myself, but I had never really done that before. It was a new experience. Not necessarily a bad one, but it felt a lot different from the dynamic of being with my family.

Considering it was becoming a rare occasion to be in my seat at the table, I felt obligated to cherish the moment. This feeling of "this is going to end soon, so I have to be happy and thankful now" was overwhelming. It wasn't an organic happiness that flowed naturally from the situation but a forced one that I deliberately made myself feel.

It was utterly exhausting.

The food really didn't interest me, and neither did the company. I carelessly played with my food with my fork, only occasionally actually taking bites. My eyes began to unfocus, and I watched as the plate in front of me gradually became more blurred. Every once in a while, I would feel eyes on me, but when I were to look up, it would vanish. Feeling a tinge of guilt for not participating in any dialogue, I tried to focus in on the conversation that was playing out. My father and Isaiah were having some arbitrary conversation about crops that were going in and out of season, with my mom, sister, and Abagail listening intently. I watched the girls watch the boys, and I tried to emulate them. I cocked my head and placed my hands carefully in my lap in replication to everyone else. I kept my posture upright despite the shooting pains in the various locations in my back. I molded my face into a look of understanding and interest despite my not giving any sort of care for any word they said. I watched as my father altered his demeanor when he broke away from the conversation to speak to my mom. He went from speaking contentedly with Isaiah to almost belittling towards my mom, asking her for her help when he was fully capable of taking care of himself. Confused by this change, I then watched as Isaiah did the same to Abagail. She obeyed with a chagrined smile and pleading eyes. I felt as my face fell into a frown. I had only ever seen my father act lovingly to my mom. He was soft, gentle, and never seemed too demanding or lazy. Watching him practically bark at my mom for various tasks was likely not new, but it was new to my eyes, and I did not wish to see it.

"Can't you get it yourself?" I snapped. While I thought it, I didn't expect to say it. The words simply fell from my lips, and I couldn't stop what I started. For the first time that night, all eyes were directly on me. I shrunk back.

"Ema, are you okay?" he asked, his tone almost condescending, frustrating me further. "Now, what has gotten into you?"

"Hormones, it's alright, it'll pass," my mom whispered to him. He nodded, though not without a slight look of disgust. He curled his lip before smiling. Offended, I stared wordlessly at my parents. I felt as my throat began to tighten, so I pressed my lips into a fine line, stopping myself from speaking any further. Rather than saying anything else in my defense, I pushed the table away from me, causing everything that was on it to wobble ever so slightly. I stood up sharply from my seat and stomped to my bedroom.

Realistically, he could have been correct. I was far more moody than I had ever been before becoming pregnant. I cried for what felt like every single day, and every little thing seemed to get under my skin. I wasn't even exactly sure what I was mad at, the dismissal of my behavior or the feeling of separation from the rest of my family; many answers were correct. I lay in my bed as if it were my hobby and simply stared at the ceiling.

I heard dishes being put away and the sound of goodbyes from my brother and Abagail. Isaiah and Abagail. Something told me that we would continue to say their names in such a way. I could just tell from the way my parents interacted with the pair to how Isaiah and Abagail interacted with each other. There was little doubt that it would not end in marriage.

Once the noise settled, I decided to make an apologetic appearance. I had my tail between my legs as I walked out of my bedroom. Everyone had left. It was now quarter past nine, and the house had fallen silent. There was no noise at all. That is, until I began walking around the house, but even then, I was the only noise. It was disturbing. I was disturbed. I ambled around the living room and noticed the clock stopped. It said the time was quarter after nine, but I wasn't sure if that was even true. Each hand of the clock stood solemnly in its place. Thinking little of it, I walked to the kitchen to fix myself a cup of water. I absentmindedly opened the kitchen window to let fresh air in, only to do a double take. The air outside was no different than within;

there wasn't any temperature change, but more importantly, there was no wind. There was never no wind. It didn't have to take a storm for there to be a little summer breeze or simply just being able to notice tree branches sway ever so slightly. Outside held the same stillness that the house did. Growing more unnerved, I knocked softly on Judith's door, assuming that she hadn't quite fallen asleep yet. I listened intently but didn't hear anything. I knocked once more and waited. I had begun to count the seconds waiting for her to respond but was met with silence. Very carefully, I began to turn the knob on her bedroom door. Judith was awake and standing over her bed, looking as if she were just about to go to sleep.

"Jude?" I whispered. I was met with no response. I tip-toed deeper into her bedroom and tapped her on the shoulder. She might have well been a statue. Her eyes were open with a heavy glaze covering them. Her shoulders and chest were motionless, with no movement that would have indicated breathing.

"Judith!" I shouted, shaking her shoulders. She was but a mannequin, her skin plastic and expression carved. Her nightgown simply sat on her shoulders rather than being worn by a living body. Hair was lifeless and limp, and skin devoid of any details. No warmth emanated from her frame.

"Judith!" I shouted once more.

"Ema, stop yelling. What's wrong?" Judith asked with a yawn. I was standing in the center of my room with my sister standing in my doorframe, exhaustion written all over her face.

"What's going on?" I asked, completely bewildered, looking around the room. With a look of trepidation, Judith replied by telling me that I had been shouting her name for the past few minutes. I apologized sheepishly before asking her the time. She nonchalantly exited my room and slipped into the living room. As she peeked her head around the door frame she muttered in a sleep-ridden voice,

"It's nine fifteen."

I crawled back into my bed and wrapped myself in the embrace of my duvet despite it being a rather warm night. The thick fabric acted as some kind of magical defense barrier against my distorted sense of reality. It wasn't long before my body was covered in a layer of sweat, and I felt sewn into my mattress. I shut my eyes tight and tried to picture myself somewhere else, anywhere else. I thought of rolling hills and towering mountains, peaceful seashores, and calming countryside. However, no matter how hard I tried, all I could easily visualize was angry, rapid waters. The water was running at a rate that only a vast river could produce. The sight made me anxious and unsettled. What made me even more unnerved was that the only view I had was underneath the surface. As soon as I would be underwater, I would force my eyes open to be back enveloped in my duvet. This process repeated itself at a seemingly endless rate until I noticed sunlight peeking through my window. It had somehow become morning, and it felt like I hadn't slept at all.

I stared blankly into nothing. My eyes were directed to my bookshelf, but my vision was blurred, unable to focus clearly on anything in particular. I lay there with exhaustion dragging my eyelids downward. I felt my eyes begin to slowly narrow in anger. I just wanted a peaceful rest. I wanted to dream about something relaxing, something beautiful, something boring. Throughout my entire pregnancy, I was plagued with nightmares, hyper-realistic stories of dread and terror. My options were either fright or sleep deprivation. I just wanted peace.

Something peculiar caught my eye. The knob on my bedroom door looked different. A dark brass knob glistened with a newness that I was unaccustomed to. Confused about how I didn't hear its installation, I brushed it off and continued with my morning routine. As I stood up, I felt as if any last remaining bit of energy stored in my body drained out. My body even instinctually hunched in on itself. It was as if magnets were sewn into my skin, pulling me closer to the floor. I didn't feel ill; I simply felt dreadful. I simultaneously felt completely hollow and like dead weight.

After letting myself wake up a bit more, I slowly ambled to my feet. As I walked to exit my room, I realized I was unable to turn the knob. Furrowing my brow, I shook it, trying to find the perfect spot in which it'd open. My father was far better at building things simply from scratch than he was redesigning or installing. Frustrated by his mistake, I knocked on my door, assuming someone was nearby to hear. My room was at the end of the hallway, with Isaiah being my neighbor, Judith next to his, and then finally, my parents, excluding the bathroom. After a few silent seconds, I tapped my wall and shouted for Judith. I assumed Isaiah was gone at work by now, so she was my next bet. I couldn't remember if she was still in school or if school had let out for the summer just yet. It was the early days of June, allowing for it to easily be either scenario. I tapped, this time a bit harder, and once again shouted for my sister. Silence. I pressed my ear against the door and listened for any signs of life. I couldn't hear the radio playing, the dishwasher, or even footsteps. I turned away from the door and looked at my bedside table. The table that once housed a clock was now one with just my empty water glass. Frozen in confusion, I stared with my mouth agape with the uncertainty of time. I ran to my window and peered outside. The sun was soft, not quite at its peak. It looked like it could have been around ten.

Back at the door, I ran my thumb over the knob. Perplexed as to why it appeared locked, but no lock was present, I anxiously fumbled with it more. My heart hit hard against my chest and raced at a beat that felt dangerous. A warmth spread over my body as if a dull flame had been lit behind me. Sweat beaded at my temple and I whimpered as I pulled at the door. It wasn't long before footsteps approached. I gasped before holding my breath. My nerves made it hard to identify the pattern of walking. The sound of a door unlocking made my shoulders slump in contentment. As it opened, my parents faced me, their expressions unreadable. Their presence, however, felt foreboding. They had an oddly menacing energy that made my body tense up. I stared at them with childlike eyes, waiting for them to speak, expecting an apology. However, with expressions as grim as theirs, it was evident that an apology wasn't likely. I sat patiently, waiting for them to speak.

"Put in new door handles," my father said in a low, gruff voice. I nodded solemnly to signify that I both understood and didn't wish to speak. I peered down the hallway to see that my door was the only one which was altered. Every other door had its original handle. I watched as my parents walked away, my father shoving a key into his breast pocket and sighing dejectedly.

WEEK 25. MONTH 6

Asphyxia. Despite my eyes being open, I couldn't concentrate on anything as I began coughing wildly, water spilling from my lips. Gasping for air made it feel as if there was no air left in the world to engorge upon. Oxygen was a luxury, and the once simple act of breathing became a mighty challenge. My heart nearly beat out of my chest, and I soon grew lightheaded. The globe I lived in was suddenly struck by a curious child, who spun it at a wild velocity. Getting my bearings was impossible. A pat came to the small of my back. It surely wasn't expected, but I was too preoccupied with staying conscious to be any more frightened than I already was. The sudden sensation was a welcomed change, however. I tried to concentrate on the rhythmic tapping on my back, but whatever was stuck in my lungs remained stuck. My gasps came out in raspy cries as tears stung my eyes. It took one final smack to my back for me to spit up whatever ailed me. I assumed it to be more water, but this liquid was darker and had a truly vile scent and taste. I instantly began to vomit in response. Hyperventilating, I attempted to ease my body back to a calmer state. My heart rate eventually slowed, and my breathing stabilized. Realizing that I wasn't alone, I turned quickly to see who helped me stop choking.

Virginia. My jaw fell to the floor at seeing a comforting, familiar face. My nightmares have been plagued with creatures from the depths of hell, bodies distorted, and monsters angry. Seeing a friend in this world was not necessarily enough to take me out of the nightmare realm, but it was nice nonetheless. I climbed off the ground and fell into a hug. I wrapped my arms around her tight, not wanting to risk possibly losing her. Based on the distorted reality I was within, I expected her to be different in some way, lacking of the person she was. However, when I hugged her, her body was warm and soft. I felt her breath against my neck. Her hair tickled my nose. She smelled like cinnamon apples. I felt my body shake, completely overcome with emotion. It felt as if someone had inflated a balloon in my stomach, and once it finally popped, nothing but joy spread to every last corner of my body. My hands trembled, and I cried out in relief.

As I slowly pulled away from her body, I looked at her. She was exactly the same as I knew her to be. She didn't suddenly have various additional appendages, she wasn't spewing tar-like vomit, and she wasn't malevolent in any way. I felt my heart drop as we finally broke away from the hug. Virginia looked at me with sympathy. It wasn't a look of pity, but she looked worried. It was as if she were looking at a lost puppy. Her eyes scanned down the length of my body, and once they stopped at my stomach, she sighed.

"You've gotten so big," she said, her voice quiet. Her tone was unreadable. I couldn't feel what she was feeling.

"You're here," I whispered, completely disregarding her former comment. Despite looking at her and hearing her voice, it was still unbelievable that she was with me. She stared back at me, smiling softly.

"What are you doing here? How did you get here?" I asked, emotions making my voice louder and my words delivered quicker.

"I'm here for you. I've been here a while, actually," she replied, grabbing my hand. After taking my hand, she began to lead me further from the river.

"Wait, why?" I asked, having new questions pop into my head at a fantastic speed. She walked at a casual pace, taking her time as she escorted me. I wasn't sure if she was walking slowly due to my pregnancy or if she simply was in no rush. I was still so flustered by the sight of her that I didn't want to question any of her choices at the risk of her leaving.

"To guide you through." Her words felt very final, like I didn't have a choice in questioning them. I, however, had many questions, but her demeanor made it difficult to ask. We continued walking along the gritty terrain for a while in silence.

"Why did you wait till now?" I asked finally, breaking the silence. "You said you've been here, but why am I just seeing you now?"

"I've been here with you the whole time. I made sure nothing bad happened, or nothing *that* bad anyway." I brushed off whatever that meant. I didn't need to know the specifics; I was just thankful for her presence.

We walked down a winding path. She led me back up from where I originally came from, but down once again to face a different part of the river. A rather small boat sat before us. Virginia dragged it to the river and pulled me to her. Just like that, we were suddenly on a boat, crossing the waters that scared me so. My shoulders tensed, my knees locked, and my brow permanently furrowed. Virginia smiled sympathetically at my demeanor. She reassured me I'd be fine, but I had yet to experience one fine memory while being trapped here. As I peeked out over the side, I saw dozens, perhaps hundreds of bodies. Arms reaching out above the water's edge, begging to be saved. One hand grabbed the side of the boat and rocked it slightly. My hands flew up to my mouth to cover my gasps, and I looked to Virginia for help. She waved it off. She was so calm. The hand lost its grasp and descended further into the river. As I sat there in dread, we eventually crossed to the other side. Virginia helped me out of the boat once docked, and the sounds of running water slowly became more and more distant until it was nothing but a bad memory. The cool, clammy air that hovered around the river dissipated, only to be replaced with warm, stuffy air. It was similar to walking into a bathroom after someone had just taken a shower. It wasn't sweltering or warm enough to be bothersome, but the temperature difference was stark. After walking together for a bit, Virginia let go of my hand, letting it fall to my side. I stopped in my tracks, confused, but she continued forward. It took a moment for her to turn around with a quizzical expression. She motioned with her head to continue following her, and I obeyed. I figured she realized that I no longer needed her hand as a form of physical support.

The dark skies bled downward, making the world above me both never-ending and non-existent. I didn't know how far down I was from the world above, but it felt like I was on an entirely new planet. A new noise began as we approached whatever destination Virginia was leading me to. The noise was hard to place, sounding like a mixture of high and low pitches. Without knowing what was causing it, I knew that it wasn't good. A feeling of dread came over me, but I wasn't sure as to why.

Virginia and I continued, with no interesting landmarks making our location stand out. There were no trees, no bodies of water, or really anything at all, just broken stone beneath our feet. Just as I was thinking how difficult it was to see, Virginia bent down and suddenly came back up with a torch. Curious about what she did to get it and how she did it, I had no reason to question, as I was grateful for the sudden light source. Considering it was a mere torch, the world around us was not suddenly ignited, but I felt a mild sense of relief. Just as I was starting to feel more comfortable, a piercing shriek echoed near us. I choked on a gasp as my body halted. In terms of deciding between flight or fight, I was on the hidden third option of freeze. My knees felt stuck, as if someone locked them into place permanently while cementing my feet to the ground. My hands tingled and felt like my blood was moving at double the normal speed. My paralysis was broken when Virginia took my hand. I shakily followed her lead despite wanting to run away.

"What was that?" I whisper-shouted. Virginia angrily motioned with her hand to stay behind her. Virginia was taller than me and seemed tough, but whatever made the noise seemed a lot more powerful than the pair of us combined. The scream happened again, the noise being closer this time. I grabbed onto Virginia's arm as if she knew what it was. She seemed more acclimated to wherever we were, so I just assumed she knew what everything was.

It was a whirlwind of what happened next. One moment, I was walking behind Virginia, my hand gripping her forearm tight, and the next I was blinded and being pushed forward. There was some kind of cloth fabric pressed over my eyes. Not knowing what was happening and unable to see, I stumbled. Virginia was there to catch me and keep me moving fast. Wherever we were, whatever we were near, was bad. The air quickly grew hot, and I could hear something or someone moving. Instinctively, I stuck my arms out in front of my face in an attempt to gain my bearings. There was no wall for me to hug or railing to grip onto. I was merely cast out into an open nothingness, with only Virginia's grasp on my blindfold. Unfamiliar with the terrain, I wanted to walk slowly, carefully. This place, whatever it was, has had cliffs and rivers; who was to know what else one may find? Hesitation seemed wise. However, when some kind of demon-like creature was near, running was also instinctive. What, in turn, came out was this ridiculous combination of the two. I essentially was tip-toeing quickly, with my arms outward, looking quite the fool indeed.

Each step was a gamble. I had to trust that Virginia knew what she was doing and, if not, was at least someone who would help me if needed. A disgusting shriek bellowed. The thing was near. I couldn't see it, but I could only imagine. In my head, I saw some kind of bird-like creature, considering the noise it made. Some kind of half-human, half-bird with claws, flapping its wings menacingly. As I continued forward, my hands touched something. I recoiled back quickly, startled, my heart racing. Whatever it was, it was hard, perhaps part of a wall?

I felt a kick to the back of my leg. I took it as an instruction to walk faster and not worry about whatever I found. Walking further, it happened again. My hand came into full contact with the thing. The material was rough, like cement, and dense. I only had a few seconds before I was to walk past it to try and think of what it could be. It wasn't in line with the one previous, so it couldn't have been a wall. It was as if there were random cinderblocks in the middle of the walkway. A hand was placed upon my shoulder and pulled me in close. Thankfully, only Virginia, but I was worried about what we were about to encounter with her sudden change of direction. Our path became a zig-zag, no longer a straight shot through the dark. I felt her drag me away to the left and then again to the right. There were times when she moved my leg out of the way of something. I wish I knew what was happening, but being as perilous as the situation seemed, I didn't want to risk our lives.

Questioning what my reality was perhaps more frightening than what was actually there—fear of the unknown and so forth. Sure, whatever was being hidden from me was being hidden for a reason, but that didn't stop my imagination from going into overdrive. I began counting my steps as some last-ditch form of distraction. I got into the fifties before my blindfold was removed. I couldn't see anything at first. Life was but a dark blur until my eyes eventually adjusted. When looking around, the terrain wasn't all too different from before. It was still dark; fog still sat in the air. We were still on a broken stone path. The path was widening, however, so the area was changing, if only slightly. Virginia walked next to me, her face emotionless. I looked at her, my face very emotional.

"What was that?" I asked breathlessly.

"You can't look at her," she said very simply. I shook my head in bewilderment, frustrated at her simply using pronouns to describe something I wasn't allowed to see. I did not want a vague answer. I wanted details.

"Her?" I insisted. My voice cracked.

"I don't have a name for her. If you look at her, you turn to stone. Do you want to turn into fucking stone?"

"No," I replied calmly.

"Obviously." That was the last thing she said that night.

SUMMER. Summer had walked in like an old friend, casually but steadily. Each day grew longer and the nights shorter. I loved summer. It was so utterly livable. Having rather harsh winters and, depending on the year, springs. Summer was always a guaranteed hit. I would live outdoors, even with the incessant bug bites I would quickly receive. When I grew tired, I knew there was to be lemonade waiting made by some mother of the community. The sounds of children playing echoed throughout the fields, making it feel like life would always be simple. When dusk eventually broke, the younger kids would go inside, but the ones who were a bit older were allowed to play in the stars. Sunburns, mudpies, and constellations were all around us. Summer. How I missed its simplicity.

My hair was already quite long, but it seemed to grow nearly half a foot during the duration of my pregnancy. While I'm sure if maintained, it would look quite pretty, it often was wrapped up in some sweaty headband to get out of my face. I looked to my right and saw a plate of food with a note on it. I carefully crept up to the plate and examined the note.

Going to church. Will be home by eleven.

I got many of these messages, especially during my first few weeks when I was mostly sick. I got left home alone quite often and was rather used to it. I wasn't due for quite some time, so it's not like they would go to church and return to a grandchild. I undid the foil on the plate to reveal a still-warm breakfast: wheat toast (already buttered), scrambled eggs, fried potatoes and a few pieces of bacon. The bacon still sparkled with grease. The bacon and toast, however, indicated that this was very freshly made. I stood up to see if my door was unlocked. Lately, my parents would lock my door at night after I had gone to bed and unlock it in the early morning. They wanted to prevent any more disruptive sleepwalking habits I had taken up. To my surprise, the door was unlocked. I peeked around the door and saw my family tying shoes and smoothing jackets. All of their eyes instantly locked onto me. I smiled sheepishly, waiting for some kind of interrogation. *What's wrong? Why are you leaving your room? Do you need something? Do you feel sick?* It was nice to be waited on, but my presence was seen as a small emergency. I was some liability rather than my former existence of neutrality.

"Sweetie, are you alright?" my mother asked, her eyes crinkled with worry. I smiled and nodded.

"Am I going, too?" I asked quietly. Silence. It was an awkward silence. Palpable and spreading. My father's lips formed a hard, straight line. Judith looked away as if another direction of the house would save her from the conversation. My mom opened her mouth, ready to speak, but only air came out. That clearly meant no. That clearly meant, "Get back into bed and come out only when told".

"If you feel well enough," my mom said after some time. My parents exchanged glances and Judith wrung her hands.

So to church we went. My parents walked together; her arm locked in his. Judith walked beside me, giving me an oddly worried look every now and then. I suppose it was warranted. This was definitely the most amount of exercise I had performed in quite some time. Walking any distance further from my bedroom to the bathroom was unheard of. I did notice myself tiring out easily. It wasn't a long walk, nor were we walking quickly, but I felt my heart beat a bit harder than it should have. I took deep breaths in an attempt to regulate my body, but that didn't seem to help.

Being outside was oddly…odd. Fresh air. That was something I hadn't experienced in months. Not fresh air coming through a screen, but all-encompassing fresh air circling all around me. It was a welcomed change. Birds singing and the chattering of neighbors were sounds I heard from my bedroom, but hearing them closer, hearing them outside was comforting. Sunshine was by far the most loved, and skin soaked up the rays instantly. It was a kind of warmth that couldn't be replicated.

No warm blanket, no hug, or thick coat could compare to the warmth of sunshine on a nice day, especially when you have been locked indoors for somewhere around four months.

I wanted to take a moment to soak it all in, to really appreciate the moment, as I wasn't sure when it would happen again. I was feeling well enough to make the journey to church on foot, which wasn't common for me. My family was welcoming enough to let me go with them, which was even less common. Sure, it might happen again in a few days, but it just as easily may not happen until after my pregnancy.

Who was I to know?

The inside of the church was simple and quaint. I had seen photographs of larger churches throughout the world that held high ceilings, stained glass windows, and art all over the walls. None of that was at ours.

The exterior was a weathered white, likely a bright white a generation or two ago, but with time and storms came a more rustic look.

The interior was a whirlwind of oak-brown wood: oak-brown banisters, pews, walls, and floors. It was shockingly monotone. If you relax your eyes, it could look like nothing but a piece of brown paper.

Being wood, the pews weren't comfortable. I knew they hurt from coming to church for my whole life but having not been back since becoming pregnant was a different story. Pain radiated through my legs and shot to my back. I exhaled sharply. Adjusting didn't help. It didn't hinder, but it didn't help. I leaned back and waved my hand to cool myself down. A short walk felt like a long run, and finishing by sitting on hardwood was no reward. Judith asked if I was okay, to which I nodded. I grew up seeing people who were pregnant in the pews. They seemingly smiled and glowed. I suppose I was just a bit of a drama queen.

"Ema," a voice said. I casually looked around. I didn't recognize the voice. I knew the regular flock fairly well and thought I could recognize any of the voices but apparently not. I turned to my left. No one looked at me. To my right was the same. I shrugged it off until I heard my name being called again.

"Ema." The voice was low and smooth. It was rather calm, too. I felt myself grow a bit dizzy and confused. I looked around, not knowing what was happening. The lights dimmed, and the room grew quiet. I couldn't hear anything, not even the sounds of my family right next to me breathing. A low humming echoed across the walls. It was somehow tangible. The humming was warm and inviting. I understood what it meant. Salutations and instructions, affirmations and validations. It was all there.

"Ema, what's going on?" my mom said, her tone concerned. We weren't at church anymore but in my bedroom. My father stood next to her. Judith, Abagail and Isaiah stood in the doorway. I couldn't remember walking home. I couldn't remember the service starting.

"When did we come home?" I asked breathlessly. My parents exchanged worried looks. My siblings did the same.

"Ema, we never left," she said calmly.

"We were at church, and this voice spoke to me," I whispered.

"I know, you said that." Her voice grew quite concerned. I raised my brows, not remembering this alleged previous conversation.

"What did I say?" I asked nervously.

"You said God spoke to you at church today, right before we were about to leave." I sat in silence.

Everything I had experienced, or thought I experienced

was nothing but what, a dream? A hallucination? Roughly two hours of my life that I had simply made up? The sun on my skin, the fresh air, and the feeling of community from the church were not real. I was still inside, still in my room where I had been stuck for months. However, I learned something. I was told that He was not angry at me for having a child out of wedlock. I was not in trouble. I shouldn't be punished and the way my family was treating me was improper. The weight of the world was suddenly lifted.

"I'm not in trouble, Momma," I said softly with a smile.

"Trouble?" my father asked.

"With God. He said he's not mad at me for getting pregnant," I said. Pregnant. It was funny. Whenever I said the word in reference to myself, it might as well have been a swear. If it's said within the context of a wife who was expecting, it was nothing but a button to trigger celebration. Me pregnant? Bad. Others pregnant? Good. If I said the word around them, they'd react. It was different every time. Sometimes, there was a wince; other times, a negative look on their face, or occasionally, a sigh. That time in particular? A look on their face.

"God told you that?" my mother asked, her tone very confused. I nodded happily. It was clear she didn't know what to say. It was clear none of them knew what to say. I didn't understand why. I didn't understand why they weren't asking more questions, being more curious, being more excited. Each person standing in my room had dedicated their life to religion. They made the effort to follow the word of God. They all grew up going to our church, studying the Bible, and living life in a Godly way. I suppose being speechless was not necessarily the wrong reaction. I just expected something different, a more congratulatory response.

"Did you want to join us at church, Ema?" Abagail asked sweetly. My father shot her a look.

"I don't need to. I'm okay! I was just at church talking to God," I insisted. After my mom said they wouldn't be long, my family, one by one, left my room.

Just like that, I was okay. I didn't need to worry about what I had done with Ron. I didn't need to worry about the result of it either. Everything that I had done and everything that had happened to me was okay. Sure, the side effects and symptoms of my pregnancy were not favorable, but I wasn't damned. I had to trust that everything that I had been experiencing wasn't a punishment and merely a side effect. If things were to get worse, it would only be from my due date approaching.

I grabbed the plate of food in front of me. I carelessly threw the tin foil to the side, only to gasp in horror. Once covered by a regular homemade breakfast, it was now bright red and bloody, with what looked to be a few small organs strewn across the plate. I shoved it aside, and one piece slid slightly off the plate and onto the carpet—deep burgundy stained it within seconds. I went into the bathroom in an attempt to collect myself. I wasn't sure if I would be sick, but I figured splashing water on my face couldn't hurt.

The water felt freezing in contrast to my face, which I knew was burning. It was refreshing but not calming. It was a decent enough distraction, however. Within a few minutes, my face was regulated to its normal temperature. I shifted my weight and stared at myself in the mirror. I looked positively awful. There was no better way to put it other than I looked gross. My hair was greasy past my roots, there appeared to be a layer of pure sweat on my forehead, and my teeth were disgusting. I couldn't remember the last time I had brushed them. Tiny flecks of food were stuck between my teeth, yellow stains were painted throughout, and my breath was vile. Rather than reaching to grab my toothbrush, I simply stared at my reflection and grimaced. After what felt like ages, I finally began to brush my teeth, but after finishing, I spit out blood. Seeing the mess against the white on the sink was a shock. It was weird, highly unexpected and just plain disturbing. This did shock me, but it wasn't surprising. I was taking poor care of myself; this was bound to happen. Nonetheless, I had never brushed my teeth with that result. I wouldn't call it a wake-up call, but it was definitely jarring. It left me with a rather cold feeling deep within my stomach. I felt quite ashamed. I knew I needed help. I could hardly bring myself to shower regularly.

I walked back to my bedroom and headed directly for my bookshelf. A layer of dust was sprinkled atop every shelf and item. I remember when my father gave me my own Bible. It was after I was baptized when I was eight years old. There wasn't a specific passage or verse I was searching for as I pulled at its spine and wriggled it free. I held the book to my chest, hoping for something. I wanted the words to give me some level of strength, some level of stability. As I opened the book, I was met with completely blank pages. I shook my head as I flipped through every page. Not one had a single word printed on it.

It was wrong. I knew it was wrong. I had spent years reading from it, studying from it, that exact copy. Pages were dog-eared, and there were certain phrases I remember underlining. I had brought it to school every day for years. I impatiently tapped my thumb and middle finger together, my fingernails clacking softly. I set the book down carefully and stared straight ahead. It seemed as if somehow everything in the world had become distorted. There was no logical explanation for it all. I looked out the window. It was a sunny, clear day, with only a few wisps of clouds were scattered in the sky. Maybe I was wrong, though. Maybe it was overcast, and I only saw sunshine. Perhaps it wasn't even daytime, but nighttime, and my family had left to attend an evening church service. Maybe they didn't even go to church, but they went out to eat. Maybe they didn't even leave and were all in their bedrooms.

The walls vibrated. They moved in a motion like that of ocean waves. They rippled. A slow but steady rocking was felt. It was like being on a boat. It was as if the house had suddenly grown wheels and was going from left to right. I could stand still and didn't wobble, but I felt it. It wasn't dramatic or even that noticeable, but I noticed. I winced and got into bed. There I was, back with my sweat-stained pillows. No longer white and fluffy but flat and yellow. It was not something that would look, or especially smell, comforting, but it was the last thread of comfort I had. Closing my eyes and burrowing in the blankets shielded me from the world around me. An absolute litany of hair strands were scattered across my pillows and sheets. I started to count but realized it would be a number that would concern me. I swept them off the bed with the back of my hand and sighed.

"C'mon, walk faster," Virginia insisted. She took my wrist and led me through the broken cobblestone path. It wasn't long before the stone turned to dirt. The path veered downward, and a field opened up. Light shone in the distance but was still too far away to dictate what exactly was causing it.

"Where are we going?" I asked.

"You'll see for yourself." That was a complete statement, a statement not to be questioned. The further we walked, the warmer it grew. I must have become noticeably bothered as Virginia then said, "You're fine." Her tone was reassuring, but the situation surely wasn't. This was a very specific heat. It wasn't simply the climate changing, it was something I had never experienced.

In the distance were these shining lights. They seemed somewhat buried in the ground, but it was hard to tell from far away. They were everywhere. Dozens of glowing objects in the earth were just down the hill below us. There was noise, but it was hard to distinguish. It seemed like many noises were occurring at once, so it was rather hard to pinpoint each one. It was similar to being in a room full of people and trying to only hear one person and that one person only. All the sounds formed together into one large hum.

"Flaming coffins," Virginia said suddenly. She answered before I could even ask. It could not have been wood, or else the entire thing would be lit ablaze, but it was too harsh to look at directly to tell exactly what was happening. I saw the shapes of bodies inside, but the glow was too bright to make out any features. Screams came from each one. I stared in disgust at the dual sentence of being both burned and buried alive. Hands reached out, trying to grasp at something but only finding air.

Throughout the descent I had experienced thus far, the plane of burning tombs was by far the saddest. It invoked such a sullen, hurt feeling deep within me. It felt so unfair, so inhumane. There didn't seem to be many rules to this underground world, but no one bothered to help them. Then again, neither did I.

"Ema, come on," Virginia said, her tone annoyed. I hadn't realized I had been staring at one of the tombs, caught up in a complete trance by the warm glowing light and stuck in the songs of the person's screams.

I felt guilty walking away. Not that I think I could have helped any of them, but it would have been kind to try. It was the first time I didn't encounter a monster. All the other times were distorted humanoid things that I knew I couldn't do anything about. The cries that I heard, though, were so human and so scared. It was listening to the sounds of people being killed, but death never ceasing their pain. They were guttural, frightened screams on a never-ending loop. As

Virginia and I walked away from the caskets, further from the bodies, I still heard their screams. Even though I couldn't see the glow from their tombs anymore, I could still hear it.

I rubbed my eyes and saw that it was still daylight. My watch read three o'clock on the dot. Noises outside my door led me to realize that my family was home, and considering it was already three, they likely had been home for quite some time. It was louder than usual, but with sleep still clouding my mind, it was hard to determine what was happening. Perhaps more people were over. My parents hadn't hosted guests since my getting pregnant, so I was a bit confused over the ruckus. I heard my dad yelling, followed by a shriek. I was stopped from investigating as my door was locked from the other side. I tugged at the knob as if that would solve my problem. Shock to no one, it didn't open. I knocked on my door and called out for my mom. Silence. The silence lasted a few solid seconds before my father spoke in a low voice. Footsteps dispersed. One set of footsteps came towards me. It was my mom. Her eyes were tired, her expression solemn. It appeared as if she had a tough day.

"What was that?" I asked quietly. I casually peeked around her frame to see where my father was, but he was out of my line of vision. Instead, I saw Isaiah and Judith walk past into the hallway.

"Nothing for you to worry about. Can I get you anything?" Her tone was cheery and normal for her, but her face spoke a completely different story. She wasn't pouting or frowning. She didn't look as if she had just cried. She did, however, simply look worn. I wondered what had happened for my father to yell like that. What was more troubling was the idea of the shriek I heard. Did my mom make that noise? What happened for her to do so? I had never heard her make a noise like that before. I was completely in the dark.

"No, I'm alright. Thanks," I murmured. My mom smiled

before turning back into the living room. She didn't close or lock my door, so I had access to see what had happened or at least to speculate. I tiptoed down the hallway, peering into each room. Judith sat on her bed, her face red and shining. Isaiah stood by her awkwardly.

"What happened?" I whispered. Isaiah looked at me with concerned eyes. Judith didn't look at me at all.

"Bit of, uh, misunderstanding," Isaiah said. I stared at him for a moment before looking down at Judith. She held her body and breathed jagged breaths. I entered the room and walked up next to Judith.

"Jude, what happened?" I said, more angry this time. I was quickly growing frustrated with everyone hiding the truth from me. Considering she was the only one crying, however, I knew that she was the least deserving of my annoyance. Her body lurched up, and her face was suddenly at my ear.

"I kissed a boy after church, and Daddy got mad." I took a moment to process. She sat back down and held her arm, closing off body language.

"That's it? He got mad at that?"

"Really mad."

"I heard him yelling. That was at you?" I knew the answer, but I just wanted a confirmation. She nodded. Judith went to wipe a tear, revealing a bright red mark on her arm.

"Wait, so what happened?" I asked, instinctively reaching out to her arm. She looked up at me with large, watery eyes. Simply seeing her face made my throat close. She looked so sad. I touched her arm. It was ridiculously warm. Fever warm. Sunburn warm.

"He said it was to prevent worse from happening." I, clearly being "worse," shrunk back. I knew these weren't her words, so I was not upset with her. I was, however, shocked at his wild overreaction when I remembered him being oddly calm about my announcement.

"Jude, that's awful. I'm so sorry he did that." She didn't respond. I didn't exactly expect her to. Her silence made it seem like the proper cue to leave. I shot her a sympathetic smile and walked out. Isaiah followed.

"Can you believe that?" I asked Isaiah while he trailed behind me. We were now in my room. I sat on the edge of my bed, and he stood directly in front of me.

"I mean, yeah," he said coldly. I furrowed my brow.

"What do you mean?"

"Well, this isn't new behavior, right?"

"Isn't it? She's never mentioned her first kiss to me before."

"Not Jude. Dad."

"Dad?" I asked, completely lost.

"Yes, Dad. That this isn't new for him."

"Wait, wait. What do you mean?"

"Come on, he would do this all the time when she was younger. Helped build discipline and so forth."

"He did this before to her?"

"Oh, you really don't remember, huh?" I shook my head, horrified.

"How long ago?" I asked, trying desperately to piece together these memories he spoke of.

"Toddler age. Little younger and little older, too."

"Gosh, that's awful. That's so young!"

"I mean, that's kind of normal, Em. That's probably similar to how Abagail and I will raise our kids." Saying her name was his cue to leave, and he then followed up by saying how she was probably wondering what was keeping him. Isaiah turned and closed my bedroom door behind him, and I faintly heard the quiet sobs from Judith down the hall.

I stood in the center of my room, my hands awkwardly clasped in front of my stomach. I didn't know how to respond to the past half hour. It was all just a huge wave of new information, and it was a lot to process all at once. I picked through my brain for these memories Isaiah spoke of, but it was difficult to place. It was as if he were quoting a book I had never read but merely read the back of. It then dawned on me that Isaiah said he essentially agreed with him. "That's probably similar to how Abagail and I will raise our kids." His other words about discipline and so forth were understandable; pretty regular parenting as far as I was concerned, but hitting seemed so extreme. As I went to sit on my bed, I suddenly saw the memory playback of my father lifting up my nightgown and striking my backside only a few months prior. Shaking, as if I had time traveled to that exact moment, I softly caressed the side of my leg as if it were still tender from the hit. I then grew cold at the idea that if I had so easily hidden so recent of a memory. Who knows how much more I had hidden away?

"Oh, Ema, by the way," Isaiah said, my door now half open.

"Abagail and I are engaged to be married." I sat there like stone unable to think before standing up to hug him.

"Congratulations," I whispered. He told me that he had to leave to have a meal with her family, so he wouldn't be back till after. I smiled and nodded, watching him leave. I couldn't believe it. Isaiah, my brother, my first friend, would be a married man. I was happy for the couple, but my heart ached in such a unique way. It felt like yesterday we were just children playing, just yesterday, things were normal. I hated how fast it happened. We would catch fireflies, ride our bikes, and go on walks through the neighborhood. Now, he has his soon-to-be wife to do everything in life with. It wouldn't be long before he would be raising kids of his own. It wasn't fair. I just wanted the kid versions of us back.

I heard shouting again and immediately flinched. The sound of Judith leaving hadn't happened, so I imagined this to be happening solely between my parents. Perhaps my mother was upset at my father for striking Judith? I couldn't imagine her being happy about the situation. I slowly walked closer to the arguing.

"I knew I should have done something!" my father screamed. Done something? It seemed as if he had done quite a bit already today! What more was the man to do? I worriedly looked over at Judith's door. I didn't want him to hurt her again.

"You can't honestly be surprised at their engagement, can you?" my mother said, her voice harder to hear as she spoke more reserved. She did not match his yells. I cocked my head in confusion. So this had nothing to even do with Judith! My father was upset at Isaiah's engagement?

"It's not like it hasn't been months of Ema being pregnant also," said my mother. My head spun. Now, where did I fit into all of this? Was I to be blamed for Isaiah and Abagail's big news? None of it made sense.

"If the little whore hadn't gotten herself pregnant by that filthy city boy, we wouldn't be in this mess!"

"You don't know for sure." I heard footsteps draw near, and I shuffled back to my room. I tried to make myself look busy by folding some of my dresses that I no longer wore. The sounds of footsteps echoed into the living room. I heard the back door shut and cabinet doors open. I carefully treaded into the kitchen to see what the stage looked like. Momma was pulling out casserole pans, and Daddy was outside chopping wood.

"Does Daddy not like Abagail?" I asked my mother. She turned to me with bloodshot eyes and a dazed smile.

"Oh, it's just so emotional seeing your babies grow up. You'll see all too soon!" she said, a smile bleeding through her voice but not reaching her eyes. Seeing as that it was a nice day, I stepped out into the backyard. My father looked up, his eyes not filled with rage, but looking defeated. He set down his ax.

"What can I do for you, Ema?" he asked, his tone rather neutral considering.

"I was just wondering if I had done something wrong. I heard you and Momma talking," I said nervously. Normally, I'm not one to bring up uncomfortable topics, but I was just so confused.

"Well, Ema, you know what you did was wrong. I know it and you know it. There's nothing to be done now though, as we will raise this child as God intended."

"Do you not like Abagail?" I asked after a long pause.

"No, no. She's a fine woman for Isaiah, but that just wasn't the plan." His words grew more muffled, but his demeanor did not change.

"What plan, Daddy?" I asked. He chuckled nervously.

"Well, before you got…" he started, motioning to my stomach. "You know, there was a plan to be set into motion for you kids. You and Isaiah are two bright young children of the Lord and would go on to raise such…virtuous children."

"Okay."

"Well okay then, I think that cleared that up."

"No, it didn't. How is that against your plan? Isaiah is getting married. It won't be long before him and Abagail have kids, and I'll have one, too. I don't get the problem."

"Well, see, the problem, Ema, is that you got with that city boy. The plan was for you and Isaiah to be fruitful instead."

"What?" I asked, my voice small and hollow. Daddy sighed.

"You and Isaiah were supposed to be fruitful, but then you ran off with that, that boy! You dirtied our bloodlines!" His voice now raised.

I stood there in the middle of the backyard. Wind tenderly brushed my hair, and grass stood beneath my feet. I stared with directionless eyes over the horizon. As the silence grew longer, my father grabbed a new piece of wood to set up on his chopping block. He thrust the ax so viciously, causing me to jump. I averted my eyes, gazing out over the grassy fields. A brown patch sat off in the distance, breaking up the greens before me. With nothing left to say and incapable of words anyway, I slowly walked back into the house. As I entered from the back, Isaiah entered through the front. Our eyes met, and I continued forward.

"I need to speak to you," I whispered, my voice cracking. I didn't know how to start, and there was no easy way to do so. I also didn't want to be having the conversation in our parents' house, but I didn't know where else to go. We stood in my room silently. I watched his expression grow confused and impatient.

"Do you..." I started softly. "Do you know what Daddy wanted for us?"

"What do you mean?"

"Like for the future for us?" He stared at me blankly. "He wanted us to—oh, I can't even speak it."

"Ema, what is it?" he asked, perplexed.

"He wanted us to be together. Like, *together,* together!"

"Ah." Isaiah nodded once before going silent.

"Can you believe that!" Isaiah swallowed and sighed before crossing his arms.

"What, did you know?"

"Yeah," he said with another nod. My mouth cracked open and fell into a frown, my eyes strained from bulging.

"You *knew*? Oh, why wouldn't you tell me a thing like that?" Isaiah shrugged, embarrassed.

"Well, I didn't know you were gonna get pregnant by that guy."

"And if I hadn't?"

"I don't know. Wouldn't have been the worst thing, I guess."

"What? Wait were you going to go through with it?" I demanded, my body lurching forward as if ready to strike him.

"Well, Ema! You got pregnant by that stranger boy who clearly doesn't love you, and you were going to wind up some weird old lady with her random kid because no one would want to marry you, so I said I'd still do it!" Time might as well have stopped. I stood there, my mouth ajar, my eyes repulsed, and my stomach thoroughly churned.

"I can't believe you," I whispered. I couldn't bring myself to look at him. My hands cupped my mouth before caressing my face.

"Why?" I asked, unable to ask anything else.

"Why not? It's what they all want."

"Why would they want that?"

"We don't want no outsiders. The church elders weren't too happy when Dad brought Mom into the community. I guess this was his way of correcting that. You getting with whoever that guy was, is the worst possible outcome, one that he probably didn't even think was possible."

"So this has been a plan for a while now?"

"Yeah, pretty much."

"Since before I got pregnant?"

"Much before."

"And you were gonna go *through* with it." I trailed off, rubbing my temple.

"I still would've till things got serious with Abagail."

"You were to lay with me?"

"Yes." His eyes met mine, and I couldn't take it anymore. I hurriedly showed him to the door and shut it behind me. For the first time since the installation, I wished my door was locked. I went over to my bed, which I dejectedly sat upon. I felt so filthy, so betrayed. I wanted to talk to my mother and to Judith. Did they know, too? Or was this sick plan something only spoken between the men? My head fell forward and I began to cry. They really only saw me as a vessel. I was only a tool to continue their bloodline. I held my stomach in my arms. God forbid I have a girl. I couldn't let the same fate befall her.

WEEK 27. MONTH 7

The broken road Virginia and I walked along was no longer this never-ending plane with blackened skies above. The change was very much welcomed. The skies were turning red, and the air had a noticeable scent change; turning from a sulfur-type smell, it now reeked of melted iron. Although merely resembling machinery, there was something oddly sinister about it. In the distance, I was able to observe another river. I shuddered, remembering how the last one treated me.

"Don't worry, you won't fall in this one," Virginia said, perfectly on cue as if she had read my mind. I smiled but didn't believe her. This was the land where anything could happen. I couldn't put myself above any outlandish-sounding scenario. The red skies of oblivion shone down upon the river's surface, casting a dark glow that caused my jaw to unhinge. It appeared as if people were struggling to escape its currents, but we were still too far away for me to tell.

"Are there people in there?" I asked, worried, slowly increasing my walking speed.

"Oh yeah," she said rather nonchalantly. Bewildered by

her lack of care, I jogged a few paces ahead of her to inspect closer. Indeed, there were people in the river, flowing along with the natural currents and barely keeping their heads above the water. Red ran down their faces, staining their skin and tinting their hair. At that moment, I realized that the sky hadn't turned the river red, the river was made of blood. Dumbfounded by the concept, I stopped in my tracks.

"What happened?" That was all I was able to say. Virginia casually shrugged me off. I suddenly felt a surge of rage, starting from my head and spreading quickly throughout each and every inch of my body. I felt it as if I had injected pure emotion into my veins. It spread so fast. I felt so much.

"Why am I here? This place is awful, and I didn't do anything wrong! Why can't I leave?" My voice trembled. I wasn't about to cry, but I had still lost my steadiness. A look of shock momentarily graced Virginia's face before being quickly replaced with exhaustion.

"Don't yell at me, I didn't bring you here," she said, continuing on down the path.

We were now much closer to the river. I was able to see the faces of those floating and those drowning. They just looked like people. There were no distortions to their body, no monstrous or ghastly appearance. They looked like random people you would see on the street. Faces that were so nondescript they could fit into any background easily. There were no differing features, but they didn't look like clones. The look of fear, however, was universal. Each of them was putting up a fight. Blood splashed about in an almost never-ending fountain show. I knew I was simply a spectator. I wasn't meant to break the fourth wall and reach out for one of their hands. This was their reality, and I was simply passing by. All I could do was watch and be horrified. The closer I approached, the warmer it got. This, in addition to observing the river, led me to realize that it was boiling. Large bubbles shot up over one another resembling a pot of soup cooking on a hot stove. I eventually put two and two together and realized where the iron smell was coming from, only now that I was closer, it was mixed with a burnt smell. It was absolutely foul, and it was difficult to breathe. Breathing through my mouth simply made it feel as if I were ingesting their burning skin. It turned my stomach and clouded my mind, captivating me in such a horrific fog. I turned away and looked to Virginia for something, anything. Answers, stability, a hug, I would have taken anything then, but she just stared back at me. I knew there was nothing she could do, it wasn't as if she were in charge. I just wanted comfort in a world that was made to be uncomfortable.

It was growing warmer with each passing day. I had begun my journey in the days of frostbitten grass and cold noses. As the months went on, the snow melted into the earth and the birds and the bees did as the saying goes. Rabbits would pop up every now and then, seeing a glimpse of one or two from my bedroom window. A few rainy days would be interlaced between, but for the most part, it was nothing but strong sunshine and birds singing. Spring, as it does every year however, got replaced by its stronger successor. The heat was in, and it felt like it was here to stay. The concept of snow felt a million miles away. The sound of former springtime showers was replaced by the consistent humming of bugs. It would have been nice to sit on the porch, having iced tea and eating cold fruit while catching a tan and growing sleepy from the sun. These things still happened; I simply wasn't included.

Judith, being a bit older than the neighbor kids, but surely too young to congregate with the adults, played on tire swings and helped make lemonade. My parents chatted casually with our friends and neighbors, sharing food and thoughts. Every day was a party, and every day I wasn't invited.

Abagail and Isaiah set a wedding date. It would be in about five months, enough time for her to find a dress, for me to give birth, and for them to decide where to live. At the beginning of their marriage, Abagail would move in with us, but they're deciding on whether they should buy out a plot of land to build on or wait for Mrs. Meyers to pass away as she had just celebrated her eighty-ninth birthday, the oldest in the community.

When I woke up, there was the faintest taste of blood in my mouth. I reached over to wash down the faint taste of iron before swinging my legs over the side of the bed. I instantly felt the urge to use the restroom as I stood up. As I all but ran for my bedroom door, I was met with the unfortunate realization that the door was locked. It almost always was now, not just in the early mornings. I knocked softly, expecting a quick response. Usually, my mother was around to let me out of my room. As urgency grew, my knocks grew louder. I called for my mom, waiting for the moment to hear footsteps. I was met with silence. Frustrated, I knocked harder, at a level where I knew that no matter where she was in the house, she could hear me. I had lost my watch some time ago, so I didn't know the time.

Based on how the sun shone through my window, I knew it was still morning. It appeared to be around the time when she would be cleaning up breakfast. My father worked for the town church. He wasn't an official congregation member but on the maintenance side of things. Occasionally, he would make house calls for neighbors, but primarily, he would work at the church. His hours would fluctuate, but often, around late morning he wasn't home. My mother, on the other hand, was almost always home. She would leave the house to gather groceries and, every now and then, go on a walk with a neighbor. It was summer break for the kids in town, so Judith should have been home. In short, I likely was not home alone.

I banged my hands on the door until it was too late. It began to trickle down my legs and dripped onto the carpet. It was a lot, too; after all, it was the first pee of the morning. I stared down at my mess in shame. I solemnly went to my closet to find a rag to clean up the carpet. I pressed the cloth into the ground with my foot as bending over was getting less easy. I heard the sound of the door unlocking. I rolled my eyes as it was now too late for that.

"Were you yelling?" my mom asked. I stared up at her with vacant eyes before saying yes. Her eyes met mine before trailing down at the puddle on the carpet. I expected her to help out, but she simply left to return with a soapy towel. I took the towel from her and she promptly left. Better things to do, I suppose.

I went into the bathroom to clean myself off. I reeked of urine and sweat. For a moment, I was motionless, unsure of even where to start. My hair was impossible to brush as it had completely knotted into oblivion. I still felt the wetness of urine down my legs. Underneath my arms was a smell so putrid, I physically grimaced at the scent, and my skin was consistently breaking out.

A bath was a start, I thought to myself, as I carefully turned the knob on the tub and waited as the water level rose. As I stood naked on the bathroom floor, I stared down at my stomach. Purple and white marks were everywhere on my skin. It was as if someone took a crayon to my torso and simply went wild. My skin wasn't quite as painful as it looked, thankfully. I ambled my way into the tub and breathed a sigh of relief. The water temperature was perfect, warm enough to be calming without scalding. I didn't exactly bathe myself. Never once did I take a bar of soap to wipe down the layers of grime from my skin. I just let myself become one with the water. While I knew in hindsight that it wasn't enough, it was enough for me in that moment.

I had never had a haircut in my life. I knew it was a thing people did, but not people in our family or community, for the women at least. Daddy liked our hair long. My hair spilled far past my shoulders, long enough to cover my chest. From my position in that moment, pieces were submerged in the waters, dancing anytime there was a ripple in the tub. The length was quite burdensome, especially in the warmer months, but I had learned to tie it up or put it in a braid long ago. My mom and Judith did the same, and every other girl I had grown up with did as well. Growing your hair long was encouraged. Daddy always said that it was our glory and cutting it was being disrespectful to our creation as women. Seeing women come into the pet store with shoulder-length haircuts, with bangs, or even dyed hair was something that left me almost star-struck. My mom said that people would be like that the further I got from our town.

After getting out of the water, I got changed into a fresh nightgown. I no longer smelt of urine, but I still didn't exactly smell fresh. As I walked out of the bathroom, I passed by the living room. My entire family was home and sprawled out on the couch. They appeared to be in the middle of a lively conversation. I stood awkwardly in the doorway watching. It took a few beats before my dad noticed me. His eyes widened, and his lips formed a straight line. He nudged my mom and said something under his breath. She quickly looked up with a smile.

"Do you need something, Ema?" she asked. Her voice was genuine, but my heart sank. It was apparent she only wanted to cater to me to get rid of me. What food can she prepare for me that I can eat in my bedroom? What drink can she offer me that makes me stop bothering them? What can she do so I go away?

"I'm fine," I murmur softly. I was rather hungry. I didn't receive my plate of food on the floor that I was used to expecting. I felt rude for asking, considering how much she was taking care of me, so I didn't ask. I still stood facing them. They all had their necks crooked so they could stare in my direction. They weren't looking at me but waiting for me. Perform! Perform! Dance! I was their pet, their entertainment. I was their thing to talk and gossip about. I was their thing to be kept away. My nonchalant attitude as I gazed in their direction was boring. That wasn't something to spectate. As they realized I had nothing to contribute, they slowly, one by one, looked away. With one awkward transition, they were back to whatever conversation they were having before I was in their presence. I turned away and went back to my bedroom. I felt my throat grow tight and my chest grow heavy. My eyes remained dry, but my body was hurting. It wasn't the end of the world that I was excluded. Life will go on, but if it didn't hurt in the meantime.

I sat on my bed and drank my stale water as I had no other option but to do so. As I sat casually on the bed, I saw a flash of red. I jumped instinctively, and my heart thudded hard against my chest. I rubbed at my eyes, thinking perhaps something got in them. There was no feeling of irritation like when you get an eyelash poking inward. It was a complete and total vision distortion that had me questioning my sanity. It lasted not even a second, and everything went back to normal. It was haunting. It felt sinister. It seemed simply unexplainable.

Standing in my cage, I could gather how gross it was. I knew I smelled bad and I knew I looked exhausted, but I sometimes forgot how bad it all was. A stack of empty water glasses stood below my bedside table. I imagined for a moment that my family would likely be wondering what had happened to them but then realized that my mother likely purchased new ones instead of looking for them in my room. There were pieces of old food scattered. Something that was once toast was now this hard brown material that would burst into a million crumbs if you tried to crush it. The bed smelled. I knew it smelled, but oh god, it smelled so putrid. I couldn't remember the last time my mom had washed the bedding, but it felt like years. Food stains decorated my sheets, the number increasing every day. There was a spot on the carpet where I had vomited and it didn't quite wash out. That likely, too, was contributing to the overall stench. The air, despite the window being open, felt thick. Dust hung in the air as if frozen in time. It simultaneously felt damp and dry.

Cleaning my room was something that couldn't be done in a mere few hours. You couldn't cover up the smell with a perfume or a candle and call it a day. A quick run through with a vacuum would not erase it.

Laughs erupted from the living room. I instantly felt a tinge of contempt. Why do they get to have fun? Why do they have a feeling of togetherness? Why do they get to have a lighthearted conversation when I couldn't remember the last time I laughed? I didn't want to be bitter. I didn't want to feel envy; feeling it made me feel dirty and shameful. I sat at the foot of my bed and shut my eyes. I tried to pray away the feelings I was having, to be rid of such angry and envious thoughts. I whispered my pleas and prayers, feeling emotion come up through my throat. I shut my eyes tighter so no tears would escape. I didn't want to be filled with resentment. It was wrong, and I knew that. My family did nothing to deserve my anger. It was wrong of me to have such sinful thoughts. I tried to pray away my feelings, but the more I thought about what was happening, the angrier I became.

They were purposefully excluding me. Or were they? Or was I simply being overdramatic? Maybe they were leaving me alone so I could rest since my body was going through a lot. After all, I was creating life! I was doing a difficult thing that I had never done before. Letting me rest and letting me be wasn't irrational but considerate.

Well, that doesn't excuse how they leave dishes of food on the floor for me to eat as if I were some kind of animal! However, they may simply have strict eating schedules that line up for when my dad and Isaiah go to work and Judith goes to school. Perhaps they think I've grown self-conscious about my size and wouldn't feel comfortable eating in front of them. That may make sense if I had displayed behavior implying that I was unhappy with my changing body, but I hadn't said or done much of anything for them to think that way. I could understand leaving my food for me back when I was in the thick of my morning sickness, but after the first few months, I was feeling quite better, only occasionally having a bad stomach day. I was surely well enough to eat with everyone else at the dining table.

Well, in any case, none of that explains the lock on my door that no one else had. However, it was installed after I had begun sleepwalking. It was most likely that my parents didn't want me harming myself or knocking into anything that may break or wake the whole house up. It was a mere precaution, nothing more. I was just being paranoid and reading too deeply into things. Wasn't I?

I felt It kick. It's been doing it more recently. The larger my stomach swells, the harder the kicks become. It wasn't ever painful or anything to cause distress, but it was surely something to notice. What once felt like a tiny moth flutter was more like a small bird. Still small but an increase has occurred. I didn't know how to feel whenever it happened. To be frank, I didn't feel much of anything. There was no outpouring of love, pride, or joy. I didn't smile or glow when it happened. On the flip side, I did not glower. I did not curse nor stomp and pout. I simply would look down at my stomach and go back to whatever I was doing before. It just wasn't as special as I thought it would be. That made me a bit sad, and I wish I had more deep feelings about it all beyond shock and fear.

I listened as Isaiah and Abagail left, assuming to spend time over at her family's house. A wave of goodbyes echoed through the hall. Hugs were likely exchanged. I kept an ear out to see if they were approaching my room or not, but quickly received my answer when the front door shut, and there was nothing but silence. I expected it, but it still hurt. Not that I exactly wanted to see Isaiah. After our talk, I could barely look at him. I just wished things were as easy as when we were growing up. It was all so simple. Perhaps one day, when he and Abagail start a family, things may get easier as our children grow up side by side. We could transition into the next phase of our lives as parents and have an entirely different relationship.

We could laugh together, cry together, and live together just as we did when we were children.

My door was still unlocked. I took advantage of that opportunity by asking if I could sit outside for a few hours. I had a pretty good idea of my answer but decided why not. My mom was preparing lunch, and my dad was reading. I stood in my doorway for an unknown amount of time. Trepidation held me at my core, and I did not know how to proceed. After all, what would I even say? *Could I leave the house for a few hours for the first time in months?* They'd look at me like I was absolutely crazy.

"Can I take a walk?" I asked. I didn't ask any specific

parent, though my body language was directed at my mom. She jumped when she heard me speak, breaking the silence. She stared at me, confused for quite some time—almost a look of shock written across her face. My dad looked up from his book with an expression equally perplexed. It may have also been my appearance. I was simply in my nightgown and barefoot.

"You would need to dress better, and you cannot go far," my dad said, his tone a warning. I was shocked. I quickly went to my bedroom to find more suitable clothes. The last time I remembered dressing up was for what? Hannah and Adam's wedding? Church service? It felt like years. I stared inside my closet. A momentous occasion only called for my most favorite outfit: a white blouse with dotted Swiss fabric and a linen navy skirt that fell to my calves.

As I began buttoning my blouse, I realized I may need to reconsider my outfit choice. The fabric had little give, and I couldn't leave half of the garment unbuttoned. I didn't even really consider how my old clothes would fit these days. I found a worn-out shirt that had fallen loose within the stitching. It was something that I would wear to layer with during the wintertime. It fell easily over my stomach, and I quickly exited my bedroom. Despite my being tired, I felt a random surge of energy. I felt my parents' eyes on me as I walked out.

I was on the patio. Summer sunlight was brighter than I remembered. My entire face scrunched up as I squinted to see down my street. As I looked around, I suddenly felt so very small. Had the world always been this large? Had I always been a mere speck? Simple one-story houses felt like they were towering over me. Trees appeared as if they touched the heavens. I felt as though the world was swallowing me whole.

I naturally shrunk down and kept my gaze on the ground.

It was as if someone were pushing me down. My eyes darted for something to focus on, some comfort blanket to gravitate towards. I glanced behind me at my family home surrounded by flowers on the outside, but little did people passing by know that I was rotting inside. However, I wasn't rotting inside anymore. I was out. I wasn't lying in my sweat-stained bed staring at the same popcorn ceiling as I had been for the last couple of months. I wasn't begging for my door to be unlocked so I could simply use the restroom. I was outside and not just in our backyard. I could run away. I could get out. But where would I even go? Friends and family would tell my parents and I would be right back where I started. I could go see Virginia, as she was the only person in my life who had no ties to my family and knew me and only me. She was not a neighbor, a family friend, a church member, or someone who lived nearby. She tried to help me before; perhaps she could help me again or at least try to.

My car was gone. I saw my father's car parked in the driveway and Jude's bike, but my car was nowhere to be seen. I stared at the empty spot with an unrelenting feeling of dread. Perhaps I didn't have an out. I knew, that being the state I was in, I couldn't get far on foot. I could only assume that's the only reason my parents let me out of the house. They knew I would get winded quickly. They knew that my stomach would shift to where I would have to pee and have to go back inside. They knew I'd come back.

As I walked into the house, my eyes scanned for whichever parent I saw first. Neither. My father was no longer sitting in the living room reading, and my mother was no longer in the kitchen preparing food. Considering I would have very obviously known if they had left since I was standing near the house, I knew they were to be inside somewhere. I walked through the kitchen, passing by an empty sandwich tray. The backyard held Judith and a neighbor girl.

They were preoccupied with whatever game they were playing. No parent was in sight. Frustrated, I turned and walked down the hall.

My parents' door was just barely open, allowing for a sliver of light to escape down the hallway. I pushed open their door and demanded to know where my car was. As the door was fully opened, I recoiled back at the sight. My father was on top of my mother, both naked as the day they were born. A disgusted groan slipped from my lips, and I quickly turned around and disappeared into my room.

An image that I didn't want plastered in my brain was, unfortunately, plastered there. I couldn't help but let a giggle slip from my mouth. I couldn't really imagine my parents having sex at their age, considering they were done having children. I simply sat on my bed, waiting for the moment that my mom would come in to explain the situation. I sat, and I picked at the skin around my fingers. I picked at one too deep and a bead of blood showed. No footsteps were to be heard, nor the sound of doors opening. Perhaps they didn't see me, or perhaps they did and didn't care. I wasn't sure which was worse. Finally, after what seemed to be around five or so minutes, I heard the steps of my mom approaching my door. My body tensed up, preparing myself for what was doomed to be an awkward conversation. She was dressed as she was before, not a hair out of place.

"Hey," she began, seemingly embarrassed. I stared up at her with angry eyes. I had surely not forgotten about my car and would definitely not forget to bring that up. I had no interest in speaking about what I had just seen, so I was hoping we would get to the topic of my car quickly.

"So, I want to apologize for what you just saw in there," she said, her voice even but her eyes shameful. I watched as she struggled to make eye contact. I stared at her, my face fixed into a frown, not saying anything. It was weird, sure, but I didn't care that heavily. I had bigger concerns.

"I don't know if you have any questions for me about what you saw," she said, trailing off. Considering the optics of my pelvis, I didn't have too many questions about what was happening. I shook my head as the silence she created felt like a question.

"Well, that's just one perk of being married! I'm sure you will find that soon enough and be able to experience, well..." She turned away, her face written with a look of something resembling confusion.

What she said was what I was taught. Save yourself for marriage, and God will reward you with the gift of martial sex. You find a man, and you court for some time; he proposes, you marry, and then finally, after however long of waiting, you dive deep into the world of luxurious intimacy. To be joyfully available to your husband is an honor. It's something to look forward to. You, as the woman, are designed to be the help—meet to your husband in terms of housekeeping and child-rearing. That is your role and duty, and it is to be nothing short of a blessing.

I did wonder how it differed from the sex I had. What Ron and I had, a short-lived rendezvous in the back of a strangers house, wasn't exactly something to be joyful about. It was awkward, uncomfortable and somehow simultaneously went on for too long and too short. If every time was to be like that time, I couldn't comprehend how sex was supposed to be a gift. I assumed it was due to us not being married. If we were, then it would've been different. Since, however, we weren't, God punished me by making me be a young single mother. Since Ron left, I wasn't sure what his punishment was.

"Where is my car?" I asked, no longer interested in her one-sided conversation. Her face went blank, as if I had spoken to someone behind her. It took a moment for her brow to crease and give a look of concern.

"What?" she asked, her tone breathy.

"My car. When I went outside it wasn't there."

"Oh."

"So where is it?"

"Well, why were you thinking of leaving the house? Did you need me to get you something from the store?"

"No," I said quietly and confused.

"Well, if you change your mind, you let me know. You're getting far along now."

"But I just want to know where my car is."

"I know. And if you need me to go anywhere, I will, okay?" The juxtaposition of her cheery tone versus my shaking hands was odd to behold. She shut the door behind her and I heard the lock click.

The river of blood. It was everywhere behind my eyes.

WEEK 28. MONTH 7

Virginia took me by the elbow and led me away from the burning river. You couldn't help but be mesmerized. There was a river, albeit a much smaller one, behind the grassy knolls behind my parents' house. Growing up, on hot summer days, my parents would walk me and Isaiah down to dunk our feet in. It was so simple at the time, but looking back were great memories.

That was the only river I had known in life, so this took the concept of rivers and subverted it in every way you could imagine. That was the point, after all, right? To take something normal to the real world and completely alter it. Why have peaceful gravestones when you could instead have flaming tombs? Why have average people walking around, when you could have people with no faces and far too many hands chasing after you? Why have an image of your family house when you could have your family with their faces completely distorted? This world where up is down and down is up had me walking through a fairytale that wasn't supposed to be read to children.

We walked around the river. I couldn't help but stare at

each of their faces with such human looks of fear. I asked Virginia why they were there, and she didn't give me much of a reason other than that they deserved it. It was too cynical of an answer for me to understand. I didn't say anything else for a long while. What even is there to say?

Each era of terrain felt endless. At least before, there were cliffs and mountains, but after a bit, it became almost entirely flat. Where we were headed appeared to be no different. The tone of the scenery changed, however. It went from warm tones to cooler tones. The blood of the river, no longer in my vision contributed to the warmth of the world. With that gone, and nearly nothing else in our path, the world was just dark. At least before, it felt alive; now, it felt so incredibly still. It was like walking into a charcoal drawing. The skies were dark navy, the most realistic thing about the place. The ground looked like grey dirt. Clay perhaps? After quite some time, there was something along the horizon. Before us stood a forest. I was hesitant, as anyone would be up until this point, but at the same time, excited for some lively foliage. It was no longer the burnt stick trees that I had seen prior but what looked like actual trees. They had pine needles!

"Where are we?" I asked.

"The place we've always been," Virginia muttered with a hint of humor.

"No, but now there are trees. It's different here. Are we going somewhere better?"

"No," she said plainly. She said it so bluntly that I'd be lying if I said it wasn't a bit of a gut punch.

As we walked into the forest, I looked to Virginia for comfort. She looked back at me with neutral eyes, completely unphased. She acted as if she lived there. Knowing this was the land where bad things happened, I couldn't help but be on guard. My body was tense, and my eyes darted everywhere. I was ready to fight, despite never having been in a fight in my life. Better to be prepared than not, I suppose. Walking through the forest was an eerily calming experience. No monster crept out from behind a tree like I was trained to expect. It was simultaneously daunting and relieving. Good for me for not seeing a monster but bad for me because that only means it's just right around the corner. Considering the forest felt never-ending, that allowed for a lot of corners.

The forest was dark. The trees were not that tall, but there had to have been thousands. They didn't grow flowers or fruit, nor were they bright or lively. I reached out to touch a sprig and it instantly disintegrated. It was as if it were made of sand. I turned to Virginia for answers, but she only looked at the tree with a forlorn expression.

The further we walked, the worse I felt. It was as if someone had taken my body and successfully removed every organ inside. I felt lifeless. Such an overwhelming feeling of exhaustion and sorrow ran slowly through my veins. I was a corpse who could walk. Nothing really mattered. Walking drained my soul. I had to force each leg to continue, feeling as if I were to collapse at any moment. Time slowed down to where we existed in slow motion. We were in an hourglass. We were prisoners.

I WOKE up with the taste of blood on my tongue. It was becoming common, especially first thing in the morning or after meals. My eyes broke open, feeling dry and not well rested. It truly felt like I hadn't slept in months.

I looked to my right to notice the lack of dishware on my carpet—no refreshed drink. I had begun saving empty glasses in the event no one unlocked my door in time for me to use the restroom. It felt quite odd to have to kneel down, position myself correctly, and piss in a drinking cup. The first time I did it, I felt this cold emptiness run through my chest. This feeling of embarrassment despite no one looking. I had grown used to the action, but I remembered the emotion that came with it. I kept the glasses on my windowsill, always forgetting to wash them when I finally made it to the bathroom.

I don't get many visitors in my room anymore, so no one bothered to take them for me. I simply opened the window so the smell wouldn't be too strong. I guess no one had noticed the missing glasses. If they did notice what had happened, it would make sense that they would not want to reuse the glass that was previously homing fermented urine that did nothing but sit in sunlight.

My bedroom seemed darker than usual. Not dark as if it were nighttime, just as if the world dimmed a tad. Confused, I peered out the window to see if something was blocking the sun. Everything seemed to be where I remembered it and not a cloud in the sky. There was just a little less light.

As I approached my door, it creaked open. My mom stood before me, holding my plate of food. Toast. Eggs. Sausage. Orange slices. A new glass of water that was to be turned into a piss cup within the next few days. I smiled and meekly took the dishes from her. We spoke no words to each other. She looked tired and uncomfortable, like something wasn't bad, but something wasn't good. It was a shift in her usual disposition. As soon as the dishes were in my hands, she shut my door behind her. The door didn't lock, thankfully, so I had the luxury of using the restroom.

Back in my room, I examined my plate. Eggs that were once served hot, fluffy, and buttery were no longer. I furrowed my brow as I picked out pieces of shell. Once cleaned up and ready to eat, the food tasted fine. A bit cold and somewhat stale but otherwise edible and almost enjoyable. As I ate, I couldn't help but feel unnerved by my mom's behavior. It was simply so unlike her. I couldn't remember a time, really, seeing her sad. There had never been a death in the family that I was alive to witness for me to notice her not being chipper. I never remembered any of us kids misbehaving for her to scold us. Even when I had to break the news of my being pregnant, she was calm. She wasn't happy, sure, but forgiving.

Time had passed. I'm not sure how long. No more than a few hours, but a number of minutes that I couldn't keep track of. That time passing led to a knocking at my door. I grabbed my plate, ready to hand it off to my mom before Judith came in. I set the plate back down and smiled at the sight of her. We hadn't spoken in a while. She was a fresh face for me.

"Are you okay?" she asked. Her body language was stiff, uncomfortable. She was hesitant to come near me but was very aware of being far from the door. Her voice was low, almost a whisper.

"Yeah, I'm fine," I said, curious of her questioning. "Why?"

"What happened last night?"

Last night. I sat back and tried to conjure up memories. I had toast with jam for breakfast. I had listened to some birds singing in the morning. Between that time, I was simply lying in bed as usual. I had the day portion covered, but the night wasn't coming to me. I squinted my eyes as if that would help me think harder. *What did I eat last night for dinner?* Nothing came to me. *What time did I go to bed?* No idea. *What was last night?* Nothing.

"What do you mean?" I asked casually. She had my partial attention as I picked a handful of loose strands of hair from my nightgown. Judith gave me a look. A "come on now, you know what I mean" kind of look. Something had to have happened. Perhaps it was something to do with Isaiah and

Abagail and I simply wasn't informed. Or maybe there was a strange noise outside that I somehow managed to sleep through.

"All the yelling?" she prompted. I stared back at her blankly, having no idea what she was talking about.

"What was the yelling about?"

"You were the one yelling, you tell me!"

"This was last night?"

"Yes." I did not remember yelling last night. It was as if I had fallen asleep midday and woken up like usual the next morning.

"I don't remember. What was I saying?" She must have been able to be able to piece out some words of what I was yelling about.

"About your car that daddy got rid of."

I froze. So it was true. My being curious for weeks on end about what happened was confirmed. My car was gone. I wasn't angry but defeated. By the sounds of it, I had likely used up all my anger the night prior. I asked Judith about it, looking for every last detail I couldn't remember. While helpful enough, she wasn't a part of the conversation. This all happened between myself, my mom and my dad. Apparently, my parents had come to my room the night prior. The reasons for that were unknown. Our voices were low, and it appeared to be a calm conversation. After a couple of minutes, the talk grew louder and more hostile. I was trying to get answers to why they sold it behind my back, and my dad was trying to scold me. We were going round and round until it eventually stopped. I stared at Judith but then looked away. I was crying and sitting on my bed with my hands balled into fists.

"There is no reason for you to behave the way you are right now," my mother said coldly.

"You clearly aren't responsible enough, so why should

you have the honor of having a car? One that I paid for!" my dad yelled.

"But why didn't you tell me? Why was it a secret?" The words came out of my mouth like water. I didn't think them through or even feel my mouth moving. Sound just came out of me.

It went red. It was loud. The screaming all combined together until it became a hum. The noise was inescapable, to the point where I covered my ears, but that didn't do anything. Words were being spat at me, names were thrown around, and it felt never-ending. Things like "We didn't raise you this way" and "You have fallen down a sinful path" were said. They were spewed so passionately, too. Each word was such a strike to the face, it was hard not to be emotional. It was only escalating further until we were nothing but a fire tornado. Wind and debris encapsulated the space around us. Until it didn't. I was back sitting in front of Judith. I didn't say anything, as speaking felt impossible. Judith eventually left as I was not providing her with whatever information she was looking for.

My shoulders drooped and my face fell. I fell through the carpet, through the floorboards beneath, and all the way until I was back standing next to Virginia. She looked at me as if I had been standing beside her the whole time. I was back in the forest. I cautiously reached out towards one of the branches. My fingertip barely graced the wood, and it fell into ash, leaving my finger with a rusty red residue. I pulled my arm back and looked at Virginia. With a worried look on her face, she held out a hand, telling me to halt.

"Stop," she whispered. Virginia was always confident in all the memories I had of her. She was the older sister I never had. While she was quiet, she wasn't shy. What I knew of her was strength. I knew myself as more reserved, and I found myself wanting to be more like her. However, at this moment, I caught her in a rather vulnerable state. I had seen her upset, but this was different. Her eyes were somewhere where I wasn't.

"What?" I asked.

"They're people. Don't do that." I jumped back, inspecting the tree from varying angles. All I saw was a tree. All around us were trees.

"What do you mean they're people?" I asked tentatively. At that point, I was half expecting the tree to suddenly turn into a living, breathing person.

"They're people, and this is what happened to them."

"Why?"

"They were hurting." Virginia began walking further into the forest as she spoke.

"What do you mean?" I asked as I caught up to her. Something changed within the world. I couldn't quite tell if the trees were getting larger or if we were getting smaller.

"They were just in pain, and this is what happens to them and it's fucked up," she spat. I had touched a nerve that was no stranger to being touched it seemed. Being very aware of the silence, I made sure not to breathe too loud.

"My father killed himself." Virginia finally spoke. She didn't say anything after for some time.

"I'm sorry," I said softly.

"Like, he was a good person. He was a good dad," she trailed off. "And this is what happened to him. He just gets to suffer more."

I didn't know what to say, I just stared at her solemnly. When our eyes met finally, I broke my gaze and glanced to the ground. I then looked down the path where thousands of trees stared back at me. As we continued, more replaced the ones that passed us by. It began to feel as though my body was being pulled to the floor. My face was slowly drooping down as if it were made of wax. Sad. Sad was such a laughable understatement. Unhappy, despondent, lugubrious, melancholy, they were all not enough—a new word needed to be created to demonstrate the correct atmosphere of our location we were in. Sad was simply a word. It wasn't enough to convey what the trees felt.

I was standing in the middle of the living room, not knowing how I got there. I looked around, checking the windows or clocks to give me an indication of time. It was nearing dinnertime after hearing the clock chime five. As I turned to go to my bedroom, my knees and ankles cracked loudly. I had no idea how long I had been standing there. It felt like just a moment ago it was sometime around noon.

I got a plate of dinner, more than I was honestly expecting after remembering the fight. It was Shephard's pie. Sitting in bed, I bent forward to take a bite, and I felt a sudden wetness on my face. Dropping my fork back on my plate, I watched blood drip from my nose onto my lap. As soon as the droplet hit the fabric of my nightgown, it broke into multiple pieces, beaded, solidified, and rolled away. I watched in utter disbelief. The cloth was blood-free. I wiped at my face, and the back of my hand came back clean. I closely inspected my hand for any small stains or indications of blood, but nothing was there. It happened, and then it didn't.

I WAS TIGHTLY TUCKED in bed, staring woefully at the ceiling. Every night, I knew where I was going, and every night I dreaded it. I wanted dreamless sleep. I wanted peace and alleviation. Knowing what was coming, I knew I shouldn't try to stop it, but I still had a bit of a fight left in me. I widened my eyes and snapped my fingers to keep myself awake. What do you do when you need to stay awake? When needing to sleep you simply count sheep, read stories, pray, find whatever rhythm that works. Staying awake, however? I had no method available. I knew I'd eventually succumb; I couldn't stall sleep forever. One moment, I was looking lazily at the side of my bed, and the next, I wasn't.

Virginia and I were back to walking, the trees forever remaining at our ribs. I glanced over my shoulder and realized the way back looked identical to the direction we were walking. It was endless. This world simply kept going. We were moving from one room to the next, from one monster to another, from land to water, and back again. There was no finish line in sight, only more trees. While grateful not to be in the presence of something chasing me, I couldn't take the unending melancholia. We walked silently, our footsteps being the only noise to break the nothingness that lingered in the air. The forest only extended. No matter how quickly or slowly we walked, the scenery remained exactly the same. We were but two wandering travelers lost in a painting, never to see past the canvas.

I jolted back awake when I realized that I had fallen asleep. It was impossible to avoid. I had to sleep at some point. It was absolutely frustrating, the perpetual feeling of exhaustion. Restful nights were a thing of the past, and despite that being something I should have been used to at that point, I didn't want to accept it as true. Digging my nails into my skin until blood was shed to keep myself from drifting off wasn't healthy, and I knew that. Looking in the mirror and seeing purple stained under my eyes was a reminder. I felt like I was losing my mind, and no one was bothering to see if I had finally cracked. The room was getting darker.

WEEK 31. MONTH 7

The forest was cold and rather damp. The climate change was a welcomed one as most of the terrain I had encountered was warm to the point of being uncomfortable. Just as I was getting adjusted to the cool air on my skin, warmth replaced it. Even though it appeared as if there were countless amounts of trees ahead of us, we were suddenly out of the forest. Looking behind my shoulder, millions faced me, going down in a row with an almost impossible vanishing point. Just like that, we were somewhere new. Here, there was no plant life at all. It was nothing but open ground, a field to wander through. The ground was not dirt nor stone, but sand, and after adjusting my stomach to reach down and touch it, memories of playing in sandboxes as a kid flooded my mind. Billions upon billions of tiny grains stretched as far as I could see. While not quicksand, it was surely not easy to trek through. Virginia and I hooked arms so I wouldn't topple.

"We're getting close," she said.

I WOKE up to the sound of laughter. I couldn't pinpoint voices, but it was more people than just my family. Eventually rising to my feet, I looked down just to see how swollen they had become. I had stopped asking my mom about pregnancy symptoms long ago. Curiosity had a hold on me, wanting to know who all was over, but apathy clouded my mind, keeping me from wanting to investigate any further. I quickly found out that I would not even have access to investigate as my door was locked. I had a spare glass, thank God.

I didn't get served food until after the commotion died down. It was hard to tell just how long that interval of time was. One hour? Three? I didn't know. I wish I knew where my watch had gone...

Some kind of potatoes, some kind of bread, and some kind of eggs sat on the plate. It was all very cold. The bread had grown stale, and the eggs were watery. Mother's home-cooked meals had taken a turn.

As I bit into a piece of bread, I felt a slight pain in my mouth. Instantly letting go of the food, I instinctively reached to my lips. I could taste blood. Not a lot, but definitely some. I crawled over to my mirror and tried to inspect it. I hadn't bitten my tongue, but I could see a distinct redness at one of my canine teeth. I lightly traced my fingertip along the surrounding gumline. It was quite warm.

I placed my thumb at the tip of the tooth and pressed ever so slightly. I raised a brow when the tooth moved. Having not lost a tooth since the days of being much smaller, I was stunned to see the process seemingly happen again. I shifted the tooth again. While it wasn't ridiculously loose, it was surely loose enough. I swished my mouth with water and set aside the bread. In an effort to avoid that happening again, I choked back the watery eggs.

"Who was over earlier?" I asked my mom when she came to my room to collect my plate. Her wide eyes and her lips slightly parted led me to believe that she assumed I had slept through the occasion.

"Oh, I'm sorry. Did we wake you?" she asked in a sincere sounding tone.

"No, it's fine," I said softly, watching her carefully carry all the dishes in her arms. I realized she had dodged the question after she had already left. I sighed, frustrated with myself for not being able to think more quickly on the spot. She had, however, left my door unlocked again. I peered around the corner to Judith's room. She looked as if she were busy with some scrapbooking project. She looked up when she saw me and gave a small smile.

"Who was here?" I whispered. Being a good few feet away from each other, she cocked her head to the side and gave a puzzled look. I repeated myself once to which she then understood.

"Jonathon and Sarah," she whispered back.

Jonathon and Sarah were my parents' friends. They were close in age and had children who were peers and former classmates of mine. The couple lived only a few houses down, so they were practically family. I saw them in passing at Hannah and Adam's wedding, but beyond that, I couldn't remember the last time I had sat down and had a conversation with anyone from that family.

"Oh, how are they?" I asked with a smile, walking further into her room. Judith shrugged.

"If, uh, anyone asks, you're on a missionary trip," she blurted out. I stared at her blankly for a few solid seconds before realizing I had to respond.

"What?"

"Sorry. Momma and Daddy don't want people to know about you, so they said you're gone."

You never really feel your face unless it's in some kind of discomfort. It doesn't operate like hands and feet, where sensations are never-ending. In that moment, however, I felt my face. It felt as if my skin was clay and from my nose down was dragged in a permanent frown. I was used to feeling disappointment or hurt in my chest or stomach but not this. I don't know why I felt that way. I knew very well that they were unhappy with my premarital pregnancy; neither of my parents exactly hid those feelings from me. That was the moment when I knew exactly how much shame they had for me. I was something to be dusted under the carpet, to be locked away, to be forgotten.

I walked back to my room with anger in my footsteps. I scratched viciously at my temples, not caring about the dozens of strands of hair that broke from my scalp. Screaming was the only thing I could muster, so I took a pillow and buried my face in it. My angry screams turned to hurt cries, and I eventually pulled away the pillow when it became too wet. I didn't want to be seen as a burden, but there was no way to convince them otherwise. I pounded my fists into the carpeting, causing a dull thud to erupt from the ground. I wasn't being quiet, and I wasn't being consoled.

DINNER MADE my gums bleed again.

I OPENED my eyes and saw the desert. Virginia was gripping my waist, and I was holding her shoulder. Above our heads, she held an umbrella. I didn't remember her having one prior, nor did I remember us finding one, but if she was holding it, she was holding it for a reason. That theory proved correct as it began to rain. I casually reached out to touch the droplets before she smacked my hand away instantly. I looked to her for answers, but she merely shook her head. When that wasn't enough, I eventually asked what was the matter.

"The water burns."

The desert was forever. It was sand as far as the eye could see, with the rain obscuring whatever other landscape there was to see. It progressively grew darker and more red, as if we were in some kind of volcano. I thought the desert was flat until I looked behind my shoulder and saw what we had walked was facing us in the form of an incline. We were walking deeper within.

"Why do we keep going down?" I asked.

"Down is the only way out."

Out. There was an out. If we were walking further down as we seemingly had been for months, that would only mean that the concept of out was close. I wanted to hold onto hope, but the images before me made it difficult to comprehend. Little mounds in the sand wriggled back and forth. My shoulders tensed as I saw them, not having seen monsters for some time now. I looked to Virginia for an answer, but she continued forward. As she walked, I had no choice but to follow, as any hesitation would result in burns. The shapes in the sand began to resemble people, the shape and outline of ordinary people.

"Who are they?" I asked.

"They're sinners in the eyes of God. That's why they're here."

"What did they do?"

"Men shalt not lie with another man and so forth. Come on Ema, they teach you this young. Don't act like you don't know," she said.

I stared at the people writhing in pain. Skin turned to sand and life into earth. Their bodies were burnt badly. They were obviously human beings from their shape and size, but their skin was covered in sores and burns, and anywhere that seemed to be rather unscathed was bright pink or purple. They didn't die either. They were left to suffer endlessly. I watched them squirm, each one of them writhing in agony as I slowly walked past them all. They didn't seem to notice me, and for that, I don't blame them. Their pain seemed immeasurable, something that I did not know the experience of.

Getting out of bed grew more difficult with every passing day. Initially, it was simply having to get up while having a stomach ache. That was a specific kind of difficult. The nausea would consume me every day. It then grew to getting up with a rock taped to yourself. It was one thing, having trouble moving out of fear of vomiting; it was another having trouble being able to get up. Lying in bed, I felt like a cockroach stuck on its back. The room had dimmed further.

I undressed in front of my mirror. I hadn't in some time and was curious as to how my body had changed. It appeared as if I hadn't gotten sleep in ages. Shades of blue and purple were painted underneath my eyes. My hair that wasn't knotted, was slick with grease. Parts of my scalp were beginning to show. Then there was me from the neck down. Marks on my body were darker, thicker, and more of them existed. My breasts hung lower, and my nipples were larger and darker. My skin had paled from the lack of sunlight my body was receiving. I opened my mouth, my lips chapped and bloodied, showing what my teeth had become. They were covered in plaque and more yellow than I remembered. I ran my tongue behind my top set, and my right canine easily moved. I instantly shut my mouth and paced around my room.

"Mom!" I yelled as I began to redress myself. It took a few moments before I heard her footsteps. I'm glad she wasn't ignoring me.

"What is it?" She burst in like a whirlwind. She eyed me up and down, concerned. Perhaps she thought I was going to be having the baby.

"My tooth is loose." My mom looked at me with kind eyes, but I knew she would be no help.

Oh, I'm sure it's nothing, sweetie.

"Oh, I'm sure it's nothing, sweetie. Just try to relax," she murmured, her tone soothing, but ineffective.

Things like this happen with a pregnancy.

"Things like this sometimes happen with a pregnancy." I didn't even need her presence to know what she would say. She gave me an ice cube wrapped in a paper towel to alleviate any pain that I was not even experiencing. Nonetheless, I held the freezing towel to my mouth as if it would fix it. The room grew further dimmed.

I missed the enjoyment of others. I missed being at the schoolhouse, and seeing my friends and discussing arbitrary topics. The concept of easy, casual, small talk felt so distant, like it was something I experienced so long ago. Dividing my life into the "before times" versus everything that proceeded may have added to my unhappiness, but I knew no other way to categorize it. I had those memories still, memories of running carelessly through the grass on a warm summer day, of playing in the snow with my siblings and neighbors, and memories of seasons in between filled with love and laughter. While I couldn't say I had the most interesting life, it was better than what it turned into. What could be perceived as an average rudimentary school day far exceeded what life in isolation while pregnant was like. My world had shrunk. As someone who had never traveled, my world was already small. I had my house, my schoolhouse, neighbor's houses, the market, and church. The pet store was added to that list near the end there. Oh, the pet store. Without that, I may have avoided the predicament altogether. Afterall, if I didn't work there, I wouldn't have met him. Him. I couldn't even remember his name. The man who I lost my virginity to, who I had premarital relations with. The man who I sinned with. His name was not as important as what followed. If I hadn't met him, I wouldn't have to wear my sin on my stomach for my family to judge me every day. He didn't even know I was pregnant. I didn't even remember his name.

I ran my fingertips over my stomach. An uncomfortable electric energy transferred through the different parts of my skin. It had been such a long year. I knew I hadn't been pregnant for a full calendar year, but God did it feel like it.

Dinner was meatloaf and a baked potato. I didn't realize how hungry I was until I ate every last piece. Eating for two, eating for two… I watched as the fork shook slightly in my hand, as my wrist quivered. Surely, I wasn't that hungry, and surprisingly, I didn't feel ill. I stared at the fork, vibrating softly within my grasp. I set down the fork and took a deep breath. I was fine.

I was fine.

I was fine.

I was fine.

Back to the desert I was, with Virginia by my side. The further down we go, the closer we are to escaping. That echoed in my head on an endless loop, reminding myself that there, indeed, is an end. There is an exit door. There is an out. So deeper we descended.

Virginia looked at me—not a quick glance, but a full up and down assessment. She smirked and looked away. I asked her what she was thinking.

"You really are getting there," she murmured. After giving her a quizzical look, she motioned towards my stomach. I really was. It was no longer just a little roundness between my hips. I carefully placed my hand on my bump. I still didn't want to think about it.

It had once seemed as if the miles of sand were to stretch on forever, but the sand was suddenly gone out of nowhere. We were no longer in the desert, and it was no longer raining. The floor was back to a rough gravel and the skies dark. Coming up on the horizon was a bridge, one made of stone that was seemingly falling apart. The air was getting noticeably thicker. It was similar to walking into an abandoned basement. Dust and grime lingering in the air. Who knows for how long, only for it to suddenly be taken into the lungs of those who discovered it. Taking in a deep breath only resulted in me coughing.

Now, at the bridge, I broke away from Virginia's hip. I peered out over the edge. She said we were still going down, so how much further was there left? The bridge was connecting two pieces of rock with nothing but space in between. There was no running water below me, nor was there dirt. A piece of gravel sat next to my foot, on cue for my experiment. I chucked it over the edge, listening intently if it were to make a noise. I stood there like an idiot waiting, knowing in my heart I wouldn't hear the sound of impact. I looked at Virginia with concerned eyes, and she stared back at me with apathy.

"Why do you always look like that?" I finally asked. She raised both brows, and her head jerked back slightly.

"What?" she asked, completely confused.

"So used to this! You look around as if you're home. As if there aren't monsters here! As if there isn't just nothing below the bridge! Why are you so calm?" I demanded, my voice nearly shrill.

"Because I have to be."

"I feel like I'm going crazy and have been since I got here." Virginia stared at me, the way she always did. This time, I couldn't blame her. Afterall, what could she say to that? She probably agreed and didn't want to offend me. Maybe she knew things I didn't and was too nervous to say. Either way, I wasn't comforted by her silence.

"I just want to leave!" I screamed, banging my fist into the stone wall of the bridge.

"What?" Judith asked nervously from the hallway, eyeing me with worry. I was sitting on the toilet with my skirt around my ankles, but my underwear was still on. The bathroom door was wide open. My hand was throbbing in pain.

DINNERTIME.

I didn't remember being invited or even walking to the table. One minute, I was in solitude, the next, I was taking part in a family dinner for the first time in ages. I wasn't that excited for the company, but the idea of fresh food and not my tin foil servings was enough to get me to stay. I tried to be there, be present. I laughed when they laughed; I would look with curious eyes at whomever was telling a random story or anecdote, but no one seemed to care. I looked to Isaiah. He never met my gaze, his eyes fixed on Abagail. Judith didn't quite replicate this behavior. She knew not to ask me questions or to center a conversation around me, but she would look at me every now and again. She would look at me with these sad, shameful eyes. I understood completely.

Isaiah and Abagail left without saying goodbye to me. They said goodbye to everyone else and then a final blanket goodbye. I awkwardly waved as they scurried out the door. My mom sighed contently before going to clear the table.

"That'll be you next," my father said to Judith, patting her on the shoulder.

I stood there, almost in a state of shock. I was right there. Judith would not be "next." Judith was not yet a teenager. I wasn't even sure if she had gotten her period yet. What I did know was that she was not to be next in terms of starting a family when I was standing there, ostentatiously pregnant. I was there with my hormonal acne and swollen feet. I was there. Was I really there? No one took notice of me. No one spoke to me. I didn't even get a goodbye hug.

"Not me?" I asked with a hint of attitude in my voice. Now they were looking at me.

"Well," my father started. His tone was awkward. He was embarrassed, caught off guard. I wasn't supposed to talk. I couldn't sit through his attempt at recovery. I walked back to my room as I knew where I was wanted.

WEEK 35. MONTH 8

I walked across what felt like the millionth bridge with a look of pure defeat on my face. I was stuck in this world, falling deeper with no avail. I was told the way out was down, but down was not out. Down was simply further down. I wanted to grab Virginia and shake her by her shoulders, asking when it would all be over. I knew she would only give me a vague answer as she so commonly did. I was thankful to not be making my journey through hell alone, but I wanted a bit more context.

The bridges overlapped. One would lead to a slab of land that would eventually wind around and lead to another bridge. It would go back and forth for what felt like forever. As I crossed a bridge to the next island, I felt something graze my leg. I jumped with a squeal and looked around to see what happened. I didn't notice it at first, but after looking closer, I saw fingers sticking up through the dirt. I looked at Virginia, looking for an answer.

"What? You're okay," she said reassuringly. I made a face of horror and pointed at the ground. "Come on now. You've seen far worse at this point."

She was right. I hated that she was right. I wiped down my legs, trying to rid myself of the sensation of touch from undead fingers. Instead, I grabbed the blanket that was wound around my ankle. The blanket was no longer a problem when I realized the strong taste of blood on my tongue. I ran my tongue behind each of my teeth to determine the issue. The issue was the same tooth as before. I pressed my tongue into it and it moved. My heart raced instantly, and my hand came to my mouth.

"Mom!" I shouted. We had done this dance before. She came in, her hair set in curlers. This made me realize I had no idea what time it was.

"My tooth is really loose. I think something is wrong. I think I should see a nurse," I said, pleading with my eyes. After pointing to which tooth that was bothering me, my mom peered into my mouth.

"Everything looks normal to me," she whispered sheepishly.

"Momma, there's something wrong with me!" I sobbed. Her solution was lemonade and a prayer.

I went to the bathroom to fix myself up. My hair fell from my scalp in long, matted pieces. Back before, I would take excellent care of my image. I wasn't allowed to wear makeup, but I made sure to wash my face, brush and style my hair, and carry myself with a level of grace. No wonder I had been locked in my room. To be looked at in my state of being would have been shameful. As I attempted to brush out the knots in my hair, strands began filling up the brush. My hair had thinned out from the last time I had noticed. As I tucked a lock behind my ear, it exposed a bald spot. I gawked at the sight, unaware of its existence. As I ran my hands down the length of my hair in the attempt to soothe myself, I felt my fingernails get caught in knots. I hesitated before searching through the drawers. After some digging, I ultimately found what I was looking for. My father's straight razor sat in the palm of my hand, the metal cool to the touch.

I stared at my reflection, a stranger to my former self. I had never cut my hair, never wanting to disappoint my father. When taken care of, it was so beautiful. I grabbed one of the knots and began to saw at it. I winced at the pain, but welcomed it, thinking it to be deserved. Hair fell to my feet in clumps. Once I had started, I couldn't stop. I began viciously breaking apart my hair. Grunting, as I threw pieces to the floor. If my father already hates me when why does it even matter? This was just one more reason for him to be cold to me. I eventually stopped and I carefully set down the razor. Looking back in the mirror, I was a different person. My hair was now a dozen different lengths, impossible to be styled neatly. I stared at my reflection, tears beginning to form. My scalp throbbed. I wish it didn't have to be this way.

Back in my room, I began to aimlessly look through my bedside table. A few hair ties, pens, and a seashell. I had never been to the ocean, any ocean, before. I had found it at a local yard sale and begged my mom for it. It was small, about the size of my palm, and had muted tones of lavender. Underneath it sat a small book. It was my diary from middle school. I recognized it instantly. I couldn't quite remember the contents, though. I flipped to a random page, the spine creaking as I did.

You are such a whore for sleeping with Him!. He didn't love you and he never will. You're going to Hell!!!!

I stared at the page in absolute shock. My face was fixed; it felt incapable of moving. I lightly traced my fingers across the paper and felt the indentations from the words. None of it made sense. It could not have been real. I flipped to another page, closer to the end of the diary.

Isaiah and I had so much fun today! We rode in the wagon with

Jeremy and Diana after school got out. I'm excited for summer break. I want to do this every day!

I remembered that day. I felt a small smile form as I thought back to sitting in the wagon as Isaiah would push me down the road. Every family had a car, but drove rather little, so the roads were often safe. When I worked at the pet store, it was quite the opposite of the community. Cars ran up and down the busy streets, only stopping for lights. It was a bit more city-like, as folks often called that area, and we were definitely more of a small town. It didn't matter to me, I knew no difference.

I closed the diary slowly. That part of my life was gone, and it felt gone forever. I hadn't realized that I couldn't go on to do those things with whatever was inside of me. Instead, I was now the adult and no longer allowed to have fun. Fun was for children. Fun was gone. I mean, my mother surely didn't seem to have fun. Sit, serve, and obey. That was what she did. She obeyed my father, raised us children, and existed. She smiled. She smiled when Judith took her first steps. She smiled when I was able to ride a bike. She smiled when my father was in a bad mood from a bad day at work. Her existence was to be a convenience. A mother is an ease; a wife is a please.

Today was Judith's birthday. She was turning thirteen. I couldn't believe she was a teenager, as I have clear memories of changing her diapers. I felt bad for not having a nice present for her. I looked around my room, hoping desperately there was something for me to pass down to her. Sure, a new item was all good and well, but something sentimental being gifted was far sweeter. There was no piece of clothing that seemed worthy or quality enough to be a present. They were all skirts that hadn't been touched in months and dresses that were beginning to smell like someone who passed long ago. I had a few pieces of jewelry but nothing that was "her." Glancing through my bookshelf, I found a diary I knew was empty. I carefully took it in my hands and walked to the door. I tapped on the wall rather than the door and waited to hear Judith stir. Not long after, she answered with a glowing look on her face which was quickly changed to shock. I shook my head and waved her off, not wanting to explain my new haircut.

"Here," I said softly. She shot me a confused look.

"Look, I had a diary when I was younger. I don't know, it's neat to look back on. You'll think it's funny when you're older." Judith looked through the empty pages, perhaps expecting a more interesting present.

Later that day, we were all in the living room. No one asked about my hair, but looks were exchanged. Isaiah and Abagail were over, her engagement ring sparkled in the sunlight. They had gotten Judith a pair of earrings. This made me realize that I had no idea if her ears were even pierced. For the rest of the evening, I kept staring at the sides of her head to tell, but her hair was always in the way. I sat idly on the couch, listening in to random conversations centering around Judith. Everyone said similar things. "I can't believe you're thirteen. I remember you when you were this small, and it feels like yesterday you were X years old." Rudimentary anecdotes for someone her age.

"All the boys will be after her in no time!" Abagail said with a smile, and my father's face hardened.

"Well, I'll have to make sure that doesn't happen," he said solemnly. Abagail smiled sheepishly before turning away.

"Do not be hasty in the laying on of hands, and do not share in the sins of others. Keep yourself pure. Timothy 5:22."

No one looked at me when he spoke those words, but I knew. I knew I was "others." Sure, there were others in the world, but it is easy to have an example in the room with you. I watched as my mom nodded slowly and serenely. Isaiah nodded once firmly and squeezed Abagail's hand. I sat there, frozen, upset at the passive aggression, but unwilling to say anything.

"No one wants to be a whore like Ema," Abagail sneered. Isaiah chuckled, and the others verbally agreed. I looked up and focused on the conversation, physically taken aback. Abagail had never been anything but kind. This was ridiculously out of her character.

"Maybe if she didn't spread her legs for some boy she hardly knew, she'd still be good like us," Judith chimed in. I felt my mouth fall open. I suppose Abagail could do a 180 in terms of personality, but for Judith to turn on me, I was beyond hurt.

"Ema, we raised you better, and this is how you repay us?" This one was from my mom. I was a bit confused, as if my out-of-wedlock pregnancy was suddenly news. It was one thing to paint me as the bad example in the context of Judith getting older and being drawn to sex, but for everyone to suddenly attack as if I had just announced seemed so uncalled for. I knew they were upset, but I wasn't sure at what caliber.

The walls began to deteriorate. Wooded panels splintered and snapped, revealing this skin-like wallpaper. It was pink-toned, irritated, and stretched all around me. The carpeting broke into a million little fragments and swept away into dust. Each family member melted into the ground, starting from their scalp and down to their toes. They were but a candle, their flesh now wax.

"Look, it's gonna get worse before it gets better," Virginia said. She was back and so was I.

"It feels like it's been bad for a while," I whispered, still in quite a state of shock over the sudden location transition. Virginia laughed. I felt like I had never heard her laugh before that moment. It was loud, echoing around us somehow despite the lack of walls.

"What, you thought pregnancy was gonna be easy?!" She shook her head with a smile. Something inside me snapped.

"I'm going crazy! Pregnancy was not supposed to be this way! I'm supposed to be happy! I'm supposed to be beautiful! I'm supposed to pick out names with my husband and not get dirty looks from my mother! I'm seeing things, losing my hair, and I feel like I'm losing my mind!" I was gasping for air as words just kept coming out.

My family stood around with looks of utter confusion on their face. Each person varied slightly, some showing more expressions of concern, some more shock. We all stood around the room, staring at one another. I reeled back, sheepishly. The silence wasn't awkward, but it was surely palpable. I stood there, hoping that the conversation would not focus on me.

"Here," my mother said, breaking the silence and walking between everyone. "Let's all pray together. Let's pray for Ema and her feelings." I did not want the attention on me, but I was touched. She was actually recognizing that I was upset.

So we sat around together and prayed. My mother spoke about the blessings of fertility and for God to show me what a gift I was given. My eyes fluttered slightly. I paused before slowly opening them. I watched Isaiah let go of Abagail's hand and feel up her body, reaching for her breast. I immediately shut my eyes, tight enough to where I started to see colors swirl against the darkness. When I opened my eyes again, her dress was lifted, and her panties pulled to the side. With his one hand still holding my mother's, his other hand was inside of Abagail. My mouth fell, and I instinctively broke away. I got up as fast as I could, running off to the bathroom. I emptied my stomach into the toilet for some time before someone came to check on me. I felt a hand on my back, assumed to be my mom. Instead, it was Judith.

"I'm sorry I ruined your birthday," I said with labored breathing.

"Well, you're sick," she replied plainly. She wasn't wrong.

"I know. I still feel bad." Judith sat down next to me, her hand still on my back. We sat in silence. Her touch was more comforting than I expected. It was like a mother's touch. I wanted to lay my head down in her lap and cry forever, but that wouldn't be fair. I helped change her diapers. I thought of her at times as my own when my parents were too busy. I am her caregiver; she is not mine.

Later that night, my door was still unlocked, so I went into Judith's room. She was brushing out her hair with one hand and smoothing it down with the other. When she noticed me, she flashed me the smallest smile. In return, I waved the smallest wave.

"Did you have a nice birthday?" I asked softly. I sat down on her bed, my feet aching.

"Yeah, it was nice." Her reply was as boring as my question.

"You're getting old," I teased with a smile.

"I am not!" She giggled. I laughed with her. It was nice. It was an easy conversation that felt so normal. We were just two sisters giggling in her room. We were pinching our cheeks to have them blush. We were styling our hair. We were kicking back our feet in the air as we talked about boys. We bickered and laughed, shared clothes, and held hands.

"Do you think I'm crazy?" I asked. This was out of nowhere, and I didn't want to kill the mood, but I asked anyway. Judith stared at me intently, as if looking for crazy on my face. She squinted her eyes and looked me up and down.

"Only a little, I guess," she said nonchalantly. There was a real honesty in her voice that I couldn't help but respect.

"Why?" she asked.

Why indeed? Because I sleepwalk. Because time was no longer linear to me. Because I'm losing my hair, my teeth are coming loose, and because I haven't had a normal dream since becoming pregnant. Because I started screaming at your birthday dinner in front of our family because I thought I was in hell.

"Just wondering." She seemed satisfied with my response.

"Well, I've never been pregnant. So maybe you are crazy, I don't know."

"I'll tell you a secret."

"What is it?

"Being pregnant stinks."

"Really?"

"It's a weird kind of secret, I think. Like they want you to have all these kids, right? You get married, you leave your family size up to God, and He says to multiply, right? Well, did He ever say that means you have to throw up every day? It's really awful, Jude."

"Every woman I've met is so pretty when they're pregnant. Their face glows, and they look so happy. I wish I could be that, but I just can't. I'm not pretty, and I'm not happy and it makes me feel really guilty." Judith sat there watching as I poured my heart out, my voice eventually breaking and my eyes welling up. She looked at me with her big eyes. They were curious in a childlike but concerned way. I knew she didn't have the words to say, and I didn't expect her to. She was still a child. It would be wrong of me to place my burdensome feelings on to her.

"You'll feel better, though, when you have the baby, right?" she asked softly. Conceptualizing the idea of post-pregnancy felt so far away, so out of reach. I knew it was approaching. I watched my stomach somehow get larger with every passing day. I had just been stuck in the limbo of pregnancy for so long it felt like it would last forever.

"I hope so."

After leaving Judith's room, I went to use the restroom. Inside, it had a slight reddish tone, like someone with a red flashlight was pointing it at its white porcelain base. I blinked a few times, thinking that would make it go away. It didn't. Looking around the room, the red hue was cast on everything. The sink faucet, the showerhead, the window, all of it had a slight red glowing outline. I ran my hand along the faucet, as if there would be a change to its composure. It felt as it normally did like there was nothing odd about it. My bedroom was the same way. My bed was just as I had left it but with a faint red glow. I rubbed at my eyes and knew it was weird, but I felt too tired to care. I was under the mindset that if I sleep it off, I'll wake up normal.

"Hey, Ema?" Judith asked from my doorframe.

"Do you ever think about our grandparents?" she asked softly. I froze, completely caught off guard by the question.

"Not really. Why?"

"I don't know. I was talking with my friend who asked what my family did for my birthday. So I talked about everyone, and she asked about my grandparents, but I didn't know what to say."

"What did you tell her?"

"Didn't really say anything," she muttered. She looked down at the floor for a moment before looking back up at me. "Have you ever met them?"

My grandparents were not something to be really spoken of. I grew up without them. I had my parents, their siblings, my siblings, and my parents' friends from church. I didn't know something was missing until my peers pointed it out. When I was young, far younger than Judith, I had asked my mom where were they. She said they lived far away, and that was the answer I lived with. I knew it was different. The families in my town were all close-knit. Generations would often live all within the same house. If they didn't, they all lived within our community.

"No," I replied plainly.

"Are they dead?"

"No. I mean, maybe, actually. I'm not sure."

"Can we visit them?" Her steady stream of questions was beginning to get to me, and I grew less patient with each passing one.

"Jude, I do not know where they are."

"Why?"

"Because."

"Because why?" I felt my teeth begin to grind together.

"Because that's what momma told me. They're just not here. I don't know what else to say."

"You don't think that's weird?"

"I don't know, Jude. I just trust her." The words felt sticky coming out of my mouth. I wanted to believe my words, and a part of me truly did. A larger part of me, however, knew that I didn't. Not like I used to, anyway.

I went to bed not long after that, but the conversation stuck with me. The more I thought about it, the weirder it was. I didn't think about it because it was never something to bring up. Now that it was brought up, it was up. Up was noticeable. It would be one thing if it were just one set of grandparents, but it was both. Did all four pass away? Were all four bad?

"You're getting so close," said Virginia. Her voice was low and serious. Her tone was sinister, which unsettled me deeply.

"You already said that," I grumbled, annoyed. Virginia hid a smile.

"Well, you are."

We faced a bridge that led down. It wasn't a steep decline, but I could tell it was a descension. It was another stone bridge covered in gravel. The gravel seemed to be trickling down the path with us, but upon closer inspection, it was bugs. Centipedes, cockroaches, spiders, and every bug you could think of crawled along the stone path. I was no stranger to them, having spent many warm autumn days outside in their company. I didn't particularly like them, but a fear wasn't there. However, I would jump if one began to crawl on my feet.

"Well, you'll be out soon," Virginia said.

I was back in bed, but dawn hadn't quite broken yet. With my back hurting and having few sleeping options, due to my stomach, I succumbed to the idea of being and staying awake. I adjusted myself and turned on my bedside table lamp. As I pulled off my sheet, dozens of cockroaches ran up and down the sides of my mattress, some crawling over my legs. My heart nearly exploded and I began brushing my legs manically as I tried to climb out of bed. Getting out of bed wasn't the easy task it was eight months ago, so it took me a moment before I got to my feet. I could feel their hairlike legs crawling on mine. They were on me and then they weren't. My body was clean, and so were my sheets. My heartrate was still not back to normal, and I stared in shock at my wrinkled blankets. After careful consideration, I sat back down on my bed, casually smoothing out the sheets. I ran my hand through my hair, feeling as my fingertips grew slick with oil. I held my hair in my fist, staring blankly at the carpet. In times like those, I would have started a prayer. Times were different as I felt no urge. I had no urge to do anything at all. I just wanted to feel better. The room was still red.

The sun eventually rose as it does every day. A bright

pastel orange painted the sky just over the trees. The birds began to sing softly. There weren't many, so the ones who did broke the stillness of the early morning. Living in a neighborhood where there are few cars and other distractions, the birds are the music of the community. The sunshine came in from my window, casting a beam of light across the carpet. I stuck my hand over in front of the light, lighting up my palm. Its creases ran miles across my skin with some breaking off into tiny fragments.

With nothing to do as I was too awake to go back to bed, I slowly rose to my feet to go to my door. It was locked. I hadn't sleepwalked in weeks. I thought I was doing better. I thought I was to be trusted. I mindlessly toyed with the doorknob until I heard a click. I froze, scared. I didn't know why I was scared but I was. I was too frightened to open the door, so I simply stood facing it. I didn't have to open it as it simply did on its own. I backed away to see Judith on the other side. I felt my shoulders relax.

"Why'd you unlock it?" I whispered.

"I don't know why they lock it," she whispered back.

"It's because I sleepwalk and stuff."

"I used to sleepwalk too." It took a moment before I remembered what she was talking about. When she was a bit younger, perhaps around seven or so, she did, in fact sleepwalk. It didn't last long, and I didn't remember ever witnessing it firsthand, but I remember people talking about it.

"And they never locked your door?" I asked despite really having no recollection of my parents doing that.

"No. Momma would bring me into the living room for some water and read me a story sometimes."

I sat in the living room, knowing my parents were to get up shortly. There was a bookshelf across from a chair that stood tall with photographs. My parents' wedding photos were, of course, on display. They both looked so young, but they looked happy. A photo of us three kids was positioned off-center. Isaiah was likely twelve, me ten, and Judith about four. Judith and I had matching dresses while Isaiah was in a suit. It was for some event, but I couldn't quite remember. As I was looking, I heard my mom walk from her bedroom to the kitchen, her heels tapping against the floor. I heard her pause as she saw me but then continued walking as if everything was normal and fine.

"Why aren't there any pictures of our grandparents?" I asked. Silence. Heel clicking. My mother stared at me.

"What?" she spoke as if she didn't hear me.

"There are pictures from your wedding. Pictures of us but none of our grandparents."

"Oh. I probably have some somewhere." Her tone was off, dismissive. I watched any interest leave her face as she walked back to the kitchen to start breakfast.

"Why don't they visit?" I asked, following her as she started to take items out of the fridge.

"Well, they live far away, honey. They're older. They can't travel like that."

"Well, can't we visit them?"

"That'd be nice, but that's really a lot of money."

That was the first time either parent had ever mentioned money, or at least in that context. When I first applied to the pet store, my mom said it would give me a sense of finances while giving me some extra pocket money for shopping. The money was paid out in checks and never that much, but enough to get a new dress if I wanted. I had never heard about the status of my parents' wealth before. I sat on her answer for a while.

Abagail came to visit for a few hours. I heard her and Isaiah from my room, chatting happily with my parents. Judith was outside playing with friends, their laughter drifting through the windows. I lied on my sweat-stained bed with a wet washcloth on my chest as it was so hot out. Eventually I heard a tapping on my door. I sighed before throwing my legs off the side of the bed, the washcloth falling to the floor. I felt strands of hair stick to the sheen of sweat on my forehead. I opened it to Abagail and Isaiah.

"Hey, how are you feeling?" Abagail asked in a soft voice, the voice you use when you speak to a child.

"Oh, fine, Abagail, just a bit tired," I muttered automatically. As soon as I spoke the words, I instantly forgot saying them. Isaiah walked into the room, his nose wrinkled as he drew closer.

"Hey," I said as he made eye contact with me. He nodded in response.

"Can I ask you something?" I asked. Abagail shrunk down and took a step back, looking ready to give us privacy. "No, it's okay. Stay." She smiled sheepishly and looked to my brother for approval.

"What is it?"

"Our grandparents. Did you ever meet them?" Isaiah made a thinking face, really contemplating my question, and sighed.

"I don't think so," he said after a moment of deliberation. "Why?"

"Oh, I mean, it's a long story, but Jude was playing with friends, right? They asked her about her grandparents, like if they were at her birthday dinner. It just is weird that all three of us don't really know them. From either side, too! Mom's or dad's."

"Do you know where they live? Any of them?" Abagail asked.

"No. Mom just says far."

"A telephone number?"

"I don't know."

"Check mom's contact book?" The three of us stared out into the hallway. I looked at Isaiah with pleading eyes. *Please. They don't trust me anymore. They trust you. Please.* He met my gaze. *Please.* He sighed softly before exiting the room. Abagail waited in my bedroom with me.

"So, did you think of names yet?" Abagail asked, breaking the ice. A giggle broke from my lips, and I shook my head.

"No. She'll be here soon though."

"She?" Abagail's eyes perked up.

"Oh, I'm not sure, actually, my bad," I said with a nervous laugh. Isaiah was back with a small leather book. Flipping through was interesting. I knew every single name. Next-door neighbors, school house teachers, the local doctor. Everyone I knew the name of was in there. It had just about everyone in town, minus a few random blurry faces here and there. It was alphabetized which was helpful. I flipped to M first. Mom. I read from Maryanne to Mona with no "Mom" in between. No mother. I flipped back to D. From David to Dorothy. No dad. No father. No grandmother, grandfather, anything. They simply weren't there.

"Well, we have to get going soon, but I can ask around town if you want," Isaiah said nonchalantly. I shrugged. A part of me was going mad with curiosity, but the other simply seemed defeated. If there were no leads, where was there to go?

Behind Abagail, a centipede crawled on the wall.

Later that evening, I heard my father flipping through a book. My bedroom door had been left unlocked by Abagail and Isaiah, so I took advantage of the moment. As he heard my footsteps approach, he looked up from his reading and greeted me with a thin lipped smile. It did not feel genuine. I hoped he was in a good mood.

"Hey, I have a question," I said slowly, sitting on the chair opposite him.

"What's on your mind?" he asked, his tone a bit lifeless, but not angry.

"Where are your parents?" I asked. Sorrow crossed his eyes, and he sighed softly.

"Oh, Ema, they're not with us anymore." A silence began to spread. This was surely more information than before.

"What happened?"

"Well, my father was in an accident right before Isaiah was born. Like me, he worked for the church doing construction. Well, construction is surely not easy work. When working on a repair, he fell, and there was nothing to be done about that."

"Oh."

"Yes, well," he trailed off, his lips turned to a frown. Guilt ate through my stomach. I didn't mean to make him feel bad.

"Your mom?" I asked.

"Oh, well. She didn't take the news well. She found herself pulling away from the Lord; she didn't believe anymore. She took her own life." This silence was far louder.

"I'm sorry."

"Nothing for you to be sorry for. Her sin will follow her."

"And Momma's parents?" I asked after a long pause, my voice meek.

"Oh. Well, to my knowledge, they are still around, but they don't live around here."

"Where do they live?"

"A good distance away." I nodded in understanding, knowing I wouldn't get any more information out of him. I was happy to get the context of his parents, something I honestly wasn't expecting. Daddy went back to his reading, and I decided to get a bit of sun while I was still allowed to be out of my room.

~

I STOOD IN THE GRASS, letting the sun kiss me on my face. The sunset had painted hues of orange and lavender across the horizon. It was a beautiful day. I slowly walked about in the grass, the humming of cicadas and buzzing of fireflies keeping me company. A patch in the backyard had a different kind of grass growing atop the earth's surface. I remembered the patch being brown a while back ago, but I assumed Momma was going to plant some flowers there or maybe some kind of summertime crop. I ran my foot over the grass, and it felt denser, with the blades being far thicker than its comparison. As I dug my toes into the dirt, I felt something. It felt hard, like metal. I knew it would be difficult to bend over and pick it up, so I slowly worked it up with my foot to the surface in my line of vision. It appeared to be a necklace with dog tags. Furrowing my brow, I lowered myself to the ground to inspect it closer. Dirt and mud were caked within the grooves. It was a truly unique find, as I didn't know of anyone within our community to have been in the military. As I held the necklace in my hand, I felt a strange feeling pass over me.

I was in bed. The sun had set hours ago, and I was only able to see through the moonlight. The room was blurry; it was hard to make out the objects around me. Until I saw him. Him. He climbed on top of me. I was not in my bedroom. He kissed my neck, and I felt something hard and cold hit my face.

I held the necklace in my hand, letting it grow warm from the warmth of my skin. He never went to my house, not my backyard, at least. He picked me up on the road. I stared at the mismatched grass patch. I slowly knelt on the earth and placed my hand on the ground. In doing so, I felt a kick.

I stood up as fast as my body would allow, and my blood ran cold. I looked back behind me at my parents' house. I could see the dining room through the windows. My mother and father laughed with Judith and Isaiah. They were playing the loving, happy family so well. Feeling all of nothing and all of everything, I felt my body as it carried itself through the back of the house like a storm blowing in. Each of their faces dropped in a different way as they saw me approach. My eyes directed to my father, and I began to scream.

"What did you do?!" I held the dog tags in his face, his skin drained of blood.

"What the fuck did you do?!?"

DAY? WEEK?

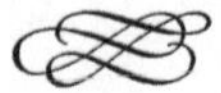

We were walking along a bridge when dust began to fall. The world began to move. Something had changed. The air was different. I looked to Virginia for answers, but she only stared ahead, ready. A figure stood in the distance before us. It was far enough away to tell it was something like a person but close enough to know that something was definitely wrong. There was no way to escape it. We were at the midpoint of the bridge, a bridge that was slowly disintegrating behind us. Pieces of rubble were falling every few seconds. The only way out was down, and down was forward, and forward was the thing. My pace slowed, not knowing what to do. There was no escape and I did not know how to fight it. Hell, I didn't even know what it was.

I didn't stop walking. It hadn't noticed us yet. It seemed to walk aimlessly around in circles. It didn't seem angry, if anything, it seemed confused. A small, hurt animal had a similar demeanor. I felt my body shrink down the closer we approached. And then I saw it.

Two people, actually. A man was on one side and a

woman on the other. They were stitched together back to back, their skin red from the shoddy incision. The man had hair the color of sand, short and unkempt. The woman had strawberry blonde with ribbons tying it back. I recognized them instantly. Their jaws were broken somehow, their mouths so unnaturally agape. He walked, her feet dangling a bit above. Both of their bodies had skin that was pale and greying. Something was wrong with their eyes, but I couldn't quite tell. I was still too far. As much as I wanted to run far in the opposite direction, I continued forward. As I did, they vanished.

My body hurt. For the duration of the pregnancy, I had always been uncomfortable. Whether that be nausea, vertigo, or whatnot. However, I had upgraded to pain. My stomach physically hurt. It felt that at any moment, my skin would snap, leaving everything being guarded inside to come rushing out. I had stretch marks that were bright red from hipbone to hipbone. There was no position anymore that was comfortable. Laying on my back and sides felt so cumbersome. You could absolutely forget about laying on your stomach.

I stood beside my window. Everything about the outdoors felt so discolored. Sure, there was blue in the sky and yellow in the wildflowers, but they both seemed dimmed. I would blink, and they would only get darker and redder in tone. It grew painful to look at. It wasn't too bright, but looking made my eyes water. I turned my attention back to my bedroom. Visually, everything was too much pressure behind my eyes. I squinted and looked away. As I walked to my bed to lie down, a sharp pain struck me in my stomach. I let out a whimper like a hurt animal and instinctively sank. My palms flat on my mattress and head down, I took a deep breath, as if exhaling would relieve me of my burdens. I slowly rose to my natural height, but as I stood normally, a gush of fluids fell out of my body and to my feet. I gasped in horror. It was like I had wet myself without even trying. Twice. However, I knew what it meant, and I instantly started to fret. My eyes darted around my bedroom, my bedroom that I had always managed to find comfort in. My hand instinctively flew to my bookshelf and grabbed my personal Bible, the last book remaining. As I flipped through pages to find peace and consolation, I was met with blank pages. I stared in horror at the wordless paper on each individual page. I blinked hard and brought the book to the window where natural light was spilling in. I flipped maniacally, trying to find something but was left with nothing more than a leather-bound journal.

The pain struck my stomach once more. I groaned and squeezed my eyes shut.

"Momma!" I cried, hoping she would hear me. "Momma!" Tears welled in my eyes. I needed her. Why wasn't she coming? Why didn't she want to help? I managed to carry myself to my chair without too much of a struggle.

"Dear Lord, please," I cried. Pain struck me once more. I gagged and nearly vomited from the sharpness and suddenness of it.

"Dear Lord. Please. I beg. Please make the pain stop. Please don't let this hurt too bad." Some other kind of liquid was secreting from me. "God, please, I don't want to do this. I'm scared!"

As the tension in my jaw increased, I felt my tooth move completely out of place. Without thinking, I reached into my mouth and pulled it out. It was far different than losing your baby teeth. This one had roots. The taste of blood quickly filled my mouth. Not wanting the taste to linger, I spit out whatever I could, letting my bloodied drool run down my chin.

I heard the sound of footsteps approaching. Fucking

finally. A key turned, and a lock sounded. What a day for locked doors. My mother and Judith were on the other side. Jude's eyes went large with shock, with disgust, I couldn't quite tell. My mother's expression was even harder to read. It wasn't excitement. It wasn't joy. It wasn't fear. She seemed so oddly neutral.

"The baby's coming," Judith muttered.

"Okay, let's bring you into the living room here," my mom said. With the help of the two of them, they got me onto the family couch. I leaned back my head and tried to pretend like everything was fine, like my entire life wasn't about to completely change for the worse in a matter of hours. I let out a sob, such a raw, guttural cry. It was a cry where you feel it in your chest like your sternum is breaking. Snot ran down from my nose and into my mouth, but that was far from the worst of the sensations I was experiencing. Judith sat with me and held my hand tentatively. You could tell she was uncomfortable but still wanted to be there. It was kind, and I needed her kindness. My mom came back with towels and a glass of water.

"Shouldn't we get going, Momma?" I said weakly after taking a sip of water.

"Go where, baby?" she asked, rubbing a strand of sweaty hair off my forehead. I paused cautiously. I felt uneasy needing to spell it out for her.

"The hospital? Or calling a doctor?" I asked. I didn't know how delivery worked, but I remembered going to the town's doctor as a kid every now and again.

"Oh, don't be silly. We can just do this here," she said. My eyes widened with fear. My mom is not a nurse. Sure, she had three kids but had never been trained on how to assist with birth. Judith was just a child. She shouldn't have to be an acting adult in such an adult situation. It simply wasn't fair to her.

"Why?" I asked in a small voice.

"Oh, that's just something that they tell you. Having your children born in your home is what God intended."

"What if something goes wrong?" I asked. She didn't answer quickly enough, so I asked again.

"Nothing will go wrong. You'll be fine. God will protect you." I looked to Judith for comfort as I had no one else to. She gave me a smile and a shrug. It wasn't that comforting. A much stronger wave of pain came over me. I groaned through my teeth, feeling another one grow loose, and gripped Judith's hand.

"Momma, I want a doctor!" I yelled angrily. I was angry and loud, and no one was listening. My mom simply smiled as if I wasn't speaking at all. She just drowned me out. Another wave of pain and my groans turned to screams.

"Momma, I think she needs a doctor," Judith said. Good. Validation. It meant nothing if it garnered me no results, but the intention was fine. At least I wasn't crazy.

"Judith, the idea of needing a hospital or medicine for birth is simply a worldly lie."

"Wouldn't the medicine make it hurt less?" Judith asked curiously.

"God made birth to feel a certain way." And what a way it felt.

Judith would ask me questions that I couldn't quite hear. Whether she was genuinely curious or simply trying to ease my stress, I wasn't quite sure. In any case, I couldn't really pay attention to her. Her voice merely echoed back behind me, bouncing off the walls and disappearing into the air.

The path before me was simultaneously dark and bright. The duality of it was oddly sinister. Virginia was right next to me, oddly cheerier than before. I looked at her, and she looked at me. Her eyes were encouraging, proud. It was like a mother sending her child to the first day of school. I fully embodied that child: the trepidation, the anxiety, the desire to hold on to any kind of familiarity. I wanted to hold onto the hem of Virginia's clothes just as I had my mother's when I was small. To be a child and think your mother's calves could protect you from the world. If only. I still carried that same naivety all those years later. Some things never change. I felt Virginia's hand on the small of my back, encouraging me to move forward. I had slowed down. I didn't even notice. Nevertheless, I continued forward, downward into the glowing darkness.

"Do you want water?" Judith asked. I blinked back to my living room and shook my head weakly. I wanted it all to be over.

"Come on, Judith, let's pray for your sister," my mom said. I didn't even know where she was; her voice a phantom. Judith's expression didn't change, she simply moved with my mom in a mechanical motion.

"Lord, as Ema begins her journey into Godly motherhood, we ask that you deliver her this baby safely. Please watch over her in this process of delivery. I pray that he or she knows you and follows your word through every day of life. We ask this in the name of Jesus Christ, our Lord and Savior."

I stared at the both of them arduously as they spoke and finished their prayers. I had given up hope that a medical professional was to step in. I knew the pain was only increasing, and the duration between the large bursts of pain was growing shorter. I didn't remember being stripped down, but I, in that moment, realized that I had been. My eyes fluttered around the room. The walls were melting. The sky was red.

"What does it feel like?" I heard Judith ask. Her voice felt so far away. I knew she was only an arms-length away, but it sounded like she spoke in a tunnel, her voice bouncing everywhere and eventually landing on me. I might have managed a groan in response. I knew I wasn't capable of a verbal answer. Looking up, I saw the face of Abagail. An excited grin stretched across her rosy cheeks. I think I managed to smile in response.

At that moment, I noticed the gowns. All three of them, my mother, Abagail, and Judith, all wore floor-length gowns, off-white in color. I was unable to focus on whether they were truly identical fabrics, but from my blurred vision, they were all matching. They moved around the room like faded wraiths, assembling the room best for the occasion.

"I don't want to," I whispered faintly. I didn't even know why I said it. There wasn't a thing to do to change my current situation.

"You'll do great," Abagail said encouragingly.

I was scared. Genuinely and utterly scared. There was no doctor present or any medical equipment. I couldn't imagine actually having to deliver. I didn't know how big it was, but it felt impossible. The idea was preposterous. How was something so large to come out of something so small? It didn't make sense. It sounded like torture. It was hard to conceptualize as I lay there writhing.

The world as I knew it prior had red skies, that of the most dreaded planes of oblivion, or the darkest, most looming black clouds. As I approached the newest territory, I was met with an all-encompassing light grey. It was foggy, like that of a crisp winter morning. There was no moisture in the air, however, but quite the opposite. A dryness ripped into my face and burned my eyes. The fog wasn't too dense to where I couldn't see through it, but I couldn't see far beyond it. As I kept walking deeper within, the temperature noticeably dropped. The finest of hairs on my body stood to attention. It was such a penetrating cold; one you feel right to the bone.

"What happened?" I asked Virginia. Cloud smoke fell

from my lips as words escaped me. It had to be somewhere near freezing.

"It's okay, it's normal," she whispered, the same cloud of smoke coming from her. The environment was dizzying. It gave me such an overwhelming, disorienting flood over my entire body. Pinpricking sensations ran through my fingertips to my veins, carrying throughout the riverways underneath my skin. My limbs felt limp like I was to collapse at any given moment, but my body never did. My knees, although wobbly, never gave. I just wanted to sleep, it was what my body craved. A peaceful escape for a few hours. It just kept going. It just never stopped.

Abagail placed a damp washcloth on my forehead. Random strands of hair molded into my skin from the pressure and moisture of the cloth. I tried to adjust it, but she kept it held in place. She smiled casually as she did. I looked around the room to find my mother and Judith but struggled to keep my eyes open. Who knew that the process of labor was so tiring? Rhetorical, of course, now, but who was I to know?

I peered around the room to see what was making me so cold. However, it looked to be daylight, perhaps noon or so. All the windows were opened, even a standing fan was going. Goosebumps ran for miles across my skin and I felt my teeth begin to chatter.

"Why is it cold?" I whispered. My voice was strained, labored. Abagail and Judith exchanged confused glances.

"It's all normal," my mom said soothingly. Of course, it was. Of course, all of it was normal. Every ache and every pain and every moment I felt like I was going to die was normal. The fact that the baby had almost arrived and didn't have a name was normal. The fact that I felt so little attachment to the baby was normal. The fact that a part of me wished I would die so I didn't have to live with everything to follow was just so normal.

"Ema, put your legs up," my mom instructed. Something churned in my stomach. It felt wrong, improper, and inappropriate. I didn't want to reveal myself. I knew it was for medical reasons, but it didn't nullify my unease. I hesitated before ultimately complying. I grimaced as my mom checked the placement of the baby, strawberry blonde strands falling in her face. She was no professional. I wanted her just to hold my hand and stop pretending to be a doctor. I wanted my mom.

"You're getting there but still have a bit to go."

That was both the best and worst thing she could have said. Good. Relief. I still had time before the big thing. However, that meant I still had to exist within the world of arduous labor and contractions. The pain was coming quicker but still taking its time. I wasn't ready for delivery, but hell did I want to be done with labor. The only way out was to find a time machine and go back nine months or skip way forward until after my body healed. No option was realistic, and all I had left to do was suffer. Not that I had much room on the couch to stretch and situate, but there was no position I found to be more comfortable. Everything simply hurt.

Abagail took a towel and wiped at the inside of my thigh. I hated it. I hated the feeling of being so exposed. However, I knew if I were to say anything, I would only be questioned on why I was comfortable with it when I had slept with Ron. When she pulled the towel back, it was covered in a diluted bloody substance. I didn't want to even bother asking since I knew what my mother would respond with. I simply accepted the fact that I was bleeding, and everyone seemed totally fine about it. If I was dying, then so be it. I was scared but too exhausted to be too scared.

Cool, misty air enveloped me. The world around me felt so still. No sound of rivers running, of monsters prowling or any other thing that could possibly make noise. It was difficult to see my surroundings well. The ground below my feet was tough like stone but smooth, with no loose gravel. The air felt rather crisp and clean, unlike other environments that were far more musty and decrepit. A shadow began to form in the distance the further I walked. Virginia was still with me, but she now followed behind rather than her being ahead of me. I looked back every so often to ensure she was still around. The shadowy figure was not a person I quickly came to realize. It was an object, rather short length-wise and long width-wise. It was likely another rock formation, so like that of many others I had seen in this world.

"What's going on?" my father asked, a worried tone to his voice as if it wasn't completely obvious as to what was happening. What a silly thing to ask. One of them filled him in, and I watched Isaiah rush to my side.

"I'm going to be an uncle!" he exclaimed loudly in my face. His enthusiasm, truly, was adorable. However, he spit in my face. His breath smelt of lunch, and I never forgot the fact that he was willing to have sex with me. What a kind boy. How unfortunate that he made me want to vomit.

So there we all were: my parents, my siblings, and Abagail. They all stood around me as I lay uncomfortably on the living room couch with my legs sprawled open. For as long as I had lived until that point, I was instructed to be modest. Wear long dresses, wear high collars, and if you go out of the town, don't question why other girls are dressed differently. Protect your virtue and protect your body. If you follow God's teachings, He will bless you with a man that you are allowed to have sex with. It is supposed to be good, but also a duty of the wife to satisfy her husband. Sex is a gift for both of you, but really, truly, it's just for the man. You are there to satisfy his needs, not him to yours. So there you are, a good, godly woman who followed all the rules. Congratulations, you get to lie there as your husband lies with you carelessly, not caring of your comfort in the matter. That is your prize. You also better hope that endeavor results in a pregnancy, as it is up to you to build up God's kingdom. It was drilled into my head from as young as I could remember. Don't let just any young boy smell and pick your flower; give it to your husband. There I was. Truly, barefoot and pregnant, legs open and baring. I was not made up of roses. My skin was precious, too.

It was a couch, not a rock. It was off-white and quilted, just like my parents' because it was their couch. As I peered over the backing, I saw that the cushions were soiled with blood. Resting on the arm of the couch was our family Bible. I cautiously grazed my fingertips against the bound leather. Delicately picking up the first few pages, I looked to see that everything appeared normal. The pages were how they always were to look, the text correctly printed, with nothing seeming to be out of the ordinary. My fingers trembled, not out of fear but from the cold. I looked back to see Virginia still there but a few paces back.

"What now?" I asked. My voice echoed off the cave walls.

"This is the end," she replied. I looked around. Fragmented pieces of rock hung from the ceiling. The room was misshapen, similar to that of a square but with a side caved in. It was by far the smallest area I had explored. Everything else felt far more open, more free. This was confined, tight. It made me nervous to even think about it.

"This?" I asked, fed up. All the running away from monsters, all the falling into rivers, of being in the most nightmarish realm. It all comes to a head with a small corner room with a piece of furniture and a Bible.

"I thought they'd save the worst for last!" I exclaimed.

"You think this is good?" Virginia asked genuinely. I swallowed hard and nervously looked around. I was then paranoid of something jumping out of the corner, someone or something coming to tackle me to the ground.

"How much longer now?" Judith asked, boredom bleeding through her voice. I did not have the tolerance for such a statement. I gritted my teeth and the familiar taste of blood was back on my tongue.

"It's hard to say. Could be quite a few more hours," my mom replied softly. My jaw tensed further. Abagail was folding up piles of laundry, blankets, and small pieces of clothing.

"It's getting worse," I said weakly.

"Well, it has been a few hours already," Judith chimed in. I wanted everyone to simply stop talking. It wasn't that hard. We did not need to talk or comment on things. I just wanted to be in a hospital, talking only to people who knew what they were doing. Only if someone in town got really sick or hurt would they drive out of town to the nearest hospital. Otherwise, people usually just saw the local doctor. I think a few of the girls I went to the schoolhouse with talked about becoming midwives. I never asked a woman who had a baby what they did when it was time.

Dust began to fall on the couch. It wasn't much, but surely enough to be noticed. I glanced at the ceiling and cautiously took a step back. I looked over my shoulder at Virginia. She nodded once at me. More dust began to fall, and I fell back in pain. God, it was happening. It was really happening. The world was so much darker and so cloudy. I reached out to my mom, but she did not hold me. She stood there, menacingly. She had such a wide smile on her face with joy in her eyes, but she felt so cold. I wanted comfort. I wanted the comfort a mother could give when her daughter was entering motherhood. I thought she would read my mind and know that I wanted her hand to squeeze and for her to tenderly brush the hair off my forehead. I wanted her to reassure me that I would be okay. Not that my child is a gift from God. Not that the pain is my punishment for my sin. I wanted genuine motherly love. Rather than holding my hand, she clasped hers together and bowed her head forward. I just wanted my mom. She just wanted her God.

The pain was becoming unbearable. I tried to control my breathing, but it was all too much. The crushing weight of the world fell upon my midsection. There was nothing else around me. Pain was all that existed. Someone grabbed my legs and held them up. I deliriously let them, as my body was nothing but a rag doll.

Everything was now completely red. The walls stained in blood, the ceiling fiery skies. The knife in my stomach twisted, and the pain sprawled throughout my body. I couldn't help but let out the most guttural scream. My life was lit aflame, and my audience only watched me burn encouragingly. I screamed until my voice became raspy and broken and turned into jagged sobs.

"You can do this!" Abagail said sweetly. My throat ran hoarse, and snot fell between my lips.

My body was being torn in two. I was being cut from between my legs and up. What my body was doing did not feel natural in the slightest. It felt nothing short of human torture. I had to be dying. The sensation of never-ending burning would never cease. Was I in hell? Did I die, and this was what I got for having premarital sex? The lines between hell and reality were too blurred in that moment to know where I even was. I was strapped to a bed, my vision going in and out as scissors began shearing through my skin. I rip and tear as if I'm a mere piece of paper.

I screamed for God to help me.

And then I heard it.

The sound of a baby crying. It was actually here. After all it had put me through, it was here. And I was there. My hair sparse and balding, my teeth rotting and missing, and my body completely violated. I, in a daze, looked over at my parents excitedly being excited. Them. It was their fault. Because I watched them have sex, and she didn't get pregnant, meaning you can have sex without getting pregnant. Even if you do, Virginia said you could make it stop. But because of my parents, I was bleeding on their couch with a newborn being pulled out of me. As absolutely tired as I was, I had never been so angry. I didn't have the energy to feel a normal rage; this was slow and bubbling like the fires rivers from hell.

I lay there in my cage with visitors watching over me. People passing by tapping on my glass with a stretched-out grin. I was somehow still so cute as I lay there, writhing. Ever so slowly, so carefully, a baby was placed in my arms. Echoing voices in the back told me to place my breast inside the baby's mouth, just as I had done to the father of the child when conceiving it. I am mother, I am whore. My body provides for others. The baby, a mere silhouette in my arms, wriggled ever so slightly. I placed a paw on its head, my whiskers tickling its face. I stared blankly before opening my mouth and eating it whole, its blood mixing with mine.

I am mother, I am hamster.

We moaned while we bled.

ACKNOWLEDGMENTS

To my team of hamsters, Daisy, Lana, Slash and Vaughan, I can't thank you all enough for the amount of work you contributed into bringing this book to fruition. This project would be lifeless without you all.

www.ingramcontent.com/pod-product-compliance
Lightning Source LLC
Chambersburg PA
CBHW060755310726
48980CB00002B/106